It was like looking at a gaily wrapped present—one he wasn't permitted to unwrap.

She was dressed in royal blue, trimmed in fur, with a jeweled girdle hung low about her hips. Her neckline was square, with the curves of her breasts visible beneath a scrap of sheer lace that might be a sensual undergarment. Daring, sexual, and marking her as less than a wife, and more than a common prostitute.

"Do I meet with your approval?" Juliana asked dryly.

"You'll have to consult me every day," he answered smoothly.

After hiding their finery beneath cloaks, they went outside to the waiting horses. Paul considered the open gate, where anyone could see them, and decided to launch into his role. When he took Juliana's gloved hand in his, she allowed him to bring it to his lips.

"Mistress Juliana, permit me to help you mount."

"I am your concubine, not your wife," she said with exasperation.

"Regardless, I am a man who treats well what's mine. And you are mine, for the near future."

Romances by Julia Latham

Sin
AND
Surrender

Julia Latham

AVON

An Imprint of HarperCollinsPublishers

AVON BOOKS
An Imprint of HarperCollins*Publishers*
10 East 53rd Street
New York, New York 10022-5299

Copyright © 2011 by Gayle Kloecker Callen
ISBN 978-0-06-178348-7
www.avonromance.com

First Avon Books paperback printing: January 2011

Avon Trademark Reg. U.S. Pat. Off. and in Other Countries, Marca Registrada, Hecho en U.S.A.
HarperCollins® is a registered trademark of HarperCollins Publishers.

Printed in the U.S.A.

10 9 8 7 6 5 4 3 2 1

To my dear friend, Laurie Bishop:
Thank you for all the help you've given me
through the years, making my books better
than I thought they could be. Now that you've
begun a new stage in your life, I hope you
find the joy of rediscovering yourself.

Sin
AND
Surrender

Chapter 1

London, 1487

Sir Paul Hilliard almost rejected the summons by the League of the Blade, the legendary knights who secretly fought injustice on behalf of the innocent. And although others would be flattered, he felt only anger, indignation, and disgust, the same feelings that had led him to renounce his place in the League, and driven him to Europe several years before. But he could not escape their shadow without confronting them one last time.

The house in a small neighborhood off the Strand looked like any other merchant's house, surrounded by a high wall to keep others out—and to keep secrets in. He was admitted through the front door by a short, stocky man with a heavy beard that partially hid an old scar. The guard escorted him through another door and into a larger room, furnished simply with benches, stools, and a cupboard decorated with plate. Three men stood about a long table that occupied the far end, scrolls and books piled haphazardly. Behind them several more men stood talking together. All looked up at Paul's entrance.

Sir Timothy Sheldon came forward first, his lined face creased with a welcoming smile. He was a short man, barrel-chested, with brown hair more streaked with gray than Paul remembered. Timothy had been Paul's foster father, his own father's best friend, who'd spirited away three frightened little boys when their parents had been found slaughtered in their bedchamber. This was the man who should have protected them himself, instead of delivering them into the hands of the League.

Paul stiffened as Timothy reached him, and the older man drew to a halt, his smile fading.

"You look well, Paul," Timothy said.

Paul nodded. "You have changed little."

"That is a compliment to a man of my middling years. I accept it gladly."

"As you wish." Paul could see Timothy's eagerness, and it made him uneasy. How could the man believe that Paul could ever forget the wrongs that had been done him?

Timothy cleared his throat, then stepped back to include the other two men who'd been standing with him. "You remember Sir Joseph and Sir Michael?"

Paul nodded, recognizing them both: Sir Joseph,

black-haired and so handsome that women followed him about with moonstruck eyes; and Sir Michael, a freckle-faced redhead, the first one to show a faint hint of disapproval upon seeing Paul. The three other strangers remained at the rear of the chamber and simply watched, which wasn't unusual. In the League, Bladesmen kept to themselves, their real lives a secret.

"What do you need from me?" Paul asked.

"Very well then, sit down, my boy," Timothy said, his voice still gratingly pleasant.

"I'm not 'your boy.' You made that clear when I was but a child."

Timothy had great control of his expressions, but Paul could tell his barb had struck home. He felt no regret, for his own life had been damaged by Timothy's actions.

"Ungrateful, aren't you?" Michael said coldly.

Paul raised an eyebrow. "Do you know my story?"

"Much of it."

"You are quick to judge." Paul turned back to Timothy. "So much for keeping secret a Bladesman's real life."

"There are reasons you do not yet understand," Timothy began.

"Paul wants to know why he was summoned," Joseph interrupted affably. "Let us tell him so that he can make his decision whether to help us."

"You mean help the League," Paul countered.

"We mean help all of England," Michael said, his eyes narrowed.

"I understand this involves the king." Paul glanced at Timothy.

"And men contemplating treason." Timothy sank down on the wood-backed settle beneath the front window.

Michael and Joseph took stools nearby, leaving Paul the bench. He gave a last glance at the men at the far end of the room, but none of them moved. They were a small group, clustered together, and for a moment, Paul thought he sensed a feeling of . . . familiarity. When he could not place it, he gave them his back, then reluctantly sat, his hands resting on his thighs.

"Surely the king has an entire army to protect him," Paul continued.

"He does, but this is a delicate matter," Timothy said. "Before I explain all the details, let me assure you that you will not be working alone. Since you will be portraying a man rather easily led"—he held up a hand when Paul began to interrupt—"you will have guards in your retinue, as well as someone at your side at all times to defend you."

Paul practically bit his own tongue to keep from insisting he could defend himself.

"Your guard will be your concubine," Timothy said.

"A concubine?" Paul echoed, finding himself on his

feet. "You expect a woman to defend me when I am perfectly capable of doing so myself?"

"A Bladeswoman," said a cool voice from behind him.

Paul turned around, and one of the men at the back of the chamber separated himself from the others and walked forward. From his height to his manner of walking to the way he held his lean frame, Paul could see nothing different from any other Bladesman.

And then the light coming through the window fell on the upturned face, smooth of whiskers, hollow-cheeked. No man, but a woman.

Paul stared at her, but could think of nothing to say. She'd blended in so easily with the others, that he hadn't even guessed her sex. Now that he'd been alerted, he could see the curve of her hip and breast beneath her simple tunic and breeches, but she managed to disguise it without even hiding it. It was obscured by the veil of her bold manner, the swing of her arms, even the tilt of her head. She hadn't bothered to hide her hair, black as soot, only pulled it back with a leather tie. There was something stark and yet exotic about her face, her jaw too square for a woman, yet softened by a lush lower lip.

"Do you not recognize me, Sir Paul?" she asked, one brow lifted.

He looked into her eyes, faintly slanted, centered with black as if to conceal all her thoughts.

She was a Bladeswoman.

"Juliana." He said her name in disbelief. "You've changed."

"You only knew me for a few months," she said.

Was that disapproval in her voice?

Yet he remembered her well. He did not know her story; such was the way of the League. But like the Hilliard brothers—and unlike every other Bladesman—she'd come to live permanently at the Castle, the League fortress, well hidden within the mountains. She'd been sad-eyed and lost when he'd first seen her, and he'd learned that her parents were recently dead. But the rest was her past, part of the outside world, and she had seemed to relish the anonymity of her new position. Surprisingly talented with a dagger and sword, she'd behaved more as a young man than a woman, and he'd tried to treat her as any other recruit, fighting feelings of protectiveness because of her tragedy. During those few months he'd known her, when a rare glimmer of attraction hovered between them, he'd firmly buried it. She'd been his student—but not anymore. He found himself wondering how she'd adjusted to life in the League, how it had changed her. There was an air of confidence—of power—about her now, and he found it far too appealing.

While he studied her, Juliana said nothing, simply watching, waiting, a new maturity and awareness in her gaze.

Paul felt . . . off-balance, and needed to reassert himself. "I see you learned at last the art of silence."

Though her eyes lightened with amusement, she said, "I learned much after you left. 'Tis a shame you did not remain to work with the recruits assigned to you."

He'd never told her why he'd left—he hadn't told everything to his brothers, either.

"Such service to the League was no longer my path, brat," he said. "Perhaps you should look into your own heart."

She did not flinch at his old pet name for her. "The next few weeks will reveal much."

Paul turned back to Timothy. "I have not yet agreed to anything. I need details."

Timothy nodded. "You know that since Henry won the Crown in battle from Richard—"

"Killed him for it, you mean," Paul pointed out.

"Defeated him in battle, aye. Since then, there have always been rumblings of discontent, especially in the north, noblemen who don't always come to London when the king calls. He put down a rebellion in York last year, and then earlier this summer, his army came to battle against traitors backed by armies from Ireland and Flanders. But not all of the traitors were discovered. Henry is determined to march north, wanting his people to see him and benefit from his generosity, the better to bring peace. 'Tis our duty to make the way safe for him.

There are still whispered rumors of treasonous plans to claim another with better bloodlines as rightful king. We need to find these traitors"— Timothy's voice grew cold—"and expose them for what they are."

Paul spread his hands. "The king's own men aren't able to discover this?"

"They suspect some," Michael offered. "But mere suspicion and then arrest will not placate the king's people. Henry wishes to be certain."

"And why do you need me for that? Send in Blades-men in disguise. Or Juliana here, since she is so eager."

She only gave him a bold smile. Apparently, she was quite willing to offer herself into danger. The League had worked its illusions well.

"You have the perfect appearance for the man we need," Timothy said.

"So you need someone fair-haired?" Paul asked with disbelief.

"You are of noble blood, and that essence is often difficult to falsify. Your hair and eyes are the right match for one thought dead."

"You want a ghost from the grave?"

"We want Richard, the Duke of York."

Paul took a deep breath. Richard and his brother, Edward—who would have been crowned Edward V— young boys when their father died, were taken into protective custody by their uncle Richard. He was named their Protector until it came to light that their father had been legally betrothed to another woman before marrying the woman who eventually became Richard and Edward's mother. This conveniently made them both bastards, leading to Richard's assumption of the Crown as Richard III. The little boys disappeared into the Tower of London and were presumed murdered. Richard only ruled for eighteen months before the Battle of Bosworth, where he lost first his crown, and then his life.

"No one would believe that I am Prince Richard," Paul said with exasperation. "I would be only one of several fools claiming such a thing. The late King Edward's sister is constantly backing a new challenger to the throne."

"But 'tis your skill that will make them believe," Juliana said. "If you have it."

Paul grinned. "The League brought me here, brat, did they not?"

"The villains will not believe you the prince," Timothy interrupted mildly. "And you will not even claim such a thing—openly. But they'll think they can use you to persuade others in the north that there is someone with more right to the Crown, someone to rally around."

"As a figurehead," Michael said. "You would do well in such an illusion."

Paul glanced at the other man. Was that a taunt? How

unusual for a Bladesman. He turned back to Timothy. "And my mission would be to find proof to convict these traitors."

"Our mission, aye," Timothy said.

"*Our?*" Paul echoed, his eyes narrowed.

"I will be accompanying you, as will several other Bladesmen. You will portray a man used to the finer things in life, not quite strong in battle, nor in intelligence. You need a retinue of guards if you are to maintain the illusion of a man raised abroad in wealth and secrecy who has returned home to claim his birthright."

Paul stared hard at the man who thought himself his foster father. He did not believe it an accident that Timothy had been assigned to this mission. Paul well knew that Timothy had the ear of the Council of Elders, for Paul had managed to listen in on more than one meeting he shouldn't have.

"Do I have a say in which Bladesmen are used?" Paul asked coldly.

Michael was equally cold. "You do not. You will be the focus of many, an object of salvation to some, a threat to the unity of the country to others. You'll be in danger constantly."

"If you know any of my past as you claim, then you know I'm used to that." He turned to Timothy. "I understand your plan in theory, but there is one problem. *Juliana* will play a concubine?"

He glanced pointedly at her male attire. He knew he might be offending her, but that faint, amused smile yet lingered on her full lower lip.

"I imagine you are right," Juliana said. "It will be far easier for you to be the fop than for me to play a concubine."

Paul heard more than one indrawn breath among the Bladesmen. Michael openly grinned his satisfaction, and Timothy looked away, hiding a smile.

She dared to openly challenge him? Paul thought, intrigued.

Chapter 2

It was no longer difficult for Juliana Gresham to conceal her thoughts. The League—and Paul—had taught her well. Now she stared up into the impassive face of this hard-eyed man and felt a tremor that shook her soul rather than her body. He was still so tall, deceptively light haired, but not lighthearted. His blue eyes were mirrors, reflecting the world but never his own thoughts. Handsome, masculine, he had a strong nose and square jaw with a cleft in the middle.

But he was a stranger now.

There had always been an edge to him, a young man thinking of other places, restless for his future. She'd tried to befriend him but he'd kept a distance between them that she'd never understood. His departure had caused a void of protection she'd little realized until it had almost been too late.

She felt slightly disgruntled that Paul had not seen her femininity, but quickly submerged it beneath pride in her abilities at deception. Her fellow Bladesmen could not be allowed to think of her as a woman and assume she was weak. She'd sworn a vow to herself that she would never become ensnared in a relationship with a Bladesman; it would only hurt her standing with the League.

She'd found herself taunting Paul, and knew it was out of disappointment. He was proving himself, like so many other men, wary of working alongside a woman, skeptical of her, judging her.

He didn't know her—he'd abandoned her training to run off and make a new life for himself, never explaining his reasons. How could he so easily forsake the society who'd saved his life? They'd given her a place to belong, a chance to feel useful.

Now the silence in the room was almost deafening, and she realized they all waited to see Paul's response to the slur against his manhood.

"I've had encounters with fops in the royal courts of Europe," Paul said pleasantly. "And I've had much experience with their concubines."

Juliana heard a chuckle behind her, but she didn't let her smile fade.

"Take no offense, brat," he continued, "but you do not look as if you'd allow a man to purchase you."

"That was a kind way to phrase your doubt," Juliana said.

He sighed, then lifted his head, his gaze encompassing all the men in the room. "And I have much doubt, believe me. I do not look like a fop, and you don't look like a concubine."

"That is easily remedied," Timothy said briskly. "A little padding about the waist for you, Paul, and a gown for our Bladeswoman. Pick the one that is right for your part, Juliana."

"Pick the right padding for Paul," she said over her shoulder as she sauntered away. "I know he'll want it in the codpiece, and much as it would help, it won't fit our purposes."

She didn't look back as several men exploded with laughter.

Paul found himself laughing with the others, impressed with Juliana's boldness. He saw Timothy's relief at his response, and Joseph and Michael exchange a surprised look. Let them wonder about him; he would not prove predictable.

To Timothy, he said, "I believe I should simply alter my carriage to a slouch, rather than use padding. It would be too difficult to don at a moment's notice."

Timothy nodded even as his smile faded. "Then you will join us on this mission?"

Paul noticed that Juliana paused in the entrance hall, waiting for his response. Her eyes met his, full of challenge. And much as his curiosity about her was an incentive, she alone was not the only influence on his decision. Nay, the League had been instrumental in aiding his brothers to unmask their parents' murderer. At last, Adam had been able to reclaim his position as the long lost Earl of Keswick, and the news of that had persuaded Paul that it was time to return home. Paul felt a reluctant debt to the League.

"Aye, for my king and country, I agree to this mission," Paul said, then coolly added, "but after that, my part in the League will be finished. I threw away my League medallion. I am no longer one of you."

Juliana caught her breath, and he saw the censure in her eyes, the disappointment. He forgave her the emotions, knowing she didn't yet realize the truth of the League and its ruthlessness. She felt rescued, valued, when in truth, she was merely another pawn to be used.

The silence was stark and uneasy, but at last, Timothy nodded. Juliana closed the door to the entrance hall behind her. In short order, Paul was introduced to the last two men who would be accompanying them. To his surprise, Sir Roger was an older man, with more than sixty years, grizzled and gray, yet with an unbent body that hinted at a wiry strength.

"He is to be your companion since your youth," Timothy explained. "He is well versed about the Tower of London, and you can tell the traitors that he'll be able to give voice to your past, to spiriting you away from London on behalf of King Richard."

"So Richard supposedly saved me, his namesake nephew?" Paul asked dryly.

"Our enemy will know the truth. But they will want as much evidence as possible to spread word that you're their prince restored."

"A good plan," Paul said, turning to the other man.

He came out of the shadows, and Paul hid his surprise.

"Sir Theobald," the man said gruffly, briefly bowing his head.

He was as big as Paul himself, a man in his prime— but with a mask tied over the left side of his face, from his blond eyebrow to just above his jaw.

"Sir Theobald will be Juliana's personal guard," Timothy said.

Paul silently arched one brow.

"Aye, she'll be with you much of the time," he added, smiling. "The two of you will be able to protect each other well. But I don't want a threat to her used against you."

Paul looked around at his retinue of guards: Timothy, whose very presence reminded him too much of the past; Joseph, bland and almost pretty, unreadable; Michael, who did not hide his contempt; Roger, old yet eager to prove useful; and Theobald, an enigma, yet the man who would protect Juliana because Paul was not allowed to. Paul found himself clenching his jaw, and forced himself to relax.

Theobald suddenly cocked his head, then went to open the door to the front hall. "Mistress Juliana," he intoned, as if he were already connected to her in some mystical way. Paul didn't know anything about Juliana, her relationships with Bladesmen, or if she'd ever found her own home.

Standing nearest to the door, Paul glanced up the hall staircase—and froze. A sultry, earthy woman was coming down the last few stairs, gowned in brilliant blue, hips swaying, lush breasts molded for display.

Juliana.

She met his gaze, her black eyes knowing and sensual. Her dark hair tumbled to mid back, caressed her shoulders, softly touched her breasts. As she came toward him, he knew that he could never think of her again as boyish. She'd become a dazzling woman.

He wasn't the only man to gape. Several mouths were open, brows lifted in shock. Not Timothy though, who looked resigned and proud at the same time.

Juliana didn't stop until she practically wound herself about Paul, leaning her tall, curved body into his, one hand playing with the hair at the nape of his neck, the other resting familiarly on his chest. She felt warm and smelled delicious, of garden flowers just closing with the onset of night.

Now she'd turned him into a poet, he thought, bemused.

She fluttered her dark eyelashes at him, then murmured, "Now who has the most talent at deception?"

"Brat." He gave her a crooked grin. Juliana was more of a woman than he'd given her credit for; there was experience and confidence in her gaze.

For a moment, he drew her against him, up onto her toes, their mouths close to each other. Her eyes widened, but she remained pliable, languorous. He let his gaze promise pleasure—and sin.

Then he released her and resumed his impassivity as he looked at Timothy. "I can pretend to be attracted to her," he said dryly.

Her demeanor changed, as if he'd blown out a candle. She appeared as an attractive woman now, not a sensual enchantress. He couldn't help wondering how innocent she really was, living alone with men.

Timothy rubbed his hands together. "All is being prepared as we speak. We will leave in two days' time. Paul, you will briefly display yourself tomorrow for the merchants on the London Bridge. Then our man within the Yorkist camp will begin whispering of an arrival from a mysterious Englishman who's been living in Europe. The Bladesmen bringing word to him will casually spread the news in the countryside as well."

"You already have a man inside?" Paul asked.

"Aye, with one northern household, but he is not privy to secret conversations. And we are not certain which of the Yorkists will be greedy enough to foment a new rebellion so quickly after the last one failed." Timothy turned to Juliana. "You may change while I speak with Paul alone."

As the chamber slowly cleared, Paul watched her walk away. But the undulation of her hips was gone, and she strode with brisk purpose—like a man. But at least he would soon be treated to more of her hidden femininity.

When they were alone, he faced Timothy impassively. "What else do you want from me? I've already agreed to participate."

"Can I not simply be glad to see you, my son?"

Timothy's smile was fatherly, and it made Paul uneasy. "I think you only want to ease things between us, so that your mission will run smoothly."

"That's not true, Paul. I've been worried about you. You never sent word to me or to your brothers about what you were doing, how you fared."

"Surely you used the League to keep track of me."

Timothy pressed his lips together. "Can I not be concerned?"

"If you were so concerned about me and my brothers, you would have raised us yourself."

"Paul, you know the danger you were once under. Your parents' murder in their own bedchamber was brutal—"

"You need not remind me. Adam overheard it, saw their slaughtered bodies, lived with nightmares. And he had but six years!"

"We knew not the reason your parents died so cruelly," Timothy said, his voice firm and controlled. "Adam was the heir to a vast holding. I could not protect the three of you as your father would have wanted. I made the decision that I thought best, bringing you boys with me to the League, so that I could know you were safe, and watch over you myself."

"Not your finest hour, *Father*."

Timothy flinched. "I agree. There are things I would change, if I could."

"But you cannot. Your devotion to them was such that you didn't even take a wife."

"Their causes are just, Paul. You cannot refute that. Nothing excuses me in your eyes, nor should it. I believed myself unworthy to act as your father, that I should have no voice in the hiding of such an heir as Keswick. I made grievous mistakes, but I cannot change the past. I feared for your brother Adam, so obsessed was he with a murderer. I worried about Robert, too carefree, almost losing what was important to him. And now you."

"I do not want your worry. 'Tis baseless."

"I worry that bitterness has distorted you. You have always been driven, ambitious, curious about the world.

Did you let yourself enjoy it, or did you constantly think of the past?"

"I have lived a good life away from the League, even as I missed my brothers."

"Glad I am to hear that," Timothy said, letting his breath out on a sigh.

"But I never forgot what you allowed the League to do to us—what you allowed the League to do to another family."

Timothy went still. "What are you saying?"

"Aye, I was curious. I made it a point to listen in on the private sessions of the Council of Elders."

"That could have put you in grave danger," Timothy said softly, looking over his shoulder as if someone might overhear them.

"I was not a traitor; I simply needed to know about these men who ran my life and set themselves up to judge other men, administering justice or punishment as they arbitrarily saw fit."

"Paul—"

"I know the Council deliberately destroyed a man's reputation and family, all to advance one of their missions."

Timothy's eyes narrowed. "What else did you hear?"

"Not enough to confront anyone, so do not concern yourself. The mission was apparently over and had been a success. Another traitor against the Crown identified.

And the only person who had to suffer was one man, his reputation, and then his very life. And you were there."

With a sigh, Timothy said, "You know 'tis not permitted to discuss assignments not our own. But let me say this." He raised his voice to dissuade Paul's protest. "You don't know everything, and yet you feel free to judge in the same way for which you condemn the League."

Paul stiffened. "I have enough evidence to satisfy me, the words of the Councilors themselves. The League may do good throughout the land, but there can also be a whiff of evil, when some men think they are accountable to no one."

"We are accountable to one another, and it has served to check any grasp for power. But we are not infallible."

"My brothers and I are the proof," Paul said, feeling suddenly weary. "And before you ask, I never told them a word of what I heard."

Timothy's eyes widened. "Why not? You wanted to be free of the League, and you could have had the company of your brothers."

"Nay, it would not have been that way. Adam was honored to be chosen from childhood for the League."

"Trust me, he knows the League has failings."

"Perhaps, but then . . . nay, 'twould have hurt him, and I couldn't do that. He had his own path to follow. And Robert . . . I am glad he has since found his way, but then, he was always eager to enjoy himself. He did not crave the life I did, the adventure of making my own way."

"Perhaps you acted as more of a father to your brothers than I did," Timothy said softly.

Paul frowned. "I didn't return to argue with you. I owe the League a debt, and will repay it. But do not bother pursuing forgiveness from me."

Timothy nodded, his expression as tired-looking as Paul felt. "Very well. For this assignment, we will be as fellow Bladesmen only."

Paul opened the door leading to the front hall. "Send for me when you need me. I'll pack my things."

"You will not need much in the way of garments. They will be provided for you."

"Something extravagant, I imagine."

"As befits a prince."

Paul nodded and went out through the door. He looked over his shoulder briefly, but Juliana was not standing at the top of the stairs. He'd only imagined it.

Chapter 3

The next morning, Juliana was sent to bring Paul to the League house. She rode her horse through Ludgate, the ancient western gateway to the city, and down Fleet Street until it became the Strand, following the Thames. Cramped houses gave way to palaces along the road to Westminster, each with its own access to the river.

She allowed her horse to walk, feeling no great urgency. It was early yet, and the heavy traffic of horses and carts, people and wagons streamed past her in the opposite direction to enter the city, not leave it.

This was her last day as herself. With her hair pulled back from her face, wearing a simple belted tunic, breeches, and a man's hat, she attracted no notice. Most thought her only a boy about his master's business. She liked giving people a different impression of herself, a skill she'd well mastered in her training, if Paul's expression yesterday was any proof.

At first she'd been full of triumph that she'd caused

him to be momentarily speechless. The other men had been struck dumb as well, and she hadn't liked that so much. She'd spent the past few years convincing them all that she was one of them, a talented recruit, more a Blades*man* than Blades*woman*. No one had ever insisted she hide her sex; she'd simply felt she could do her work more effectively when unnoticed. She'd been trained to be a woman, even a sexually knowledgeable one, but seldom felt like one. It was only a part she played, not the real Juliana.

Of course she'd dressed as a woman on past missions, but nothing so openly carnal and sensual. It had felt awkward to inspire men's lust, though she hadn't shown that revelation to her fellow Bladesmen. She had no need to wonder what they thought of her. Her dedication was understood. She would take this new part in stride, playact and pretend to be one thing on the surface, and remain herself beneath.

At last she reached Keswick House, home of Paul's brother, the earl. High walls surrounded the courtyard, but inside was a palace of windows cut into ancient walls. She knew the true beauty of the house would be facing the Thames, the main thoroughfare into London.

A servant gestured her into the entrance hall, with its dark paneling and display of the Keswick coat of arms. She expected to be led to Paul immediately, but instead was shown into a withdrawing chamber furnished with a large table and enough chairs to seat thirty people. She didn't think the servant even noticed that the chamber was occupied. Juliana stood awkwardly by the door and waited. Two women stood at one of the cupboards, putting away golden plate. Both were of much shorter stature than Juliana herself. One had brown hair, and moved with a limp as she stepped behind the other for another plate. The second woman's hair was a mass of red curls in the August heat, and freckles dotted her face.

They glanced at her and hesitated. Juliana wondered why she'd been shown into a chamber where servants were busy working, but she did not ask questions.

They must have thought she couldn't hear them, because one murmured to the other, "Paul felt certain they'd send a lady to fetch him."

"He did say he was looking forward to it."

These women called him by his Christian name; they could not be servants.

She swept her hat from her head and stepped forward. "My ladies, I am Mistress Juliana, come for Sir Paul, as he surmised."

They froze, a plate half passed between them. Then the brown-haired one giggled, even as she set down the plate and wiped her hands on an apron. It was then that Juliana noticed the faint rounding of pregnancy.

"Mistress Juliana, do forgive me. Your appearance deceived me."

" 'Tis that way often," Juliana said ruefully.

"I am Lady Keswick, but do call me Florrie. I'll call you by your Christian name as well."

Shocked that she'd been so rude to the countess, Juliana sank into a curtsy that would have done her mother proud. "My lady, forgive my discourtesy." She knew Lady Keswick was of high birth, the daughter of a marquess.

Lady Keswick reached for her hands and made her straighten. "Good heavens, Juliana, do not worry yourself. It seems we all misread each other. Do allow me to introduce my new sister by marriage, Mistress Sarah Hilliard."

The redheaded woman grinned and openly looked Juliana up and down. "So you're the lady Paul mentioned."

Juliana glanced down at her garments. "It may seem difficult to believe it at the moment, but aye, 'tis true."

"Congratulations on being a member of the League," Lady Keswick said, her voice full of admiration.

Juliana's smile died a quick death. They knew?

"Oh dear, you know we shouldn't speak such things aloud," Mistress Hilliard murmured, nudging her ladyship with her elbow.

"But . . ." Juliana began haltingly, "your husbands should never have—" Then she broke off, realizing she was speaking of an earl.

"They had no choice but to tell us their secrets," Lady Keswick said apologetically.

"Because *we* had no choice," Mistress Hilliard added.

"Forgive me, but I do not understand."

Lady Keswick smiled. "You see, I first met my husband, Adam, when he kidnapped me."

Juliana blinked in surprise.

Mistress Hilliard said, "And I met Robert when he was assigned by the League to prove me a murderess." She grinned. "And how are you connected with the Hilliard brothers?"

"I'm to be Paul's concubine," Juliana said, beginning to smile. "Although in truth, I will be his personal guard."

The two women looked at each other and burst out laughing.

"Oh, Juliana," Lady Keswick said, wiping her eyes, "our men are never dull. I do not yet know Paul as a brother, but I cannot imagine he took the news well."

"That I would guard him? Nay, he did not." Juliana felt a stirring of anger again at his assumption that a woman couldn't guard him, but put it aside.

"Come into the kitchens with us," Mistress Hilliard said.

She took Juliana's arm on one side, and Lady Keswick took the other.

"You can tell us about our husbands' brother," Mistress Hilliard continued. "You knew him for several months, I hear, where we have only known him for several days."

Lady Keswick took up the tale. "Paul said he trained you, but my husband insisted that Paul thought he was hoping to prove his talent as an instructor by making you the best."

Juliana grimaced. "Then he did not stay to do so, did he?"

The two talkative women were suddenly silent, even as they guided her down a corridor. The thought that Paul had had plans for her, and abandoned them, renewed her curiosity about why he'd so suddenly decided to leave.

And if she felt a touch of sadness, of concern that she'd done something to drive him away, she ignored it.

"I wish I had time to speak longer with you both," Juliana said, "but we have work to do this afternoon in preparation for our leave-taking on the morrow."

"We understand," Lady Keswick said, taking a sudden turn into another corridor. "Then we shall bring you to Paul. He is training with our husbands."

"They were quite excited this morn to face their younger brother," Mistress Hilliard said, shaking her head. "Like little boys, they are."

At last they opened a door that led out to a lush

garden. As they followed a gravel path, the ground sloped gently down toward the broad river, which Julian could glimpse between iron gates. But in a corner of the high walls, the grass had given way to dirt, and the three Hilliard men fought each other, all at once.

The two women on either side of her froze, and as swords slashed through air, barely missing vital body parts, she heard the women gasp or groan. Lady Keswick once even shielded her eyes.

The men—especially Paul—displayed a competitiveness that still surprised her among siblings.

He grinned when he would have struck a killing blow to Adam were he fighting an actual enemy.

"Well done!" Robert shouted, laughing at Paul's triumph.

Adam glowered. "That is a fine move you've mastered. You must teach us."

The two older Hilliards looked like duplicates of each other, both tall and dark, with the same cleft in their chin. Paul shared the cleft, but his coloring was much lighter.

At last the men glanced toward the women, and Juliana saw a softening in both Adam's and Robert's faces upon seeing their wives. But Paul only glanced impassively down her body, as if he thought she'd be gowned. She would be wearing such restrictive garments soon enough.

They sheathed their swords and came forward. Both Adam and Robert now looked openly at Juliana. Much as they had not lingered more than a few months at the League fortress after their brother had gone, she saw them often enough to feel an easy friendship.

Adam, the Earl of Keswick, gave her his winning smile. "Juliana, 'tis good to see you again."

"And you, too, my lord."

He arched a brow.

"I must treat you as what you are in London, must I not?"

"No wonder we keep our real identities from each other," Adam said. "This becomes too complicated."

While she spoke to Adam, she found her gaze wandering to Paul. He had reached for a bucket, and even now lifted a dipper to quench his thirst. In the sun his hair shone, just as it had when she'd first been introduced to him, like a beacon of hope in her new life that day.

"I miss the gown," he said to her.

The others stared back and forth between them with interest.

Juliana lifted her chin coolly. "Do not rush me into such confinement, Paul. I like my breeches."

"I am surprised that you dress so when you are in London. People will talk."

"Let them. They think I'm a boy most of the time."

"With even a codpiece?" he shot back with faint sarcasm.

Lady Keswick gasped. "That is crude, Paul," she said, though she spoke with only a lighthearted, chiding tone.

"What if little Francis had heard you?" Mistress Hilliard asked. To Juliana, she said, "Francis is Viscount Drayton, our ward until he reaches maturity."

"Francis is a little man," Paul said, grinning. "He understands about codpieces. Even Juliana does."

She gave him a withering stare, knowing he referred to her taunt of yesterday.

"Come, Juliana, show me what else you know," Paul said, walking backward even as he urged her with both hands. "You'll be giving me my last rousing match for some time. Our small tiltyard awaits."

It was hardly a true tiltyard, with no lists on which to practice jousting, no quintain to unseat an unwary knight. But she had her sword buckled at her waist, and she knew how to use it.

She pulled it from its sheath, causing Lady Keswick and Mistress Hilliard to step back, eyes wide. But she knew admiration when she saw it; these women would not disdain her for her talent.

She attacked at once, knowing that Paul's size put her at a disadvantage. When they crossed swords high, she yanked on his elbow, throwing him off balance. He grinned at her and sliced a deft cut out of the skirt of her tunic. The grin alone was enough to make her look at him twice. He was blindingly handsome, his blue eyes merry with intrigue and too much interest as he parried the moves she made. She began to wonder what was in store for her, being with him day after day—and night.

Soon sweat dripped into her eyes, and her breathing quickened. When she maneuvered him into pivoting to block her sword, she pulled her dagger out of its hidden spot in her boot, to simulate a thrust into his armpit.

He challenged that as well, calling, "Well done!"

She squelched the little thrill of pride his words caused. She should not care what he thought. But even though she'd only spent a few months learning from him, he'd been her first teacher, and had commanded her respect with the fair treatment he granted her. She thought of his disparagement of her sex just yesterday— had he changed, or simply hidden his true self from her?

At last she gave a mighty heave to his chest, and as he stepped backward, his boot caught on a rock, and he tumbled onto his backside. She well knew if they'd been fighting for real, he would have defeated her within the first minute, such was his knowledge and skill. Skill granted him by the League, though he disdained them.

As the ladies applauded wildly and the men cheered, Juliana sheathed her sword and reached down a hand to Paul. He took it, sprang to his feet, but didn't release her immediately. His hand felt warm, rough with calluses, so large compared to her own. The touch of him reminded her of their playacting yesterday, when she'd been the concubine, and he'd been her very interested lover.

She pulled her hand away, not wanting to think about that.

Paul grinned, his gaze intent on her face, as if trying to read everything about her. And although Bladesmen were taught to read expressions, they were also well trained to conceal what they wished. So he was deliberately trying to tease her, to throw *her* off-balance.

"What skill you have, Juliana!" Lady Keswick cried.

"And next she'll wear a disguise," Mistress Hilliard added. "It seems so exciting."

"'Twill not be exciting," Juliana said, sobering. "Living every moment of the day pretending to be someone else is exacting work."

"And I will be a difficult commander," Paul said.

"Then 'tis good that I will not see that side of you, for Sir Timothy is our commander."

She thought the jibe an apt one, but he didn't seem to see the amusement, for his smile faded. Adam and Robert glanced at each other, but revealed nothing else.

Late that morning, after their return to the League house, Paul removed a bound book from his saddlebag before a guard led his horse away.

Juliana eyed it with open speculation. "Did you have a chance to read much?"

"I read it all, even managing to stay awake, too."

The League had asked him to familiarize himself with Edward IV, late father of the queen and the little princes, one of whom Paul would impersonate. Paul had been surprised at the details the League had discovered about the last days of the boys, locked in the Tower of London, unable to see their mother or sisters, who were closeted at Westminster Abbey.

Once he was with Timothy and the rest of the Blades-men in the house, he patiently let himself be quizzed on his knowledge.

When it seemed to go on too long, Paul said, "Surely you can see that my skills at memorization are functioning. I'm prepared."

Michael gave him an arch look. "Are we not right to be concerned? Should things go wrong, our heads would end up beside yours on pikes on London Bridge. The king would not claim us if it would reflect badly on him."

With a heavy sigh, Paul launched into a sad narrative of Prince Richard's time in the tower, as if it were his own story, his confusion over why his uncle had taken the throne, his longing for his mother, his grief over his father's death. Soldiers had later spoken in whispers of how the boy expected death, and knelt day and night praying for his soul. It was a sad ending for a child, although there was no proof *what* had happened. But the boys were gone, and King Henry, their brother by marriage, wouldn't want them to return. Throughout his speech, Paul saw Juliana watching him, her expression impassive, her dark eyes alive with cool intelligence.

"Enough," Timothy said at last. "I am impressed, Paul, for you had little time to study the material."

Paul found himself ready to answer with sarcasm, to say such was the training of the League. But he didn't need to remind his foster father of his bitterness and disappointment. "What next do you wish of me?" he asked.

Timothy sent the two of them up to the first-floor bedchambers, where their new wardrobes awaited them. Paul was surprised by how well the garments fit him, though he hadn't been measured by a tailor. There were doublets and tunics of vivid colors, patterned and multicolored hose to match, capes and belted coats trimmed in fur. Several hats were adorned with large feathers, and chains glittered with pendants.

Paul practiced his slouch, and found himself sighing.

"Vain?" Michael asked from behind him.

Paul frowned. "Put yourself in my place, forced to be weak and soft, an easy target."

Michael only shrugged, as if he didn't want to offer sympathy. He'd been assigned to act as Paul's manservant, and his faintly disapproving air would most likely grow tiresome.

Paul buckled on his sword, still angry at playing a part that left him so vulnerable to attack.

They met up with the rest of the party in the front hall below. Paul distracted himself by eyeing Juliana, and she did the same to him.

Considering he'd just fought the woman several hours before, he was amazed at the transformation. Would he ever become used to this? It was like looking at a gaily wrapped present every day—one he wasn't permitted to unwrap.

She was dressed in royal blue, trimmed in fur, with a jeweled girdle hung low about her hips. Her neckline was square, with the curves of her breasts visible beneath a scrap of sheer lace that might be a sensual undergarment. Daring, sexual, and marking her as less than a wife, and more than a common prostitute.

"Do I meet with your approval?" Juliana asked dryly.

"You'll have to consult me every day," he answered smoothly.

After hiding their finery beneath cloaks, they all went outside to the waiting horses. Paul considered the open gate, where anyone could see them, and decided to launch into his role. When he took Juliana's gloved hand in his, she allowed him to bring it to his lips.

"Mistress Juliana, permit me to help you mount."

"I am your concubine, not your wife," she said with exasperation.

"But some might think a concubine treated better than a wife."

"Then that is a sad, cynical state of mind."

"Regardless, I am a man who treats well what's mine. And you are mine, for the near future."

He could tell she gritted her teeth, but she nodded her acquiescence. "How do you wish to—"

He picked her up by the waist, and she gripped his forearms. Though tall enough to be a man, she felt surprisingly light. She was able to put a foot in the stirrup, then gracefully slide her other leg across the saddle. When he released her, she settled her voluminous skirts so that only the toes of her boots showed. She'd adopted masculine footwear, but again, a concubine could do as she wished.

"No sidesaddle?" he asked, looking up at her.

"I do not wish to have someone leading me. If we're chased, I need to be able to control my own horse."

Before Paul could respond, Timothy called abruptly, "Let us be off."

Both Paul and Juliana pulled their hoods up, and the entire party set out through the rear entrance into the alley, meandering slowly through crooked streets while the horses picked their way through refuse. It wasn't until they neared the London Bridge that they cast off their cloaks in the sun and rode almost royally through the crowds, drawing gawking attention from fishwives with their loaded panniers to bakers holding pies over their heads. They followed a flock of geese being driven up the narrow path of the bridge, between the merchant shops and homes built on its two-hundred-year-old span.

It was almost a parade, Paul thought, keeping a faint, noble smile about his mouth.

And then there was Juliana, the queen of the parade. She dazzled every man on the street, her expression serene and confident, her black hair hanging in long, gentle curls about her body. She looked like a woman of leisure, a woman of sin.

She saw him staring, and the smile she gave him was full of raw intimacy that was as physical as a punch to the gut. Her knowing eyes slid down his body with open possession, promising much when they were alone that night. She was making their disguise far easier than he'd imagined it would be.

"Paul, my love, do you not see the children?" she asked.

He was too busy thinking of an answering endearment to understand her intent. "Your pardon, my duckling?"

She arched her brows, and he thought the corner of her lip twitched slightly, but all she did was point ahead of them. "The children? Perhaps you should wave?"

And then he saw several scruffy children out for a day's adventure. They gaped up at the closely formed entourage, eyes wide with wonder. Why was he supposed to wave? But he did so with gusto.

"Do you have any pennies?" she asked. "Do offer some."

He gave her an appreciative smile, then reached into the purse on his belt and tossed a few to the children. They gasped and cried out, scrambling for them. And when one small boy was left with his hands empty, his lips trembling, Juliana reached across from her horse, plucked another coin, and tossed it to the boy. Wearing a new grin, he touched the brim of his cap and ran.

The party reached the summit of the bridge, where another tower rose into the sky between the buildings. The road narrowed even further, until Paul's and Juliana's knees touched occasionally as they rode. They were now a spectacle, people gaping as they approached, a growing crowd following from behind. There was no way to escape down the crowded thoroughfare, no room to maneuver on horseback. There should be no reason for attack now, at the beginning of the mission, but it had been instilled in him to constantly prepare for any event.

Over his shoulder, he could see Theobald bringing up the rear, leather jerkin rough and worn, bare bulging arms warning that he well knew how to use a sword.

His craggy face, with its half mask promising to hide something fearful, was enough of a deterrent for many in the crowd. He guided two riderless horses, their panniers stuffed with garments, armor, and supplies for the journey north. In front of Theobald rode Roger, giving a gap-toothed grin at the children they'd just passed, and Joseph, drawing stares, but for the opposite reason as Theobald. His handsome face had many maids sighing and waving their handkerchiefs with delight. Timothy and Michael had the lead, weaving a path through the crowd.

A fine retinue, Paul knew, but if they were attacked, he would have to sit back like a coward and allow them to defend him.

And then there were the rumors his Bladesmen deliberately began to spread. He caught phrases as Michael and Timothy spoke too loudly to each other about "showing his face in London," and "if the king hears of this." Speculation should eventually spread through London and beyond, into the north, where enemies waited.

Paul was glancing up at the three-story buildings rising high on either side of him, when he happened to notice an upper window open, and someone leaned out with a pot.

In character, Paul shouted, "Anon, Michael, look above! Do hurry! I'm not about to be tossed with filth because of your crawling pace."

Juliana ignored him, as if she was used to his sudden flares of temper. He saw Michael's back stiffen, but the Bladesman urged his horse into a trot, and more than one man on the street yelped as he jumped out of their way.

Juliana found herself impressed with Paul's mastery of his character. He'd been away from League duty for several years, yet he managed to focus on playing a spoiled, entitled man. There was an arrogance in his smile, a boldness in his possessiveness of her. As long as he didn't think the latter was true . . .

For herself, crossing the bridge as a spectacle was—exhausting. She wasn't used to being gaped at, wondered about. There were no sneers, since for all the townspeople knew, she was his wife. The sneers would come later.

She was so used to blending in, being unobtrusive, able to watch while not being seen. As the afternoon went on, she found herself longing for peace and solitude, for no voices to be ringing in her ears. But of course, then she would be alone with Paul, their first night together as supposed lovers.

Within an hour, they reached a lively tavern in Southwark where they stopped for supper. Paul spent lavishly, seeming to enjoy being the center of the party. With his blond hair and dazzling blue eyes, he commanded the attention of everyone there, man or maidservant. He flirted with the barmaids, then drew Juliana onto his lap, as if he didn't want her to think he was ignoring her. Instead of accepting his flirtation, she stiffened and gave him a cool look of simmering anger, as if should he keep this up, he would regret it that night.

It was harder than she imagined to work like this, to pay attention to any threats from the crowd, when she felt absolutely surrounded by Paul. She could feel his hard thighs beneath her backside, his arms about her waist, his hand resting on her knee. His broad chest rose against her back with every breath. It took everything in her not to shiver at each touch, and she grew angry with herself. She was a master at blending in—and yet she felt overwhelmed by the task of playing his concubine. Whenever he spoke to her, he would bend to whisper into her ear. She could feel his warm breath stir the curls on her neck.

Once, his lip touched the shell of her ear, and she almost flinched at the intimacy, but was determined not to show weakness. She had to accept the way his hand caressed the length of her arm as if to soothe her.

At last they finished their meal. The tavern owner showed sincere regret at their departure, especially after Paul, on being told their bill, handed over his purse as if it seemed too much effort to count, offering to pay for drinks for their fellow revelers. Tankards of ale were raised in cheers and toasts as they left. Their return journey to the north side of the Thames was far less crowded, now that encroaching darkness lingered in the air. Lanterns were lit along the bridge and through the streets, guiding their way.

Timothy procured them lodgings at a four-story inn overlooking the river, with balconies wrapping around a central courtyard. At last, Juliana was ensconced in one of the private bedchambers, knowing that fellow Bladesmen would sleep in the lodgings on either side. Briefly, she was alone, reveling in the near silence. Of course, she could still hear voices echoing from the courtyard below, the neigh of horses in the stable yards, the cheerfully obnoxious calls of inebriated men.

The bedchamber was cozy, with no fire in the hearth, for it was a warm night. There was a table and chairs, a massive bed, and a screen for privacy—which pleased her, considering she'd have to change here. As she hung her cloak on a peg protruding from the wall, she would not worry about the coming night; she did not think Paul meant to abuse her trust.

Yet, for a woman who'd spent the last few years surrounded by men, she felt . . . nervous, uneasy, floundering in unknown territory. Most women her age were married with children already.

Then the door opened and Paul stood there, filling the chamber with his presence. She tried not to stare at him, even as he set down the pannier carrying their garments.

Rubbing his hands together, he looked about. "'Twill do, I imagine."

"As you know, we'll surely encounter worse the farther north we journey."

He nodded, but he was studying her now, as if he wasn't really hearing her words. She wished she had something to putter with, some task—except preparing for bed.

"I like your hair down," he said abruptly. "You shall wear it thus for the rest of our time together."

She glared at him.

Chapter 4

Paul enjoyed the outrage in her eyes, glad to provoke some reaction in her. She was usually so cool and composed, utterly focused in her confidence about the role she played. Gone was the young woman who'd once looked to him with such desperate awe, such eagerness to learn. And he found he missed her.

Surely a virgin would stutter or shy away from him now that they were alone. But she only flared with anger at his teasing.

"Do not assert your feminine rights," he said, raising both hands. "I simply thought your long hair made it clear you were yet an unmarried woman, so others would not think you my wife."

"You don't want people to even wonder about my place in your life?" she asked dryly.

"'Twill save time in the end," he assured her.

She let out her breath in a huff. "Very well."

There was a knock at the door, and Paul called, "Enter," in a commanding voice.

He saw Juliana's hand rest on her girdle, and wondered at the weapon she hid there. The League had molded her, made her into a Bladeswoman, taking away her natural femininity. She was serious about her role as his guard, he thought ruefully. But he, too, could quickly reach a blade if he needed one.

A round-shouldered maidservant bobbed a curtsy as she entered their lodgings carrying a stack of linens, followed by a valet burdened with a basin and steaming ewer. Paul handed out coins as they left, and saw Juliana watching him.

"Did I do something of which you disapprove?" he asked lightly.

"You are enjoying being so free with money not your own."

"I am free with my own purse as well. The service is always better." He gestured to the basin. "Would you care to wash first?"

Thanking him as easily as if she shared a bedchamber with a man every night, she carried the basin and ewer behind the changing screen, along with several garments she'd removed from their panniers.

Paul silently wished the screen gone. Though Juliana was playing his courtesan before others, she would certainly not act so brazen when they were alone together.

"Do you need help unlacing your gown?" he asked, testing her.

"Nay, thank you," she answered in an agreeable voice.

As if the indecent suggestion had not bothered her at all, he thought with curiosity. He couldn't help wondering about her, about her ease with men, with their assignment together. In the tavern, he'd been immersed in his part, enjoying himself to the hilt, while danger was yet distant in the north. Then he'd pulled her onto his lap, his arms suddenly full of willing woman, touching her as he wished. He hadn't been able to place the scent of her, exotic yet warmly intimate. When he'd been a teacher, he couldn't have imagined doing such a thing to a young woman under his care.

But their old relationship of teacher and student was gone, and a new one would have to take its place.

He could hear the faintest sound of her humming an unfamiliar tune and the splash of water as she prepared herself for the night. Even as he unpacked a clean shirt and breeches, he watched her gown appear, draped over the top of the screen.

And then she emerged in a silk dressing gown that skimmed her curves and hung to the floor. Her hair was pushed back over her shoulders, so that he could see the long elegance of her neck, her collarbones arching like the wings of a swan. She had wide shoulders for a woman, yet he found it incredibly attractive. She was no diminutive miss, with her height and strength, and *that* made him think too much about vigorous bed play. But perhaps she already knew all about that, considering what the League had assigned her to become.

He took his turn behind the screen, changing into a clean shirt and breeches for the night. When he emerged, he found her sitting in a chair before the bare hearth, combing out her long hair. She hadn't yet seen him, and he remained motionless, watching her.

He'd spent the majority of his life without women, and once he'd been released from the League, he'd learned about their pleasures with gusto. But his time with women was spent in bed, and he knew little of them beyond that. Of course a woman had to groom herself, but . . . how could such a simple thing as combing one's hair seem so alluring?

Surely it was because he hadn't eased himself with a woman since he'd been at his brother's these last two months. He'd been enjoying his reunion, and was hardly going to prowl London looking for a willing bedmate.

And now, here was Juliana, a woman of strength and skill, who obviously wanted to be treated as any other member of the League.

But her hair was simply beautiful.

She glanced up and saw him, and he waited for her to freeze, to blush, to appear awkward. She but gave him an absent smile, looked away, and continued combing, as if men watched her intimate rituals all the time.

"Is something wrong?" she asked.

And then he realized that when she played the concubine, she'd been using a lighter, more feminine tone. Her natural voice was deeper, huskier, and it made him think of a woman murmuring to him in the night. He was still too curious about her ease with this role, and he needed to distract himself.

"How many other men have you played concubine to, Juliana?"

She could have been offended; perhaps a virgin would be.

But she only continued to comb her hair as she arched a brow. "At least a half dozen."

Surely she was making a jest. But this was the League, and he of all people knew their ruthlessness. "So the League has been offering you to men now?"

She gave him a withering look. "Bladesmen are honorable; they would never expect such indecent things of me."

"You do not know them at all," he said quietly.

"Then explain them to me, Paul, since you have such experience."

She had the idealistic zeal of so many Bladesmen who believed the League could do no wrong. And he felt sorry for her.

He shook his head. "'Tis not my task to disillusion you. Stay with them long enough, and you will draw your own conclusions. Now since we'll have an early start in the morn, I'm going to bed."

She murmured some sort of acquiescence behind him.

He turned down the bed, which rested against the wall. "I'll sleep on the outside."

"Nay, allow me."

She'd come up behind him, her hair now plaited into a long braid.

He looked down at her in surprise. "I beg your pardon?"

"I should sleep nearer to the door."

He sank onto the edge of the bed, leaned back on his hands, and looked up at her, smiling lazily. "And why would you do that?"

"You know my position here, Paul. I am your personal guard. I take my responsibilities seriously."

He grinned, hiding his annoyance. "Are you saying that if a thief enters in the night, I'm supposed to stand back and allow you to defend me?"

"Of course. Someone might be testing your supposed lack of skill."

"And if I do not lie about it from the beginning, 'twill not be an issue."

Hands on her hips, she looked down at him with serious intent. "And then the traitors might believe you more of a threat to them. Sir Timothy's reasoning for your character is sound. You agreed to this."

"And you don't think anyone will be suspicious that my concubine is as skilled with weapons as any man?"

"I think it will only inspire mystery, and increase curiosity about me. But 'twill deflect suspicion from you. So move over."

He had thought she might suggest one of them sleep on the floor, and his relief that she hadn't made him put aside his annoyance. He slid beneath the coverlet, leaving an inviting space for her as he patted the mattress. "Come to bed, my fair concubine."

She arched a brow, but made no response to his teasing. To his disappointment, she didn't remove the belted dressing gown. He'd been looking forward to seeing her night rail a bit too much. She placed her sword beside the bed, then sat down to slide her legs beneath the coverlet, keeping her back to him. Momentarily, she braced herself on her elbow and blew out the candle. As his eyes adjusted, he realized that a torch on the balcony outside their window lent a faint glow to their chamber. He could see the gleam of her hair, the long slope of her hip and thigh beneath the thin summer-weight bedding.

He propped his head on his hand and looked down upon her. "You are not going to insist on marking your territory, placing some kind of barrier that I must not cross?"

Without looking at him, she said, "I trust you," then gave a loud yawn.

He wasn't sure he wanted to be trusted. And he liked her disregard of him even less. He rolled onto his back and stared at the beamed ceiling.

Juliana was far too tense from trying to pretend she *wasn't* tense. Her back began to ache from keeping herself so stiff. She was lying with a man in bed, and it felt awkward and strange and . . . exciting.

Always trying to be honest with herself, she could not deny that her senses were buzzing with Paul's nearness, her body alert and restless with an unexpected yearning to lean into him, feel his arms around her again as he'd done at the tavern. *This* was desire, this ache, this need. She'd been taught about it, warned to learn to control her own reactions, given methods to distract herself, but suddenly, her usual certainty wasn't all that certain. She hadn't imagined how it might *feel,* like an ache deep within her, a yearning to be within Paul's control. It was almost frightening, as if she had no will of her own.

There was a part of her that had worried she wasn't like other women, that she didn't have the same emotions. Now, at least that fear was gone.

Why did it have to be Paul who inspired this lust she didn't want? She'd lived alone with men for years now, and no one had ever made her feel this way. Once, a Bladesman had tried to force himself on her, but she'd felt nothing except disappointment in him and his behavior. It had been a vital discovery—the fact that she had to be so careful with men.

Paul had been so calm and controlled and respectful when she'd first arrived at the League that she'd let down her guard where men were concerned. He'd given her the time she'd needed to recover from the tragedy of her parents' deaths. But that had made her grow to depend on him so much that when he'd gone, with little warning, she'd felt almost . . . betrayed. But apparently, those feelings didn't matter to her weak-willed body.

This was her first crucial mission, one where she played a major part—her first as a concubine, regardless of the way she'd taunted him. She couldn't afford to be distracted like this, refused to be a pathetic woman who could not control herself with a man.

When at last she heard Paul's breathing settle into a regular pattern, she forced herself to relax, using techniques to clear her mind, to loosen her muscles. Yet, every time he made a movement in his sleep, her drowsiness evaporated and alertness gripped her.

How was she going to do this night after night?

She was still exhausted when her eyes flew open early in the morn at the sound of a knock. Without thought, she sat up and put one hand behind her to make sure Paul was where she could protect him, and with the other, reached for her sword.

"Sir Paul?" said Michael's voice from behind the closed door.

Releasing her breath, she let the sword go and looked back at Paul, who glanced down at her hand on his chest before giving her a curious stare that drifted down her body.

She realized her dressing gown had parted, revealing a concubine's night rail, embroidered and laced. Striving for calmness, she lifted her hand from him and closed her dressing gown. Just then, Michael opened the door.

He came up short, eyes betraying a hint of surprise before his brows lowered in a frown. Juliana felt a hot sense of embarrassment, but she didn't allow it to show. This was her assignment, she thought indignantly. No one was asking Michael to sleep beside a stranger to whom he wasn't married.

"Can you be ready within an hour of the clock?" Michael asked impassively.

"We will," Juliana said with firmness. She didn't look back at Paul, still too close to her in bed.

"We will meet here," Michael said, then shut the door.

She briefly closed her eyes, remembering his disapproval.

"His manner wasn't directed toward you," Paul said.

She looked over her shoulder in surprise. The tie at his gathered neckline had come loose, and she saw more of his chest than she would have liked. Of course she had seen many a bare chest, but certainly not in her bed. His hair was unkempt from sleep, and there was a crease on his cheek from the cushion. It almost softened her attitude toward him.

"I don't know what Michael expected—" she began.

He interrupted. "He is concerned that I will take advantage of you. I imagine you are like a sister to the Bladesmen."

"You once considered me as such," she said with regret.

He leaned closer. "Nay, I never thought that."

They shared another of those intense moments that were so inexplicable to her, where she felt his gaze as almost a touch upon her skin.

She cleared her throat. "Then I was your pupil."

"You were."

"Just another recruit?"

He hesitated. "Nay, I would not say that."

It was on the tip of her tongue to ask him to explain, but she stopped herself. She didn't want to know what he'd thought of her then. The mission was all that mattered.

He murmured, "Are you going to rise, or shall I be forced to stay in bed all day?"

She rolled her eyes even as she slid her feet onto the rush-strewn floor. As she sorted through her garments, choosing an appropriate gown for travel, Paul pulled on a tunic and his boots.

"I should have bathed last night," she muttered to herself, hands on hips. "Who knows where we shall find ourselves tonight?"

"You were distracted. I am not easy to ignore."

"You may create any fantasy you wish, Paul, if it keeps you amused."

Shaking his head, he put both hands up in retreat, saying, "I shall grant you privacy to prepare yourself."

She blinked in surprise. "You should not do that. You cannot be alone."

"'Tis early in our mission yet, my little guardian. No one will care enough to threaten me. Although when Michael arrived, I thought you were going to defend my presence in your bed with your sword."

"I am only fulfilling my duties," she said mildly, turning away. "See that you take a Bladesman with you if you leave the courtyard."

"Aye, mistress."

When he was gone, she braced both hands on the table for a moment, closing her eyes. She wanted to be angry with him, to keep her distance, to remember how little she could fathom his ingratitude toward the League. But he . . . intrigued her, even occasionally amused her.

When he wasn't offending her.

How many times had she been a concubine, indeed. She told herself it was a testament to her acting skills that he would ask such a question.

But what was he truly thinking? She had to discourage this easy playfulness of his. He was bored and restless in this assignment, anxious to be done so that he could be on his own again. He wasn't a man who wanted permanence of any sort—and neither did she.

After a valet came with water, she quickly washed and dressed for the day's journey. Paul returned before the rest of the Bladesmen, hair and skin damp. He ducked behind the screen and soon emerged as a pampered, wealthy man; even his traveling cloak was of the finest fabric.

And then the other Bladesmen arrived, crowding into their chamber. She liked the feeling of being among men, the camaraderie, the easy way of their conversation. Old Roger gave her a wink as if it were a call of good morning. Some of the others nodded and looked away too quickly. She felt a moment's unease, wondering if Michael had said something about her, but then she banished it. He would not be so dishonorable.

Their meeting was brief, as Timothy quietly said he'd had confirmation that word of Paul's arrival in London had gone north with messengers. The first part of their plan had been a success. And then when he was seen to leave London quickly, many would wonder about his intentions.

Timothy looked at Paul, who lounged against the door with lazy elegance. "Your work in the tavern yesterday eve had the correct spirit."

Paul's nod was his only acknowledgment of the compliment. Juliana watched him with curiosity, then looked back at Timothy, who met her gaze.

"Juliana, do you have any concerns so far?"

"Only one, sir. Am I to play my part throughout the journey, or only when we're in public?"

"On the journey as well. We shall take no chances."

As they rode through London, the overcast day grew occasionally misty, not enough to soak through Juliana's garments, but enough to be uncomfortable. By the time they reached the countryside, the rain was coming down in earnest. Old Roger took the first duty as scurrier, roving ahead of their party to check for problems down the road. Michael fell back to guard their rear.

The road had briefly narrowed as they forded a small stream, and to her surprise, when they'd paired up again, Timothy chose to ride at her side. She saw Paul pull up, his expression unreadable even as he slid into line beside Theobald, who guarded her back.

"And how are you, Juliana?" Timothy asked softly.

His look of concern made her uneasy. "Well, sir. Do I seem otherwise to you?"

"Now, now, you do not need to be defensive with me. 'Tis my duty to be watchful of my young Bladesmen—and Bladeswomen."

But he wasn't asking anyone else how they were coping.

Timothy glanced up at the sky from beneath his hood, eyes narrowing as the rain lightly splashed his face. She waited patiently, knowing he was trying to find a way to say something he considered important.

"You did not take offense at Paul's behavior in the tavern?" he finally asked.

She glanced at him in surprise. "Behavior, sir? I felt he was playing the part of his character well. Why should I have cause to complain?"

"Do not misunderstand me, Juliana. You have never been one who complains. But . . . this is a new situation for you."

"And I will meet it as I do all others, to the best of my ability."

"Even sharing a bed?" he asked.

"And what else did Michael say?" She kept her tone impassive.

"I knew how this would look, Juliana. I knew the risks you would be taking, closest to Paul in any danger, the last guard before an assassin can reach him."

That mollified her. "'Tis important that we give no one cause to think Paul not what he seems. I will not risk that."

"There are not many who would be as dedicated as you."

"Timothy, I mean not to sound defensive, but we're all taking the same risk. I simply happen to be a woman. But I am not your daughter, and you do not need to worry about me. I made my decision to accept this assignment to protect the Crown. 'Tis an honor, regardless of what I have to do."

He smiled at her, shaking his head. "'Tis a difficult lot you face, always being with men who try to protect you."

"As long as we all protect each other, then I will be content."

Riding behind Juliana, Paul could not hear the conversation she was having with Timothy. It was just as well. The countryside was a gray blur in the rain, fields separated by hedgerows, the occasional village clustered about a stream in the distance.

He felt solitary, even among the Bladesmen. There was always a faint sense of distance, for they knew he was reluctant to be with them, reluctant about the League. They could not befriend him if they wanted to, for that was not their role.

Surprisingly, Theobald was the easiest companion. There was no sense of condemnation or disapproval. With his mask a part of him, he was a man at ease with himself and his place in life.

Paul had thought the same of himself until he'd returned to England and realized how much he'd missed his brothers, the only family he'd ever known. He had thought he would return directly to France when this was over, but now didn't know.

It was a long, damp day, and they were all glad to reach an inn that night in Ware, instead of camping in the open. A valet started a fire when he showed them to their lodgings, and if the room was smaller, including the bed, it did not matter.

He and Juliana took off their wet cloaks, then stood side by side before the fire, letting the heat sink in to their damp clothing. She gave a little shudder, rubbing her hands together.

"We need to get out of these garments," he said.

And then he realized there was no changing screen, and saw that she did, too.

"I have to speak to Timothy," he said.

She eyed him. "You are being too gentlemanly for a man who is supposed to be vain and self-important."

"Are you talking about the real Sir Paul?"

She smiled then, something he'd seen little of since their taunting of each other just two days before.

"I am trapped here regardless of your behavior," she said.

He wanted to tease her, but he'd watched her too much today. "You never complain, do you?" he said.

Her smile faded. "You expected me to?"

"Nay, not you. I knew your bravery from the moment we met. You chose the League, when by now you could have been married with your own family, regardless of the death of your parents." It was all he'd known of her past. He'd been warned that she was an orphan, that it would hurt her to speak of it. "Surely there is someone you can return to, some way to escape their hold on you. You are practically their prisoner."

"Their prisoner?" she echoed wryly. "Paul, you make it sound like the worst of prisons to be one of the League. But they saved me when everyone else refused to take me in."

"Refused—" He broke off. This was a part of her story he'd never heard before. He felt the need to go forward gently, to find a truth about her background that made her so willing to be loyal, to live a life unlike other women. "Why would anyone refuse to shelter you? Your parents had just died."

She turned back to the flames, her dark eyes flickering with the light. "You do not understand," she said softly. "No one would take me in, but for the League. My father had been accused of treason."

Paul felt the first stirrings of uneasiness, of recognition. "Treason?"

"He was innocent, but the king's men arrested him anyway. He died in the Tower before even being brought to trial. Another prisoner took his life."

"So he was never cleared," Paul said slowly, his mind whirling with the truth of it.

"But I *know* he was innocent. I knew everything about him, and although we'd grown apart as I'd matured, that had nothing to do with my understanding of his loyalty. Grief over his arrest nearly destroyed my mother; I had a difficult time even making her eat or sleep, as if she couldn't even care for herself. When she heard of his death, I thought her weakened heart gave up rather than go on."

Leaving her only child alone, Paul thought in bitterness.

"I cannot blame my mother's relatives for refusing us—we were a scandal, outcasts. And then I was alone, soon to be destitute. The League *found* me, Paul," she said, looking up at him with shining eyes. "They saved me from a life of poverty, gave me a purpose when no one else would bother with me, when I was a burden on our servants, who wanted to risk themselves to keep me safe."

She didn't know the truth, he thought, feeling dazed.

"I am doing more with my life than I ever thought

possible. They *saved* me," she repeated, "and in return, I'm helping them save others. I do not understand how you can't see that."

He was now certain that he knew the story of her father—it was surely the same one he'd overheard the League discuss, just months after she arrived. That was why the League had taken her in—they'd ruined her father's life with a false accusation of treason, all to further another Bladesman's mission.

Chapter 5

Viscount Gresham, Paul remembered. The name of Juliana's father had been burned into his brain after he'd overheard the Council of Elders—and Timothy—discussing their regret that the man had suffered, that he'd died under a traitor's disgrace. Paul hadn't been able to remain with a League that used whatever methods necessary to further their cause. Aye, the king was saved, but the cost had been great—too great, he knew, looking into Juliana's cool eyes.

Timothy had been involved in the Gresham case, just as he'd handed over three orphaned brothers. Paul felt sick with anger and frustration. The king had taken everything away from Juliana's family—land, money, reputation—and the League had welcomed her to the fortress to hide their part in it. Now they were using her just as they'd used Paul and his brothers.

The League was all she had, and she was happy with them and proud of her accomplishments. She fully believed they'd given her purpose. It would destroy her to know what her supposed benefactors had done, how they'd assuaged their own guilt by housing her.

How could he tell her the truth? Or should it remain a secret, as the League obviously preferred? He would eventually have to make a decision. There was no one else who cared as much as he did—as Juliana did. King Edward was dead; there would be no repercussions if the truth came out about treason against him.

"I am not convincing you, am I?" she said with obvious regret.

"Convincing me of what?" He'd lost all track of their conversation.

"That I want to be here, that I see the goodness of the League. Why do you not? They took you in, the same as they did me. I always felt we had a bond because of that. They protected you."

He stalked away from her and pulled his damp tunic off over his head. "We were three small boys given no choice in the matter."

"But your parents had been murdered—you told me the murderer hadn't been caught. Who else could protect you so well?"

He thought of Timothy, and the foolish ache he used to feel when his foster father had to return to his real life, leaving them behind with the League.

"If it had simply been protection, I would have understood it better, but it wasn't."

"Then what was it, Paul?" she demanded. "Tell me."

He looked at her, at her damp, straggling hair, at the earnestness in her face, at her belief in the League's very goodness.

And he couldn't do it. He couldn't burden her with the truth, didn't want to see her dawning understanding, her pity. He hated pity.

He began to take his shirt off instead of answering. The linen stuck to his cold, damp flesh, and by the time he'd drawn it over his head, he caught her staring at his bare chest. Again, he waited for her blush, for a maidenly protest, but none were forthcoming.

Roughly, he said, "Turn your back, and I will change."

She did so, but said over her shoulder, "This is not finished, Paul. We will be together many weeks. You should talk to me."

"And speak of things that have nothing to do with our mission? I'm surprised at you, Juliana."

He stripped down to his braies, the thin, short undergarment about his hips. It felt very arousing to disrobe behind a woman he didn't plan to sleep with the same night. He was more and more convinced she wasn't an innocent, and that was another sin to lay at the League's door.

Yet, he could not regret her knowledge, the choices she'd made as an adult.

She stood near the table, where fresh linens had been

piled. He walked up behind her and reached past her shoulder, just brushing her with his arm. She didn't flinch, only glanced up at his face.

"I need a towel," he said softly.

"You are taking your time," she answered. "I am wet, too."

He paused, closing his eyes, savoring her words as if they meant something altogether different.

Though it pained him, he remained behind her back to dress. "I'll stand outside the door while you—"

"Nay, Paul."

She turned around while he was still shirtless, but to his regret, she kept her gaze on his face.

"We've left London. You must stay with me at all times."

He gave her a crooked smile. "All the time, Juliana?" He glanced pointedly at the closed chamber pot in the corner.

At last he'd coaxed a reaction out of her, as her face flamed red.

"Oh."

He went to the wall adjoining several of the Bladesmen. He rapped three times, paused, then did it once more.

"What are you doing?"

"I chatted with Joseph today, and he expressed his

concern about you. I suggested a system to give you privacy, and to give you peace about your assignment as well."

There was a knock on the door, and then Joseph leaned his head in. "You called, Sir Paul?"

"I'll be out in a moment."

After the door had shut, Juliana was watching him, a smile tugging the corners of her lips.

"Very thoughtful of you," she said. "I believe you are trying to win your way into my good graces."

Into your bed, he thought, then chastised himself. But he could torment himself by playing the lady's maid, if he couldn't seduce her. He caught her by the shoulders and turned her away from him. Gathering the thick mass of her hair in his hands, he draped it over her shoulder, out of his way.

"What—"

"Your laces are damp. Surely they will not be easy to untie."

She didn't even stiffen, simply stood there while he tugged at her garments, slowly pulling the laces apart, revealing the softness of her smock. It, too, was damp and clung to her. Every inch downward, her torso narrowed, and her spine curved inward, leading him slowly but surely toward the swell of her buttocks.

He reached the last of the laces, and he couldn't move,

though he told himself to. His hands spread out until he rested them on her waist. He could hear her breathing, even above his own heartbeat, which thundered in his chest, in his ears. His thumbs stroked her spine as he lowered his head. He could smell the damp sweetness of her skin at her bare neck. When he was but an inch from pressing a kiss to her flesh, forgetting himself, she suddenly stepped away from him.

"My thanks, Paul," she said, her voice showing no sign that he'd affected her at all. "I believe Joseph is waiting for you."

He was relieved to escape before doing something he'd regret.

When Paul had gone, Juliana's entire body sagged, shuddering, as she closed her eyes. Her skin still seemed to tingle, to hum, where he'd touched her.

What was wrong with her? Many men had touched her, adjusting her position with the bow, demonstrating grappling techniques. She'd rolled around on the ground with men, for God's sake. Yet . . . all Paul had to do was span her waist with his large hands, making her feel so delicate, so feminine, and she'd turned into mush.

She liked these feelings too much—and she despised herself for them. Having always thought of herself as a strong person, mere days with Paul were showing her otherwise.

She was forced to gather herself together when someone knocked on the door, but didn't identify themselves in the League manner. She slid her dagger out of her boot, and positioned herself against the wall, calling, "Aye, who goes there?"

A woman's voice said, "Servants, milady, with the bath yer lordship ordered."

They hadn't used titles, but Paul's very demeanor made all think him of the nobility. And now he was proving himself a thoughtful gentleman—for show or in reality? She didn't know or care.

"Enter."

She remained near to the door, the dagger hidden in her skirts, her unlaced back against the wall. Carrying two steaming buckets, a woman entered first, and two valets came behind, with a padded, wooden bathing tub between them. Juliana relaxed her tense stance and tried not to stare greedily at the tub. They made two more trips with water and clean linens, and then she was alone, stripping her garments off and sinking into the unbearably hot water.

It was delicious, stinging and cleansing all at once. She groaned aloud, closing her eyes, wishing she could submerge herself all the way, but the tub was too small for that. And she couldn't afford to take her time, either, for Paul would return soon enough.

She silently blessed him while she scrubbed the day's travel from her body. After lathering the soft soap into her hair, she stood up and poured the last bucket of fresh water over her head, letting it sluice away all the soap. Regretfully, she stepped out of the tub and dried herself with the linens, donning a fresh night rail and the dressing gown. Soon her dirty garments were laundered and hung on chairs before the fire. It wasn't a thorough cleaning, but it was better than washing them in a stream, as she might be doing soon enough. She even went through Paul's bags and washed his laundry, too.

When he returned, she smiled at him as he closed the door.

"Your thoughtfulness was appreciated," she said, from her place before the fire, where she combed through her hair to dry it.

"Selfishness, you mean." He set down the steaming bucket he'd carried in, then gave a shiver as he began to disrobe.

"But the water is filthy. I even used it for laundry."

"It will still do for a quick wash."

"But you're wealthy and arrogant. Simply send for more."

"I cannot do that. The wench's back looked bowed enough."

His thoughtfulness for a servant warmed her. And then she thought of him undressing and bathing right in front of her. She came to her feet, trying not to betray her concern by moving too quickly. "I'll dress and leave you to—"

"No need. Close your eyes if you wish."

Knowing she'd betray her nervousness and ignorance to him if she fled, she calmly sat back down, faced the fire, and resumed combing. She could hear his clothes hitting the floor, then the splash of water. He didn't sigh with pleasure as she had, but the water was barely warm by this point. At least he'd brought a fresh bucket to rinse with.

She tried to clear her mind, to calm herself and focus on nothing, but then she realized her fingers were trembling. What was she so worried about? He would hardly attack her.

"You did not need to wash my things as well," he said from just behind her.

She started to turn, saw too much bare flesh as he toweled himself, and then turned back to the fire. "'Twas not an imposition."

"So you're my servant in every way?"

"I imagine you wish so," she said dryly.

"You know men too well."

Not too well, nay, but she would not admit to that. And she didn't know *him* well, because she'd thought he might apologize for putting his hands on her with such familiarity, but he made no mention of it. And he wasn't the sort to let embarrassment render him mute.

Perhaps he wasn't sorry at all. Or perhaps it had been nothing to him, a tease, a way to fight boredom. The only thing she really knew of him was the kind of man she'd built him up to be in her youth. And that man had vanished. He was no saint, no great teacher, but a man without gratitude for what had been given him.

When she knew he was decently clothed, and her hair was dry, she plaited it, then went to bed, setting her weapons carefully on the floor nearby.

"Cover yourself against the chill," he said. "I shall be there soon."

Again keeping her dressing gown on, she lay down. He hadn't donned a shirt, she realized with a start—she'd been so busy trying not to look at him. Keeping her eyes closed proved too difficult, so at last, with great reluctance, she opened them enough so that she could look between her lashes. He was laying out his weapons, wiping them one by one. His blond hair was drying in random waves, as if he'd only run his fingers through and nothing more.

She still couldn't believe she'd told him of her father's sentence of treason. Since her arrival with the League, and their assurances that her past didn't matter to them, she hadn't spoken of her parents. She'd banished them from her mind, for the memories only brought sadness and confusion and guilt.

But she'd told Paul. Why?

Perhaps because she'd wanted to shock him, to show him that he should stop talking about the outside world as if she had a place to go there. Or had she wanted to remind him of the goodness of the League?

But he hadn't returned her honesty, had stopped himself from talking about his past. He'd claimed the League had wanted more than to simply protect three little boys, but wouldn't explain further. It was a mystery that intrigued her too much.

Perhaps he was the wise one, holding back, trying to keep his distance from her. This was an assignment, after all.

But then he'd touched her. She quivered as if she could still feel the way his thumbs had caressed the base of her spine. But she knew men, knew that copulating with women was something they did with ease, without attachment or emotion. And she was convenient to him.

She should keep her distance, as he did. If only his secrets didn't call to her . . .

At last he reached for a shirt, and she opened her eyes wide so she could drink in the sight of his body moving, the play of muscles in his back, the way the firelight flickered across his skin. She caught sight of several scars, evidence of a hard-fought life.

So much for keeping an emotional distance, she thought with a sigh, then realized she'd been too loud.

He glanced at her. "Forgive me for keeping you awake."

"Nay, you àre not." She used the first excuse she could think of. "I am simply still chilled, and hoping that tomorrow's dawn shows the sun."

"Perhaps I should warm the bed."

She stiffened, then once again calmed herself. He couldn't know how he affected her. The fire lit him from behind as he approached her. She went to sit up, but he put a hand on her shoulder.

"No need."

He knelt on the edge of the bed, sinking her against him, then crawled right over the top of her. She inhaled without too obvious a gasp, holding still as she felt the heat of him, the brush of his loose shirt across her hands, the insides of his thighs against her hips. And then he was on his own side, and she forced herself to breathe.

"A good night to you, my duckling."

Taking an unsteady breath, she said, "Can you at least come up with a better term of endearment?"

"I like it. A man wouldn't call his concubine his love."

"As I did to you."

"Ah, but you only showed your devotion to me."

She didn't like his satisfaction, as if her words had been real. "You mean my supposed devotion to your money. Without that, you certainly do not have enough to attract a woman such as me."

"In truth?" His voice was deep and husky, suddenly intrigued.

She realized she'd practically challenged him.

"Paul, you know what I mean," she said, her voice firm and cool. "My character, the worldly concubine."

There was a moment of silence between them, where she lay still on her back and barely kept from retreating to the edge of the bed. She was beginning to be afraid of her attraction to him. After spending these last few years learning the peace and satisfaction of controlling herself and her emotions, she didn't want to throw it all away lusting after a man who would be gone from her life in but weeks.

Yet her skin twitched as she waited for him to touch her, to—

He suddenly chuckled. "My worldly concubine, you need to sleep and think of better ways to flatter your man."

She closed her eyes, her breath leaving her lungs in a long, slow exhale of relief.

And disappointment.

A thump against the wall woke Paul later that same night. A Bladesman stood guard in the corridor, and no one had come inside the bedchamber, but . . . something was wrong. He took a moment to listen, ears straining, eyes seeking in the gloom of the nearly dark chamber. He sat up, only to find that Juliana was already crouched beside the bed, reaching for her dagger.

Trying to protect him already? he wondered.

She glanced over her shoulder at him, gestured with her head, and crept toward the door, her dressing gown billowing about her swiftly moving feet. He followed, but before he could take the lead nearest the door latch, she placed herself there.

Stepping swiftly, he reached for the latch. She batted his hand away, her gaze narrowed fiercely at him. Staying in the character of a weak prince, letting someone else protect him, was far harder than he'd imagined it would be. Although he felt his teeth grinding together, he put his back against the wall on the other side of the door and watched her.

Another thump sounded from the corridor, this time closer. Their gazes met, even as she carefully raised the door latch and eased the door open. She was cautious and correct in her technique, eyes sweeping as the opening door revealed more and more of the corridor. But he felt tense waiting for something to happen—to happen to her.

And then she threw the door wide and darted into the corridor. Paul followed. He caught a glimpse of a man struggling in old Roger's arms, only a moment before Juliana used the hilt of her dagger to render him unconscious.

As the intruder sagged, Roger bent and hoisted him over his shoulder.

"There's no one else?" Juliana whispered.

Roger shook his head. "The man was outraged at a threat to his king and the hard-earned peace of his country."

"Drunk," Paul said.

"Nay, though at first I believed the same. He was serious in his affront. Didn't want to have to kill him. I'll keep him well hidden and trussed up until we leave. You have my thanks, mistress."

"Do you need help carrying him?" Juliana asked.

"I think he can manage without you," Paul said dryly, tugging her arm.

She stiffened, her eyes going cool as she looked at him.

Though Paul was confused at her reaction, he ignored it to say, "We should retreat before anyone else notices."

In the near darkness of their bedchamber, Juliana calmly hid her dagger and climbed back into bed.

He studied her, sensing her shift in mood, feeling like he was missing something. But pressing her would accomplish nothing.

"Well done," he said quietly.

"I am certain you think you could have done better."

"I did not say so."

"You did not have to."

Feeling confused and wary, as if battling an opponent with words rather than weapons, Paul carefully crossed the bed, trying not to touch her, sensing that that would make everything worse.

Chapter 6

The morning did not improve Juliana's sense of balance. Before Paul dressed himself, he insisted on helping her pick out her gown. Perhaps he didn't think a woman could even pick out her own clothing, she thought, still feeling irritated about his behavior during the night while she'd been performing her duty, protecting him. He'd made it far too clear that he felt *he* should be protecting *her*, not the other way around. More than once in her short career, men had openly questioned whether a woman could be trusted in a position of authority. She just hadn't wanted to believe that a man who'd briefly trained her could feel the same way.

And now he was meddling in her clothing!

"I will be wearing a cloak. 'Twill not matter what I wear," she insisted stiffly.

"The sun will soon be up, and the sky bodes a clear day. You will be seen by many."

She watched, her teeth gritted, as he laid out three

gowns he hadn't seen. She felt invaded as his rough hands touched her delicate things.

"The bodice on the pink gown is far superior to the green," he said.

She ignored him, packing away her damp laundry, knowing she would have to lay it out again that night.

"It shows a daring hint of cleavage, but the obvious wealth and craftsmanship of the gown gives it enough refinement. Of course, the waistline of the green gown does flatter you more than the yellow."

"And why is that?" she asked with studied indifference, as she checked the edge of her blade before sliding it into her boot.

"This really means nothing to you, does it?" he asked at last.

"Nay, not a bit. The gowns are lovely, they all mark me as a wealthy concubine. 'Tis enough for me."

"Do you ever even wear gowns?"

She glanced at him. "Never, except on assignments." Perhaps her dearth of femininity was a way to make him keep his distance.

"Because you never see other women."

"And neither did you," she said thoughtfully. "Surely as a young man, that must have been difficult. Or did you take journeys away from the League fortress?"

He turned away, folding up every gown but the pink one with its fine bodice.

She'd struck deep, she realized with interest. "You did not, did you? Did you even know about women?"

"Of course I did," he answered almost crossly.

She held back her triumph at bothering him the way he so easily bothered her.

"Was I the first woman you saw—nay, wait, you'd already been on missions before I arrived."

"Robert saw a woman before I did."

He took off the shirt he'd slept in, a deliberate attempt to distract her from what he obviously wished he hadn't said.

She approached him, interested in his faint touch of wariness. "How did Robert see a woman? Did one arrive at the Castle, lost in the mountains?"

"You have a vivid imagination. As some boys do, Robert simply ran away."

"Ran away?" she echoed.

He unlaced his breeches, lowered them a bit with his thumbs, until she could see his hipbones, which framed the ridges of his abdomen. She refused to back down and turn away.

He sighed. "He simply wanted to meet girls. Adam was sent to retrieve him. Robert was quite excited to have kissed a dairymaid before he was captured."

"Surely you made him tell you all about it," she teased.

Did his face actually turn a bit red? Her good humor was beginning to feel restored.

He lowered the breeches even more, until she glimpsed a scrap of linen, and even more dark blond hair. She turned around at last, feeling a bit too breathless.

"You could ask me to give you some privacy," she said crossly.

"And you could realize when I need it."

"But what I most realize is your embarrassment. You do not need to feel so, Paul, especially not with me. I know how you were raised. Young men are drawn rather obsessively to girls."

"Obsessively, is it? What a choice in words. Did someone obsess over you?"

She suddenly remembered the Bladesman maneuvering her into a dark corridor, and the way she'd let him know with her fists that she wanted him to stop. The incident had changed all of her training.

She laughed lightly. "Obsess over me? The girl in breeches? Nay. But I live with men, Paul, and I do not idealize your sex." She didn't risk facing him, but did cock her head with exaggeration. "Hmm, so you never saw women. At all. You did tell me of the concern that your parents' murderer was looking for Keswick's heirs. So of course, they kept you well protected. But you never walked through a village when you were young? After all, who would have known your face?"

He didn't answer, and she risked a glance over her

shoulder to find him sitting on the edge of the bed, pulling on his boots.

"How did you feel the first time you saw a woman?" she asked. "What did you do?"

He set down his foot and looked at her for a moment. "Do you want the truth?"

"I do."

"The girl I first saw seemed like a magical creature, all soft, pretty hair and a secretive smile."

She couldn't stop staring at him, at his broad shoulders and long arms as he leaned back on the bed they'd just shared.

"And then she invited me to her bed."

Her smile faded and she blinked at him. "Just like that?" she asked with dismay. No wonder he had such a bad impression of women, and what feats they were capable of.

"Just like that."

"You must have been quite the young pup, all desperate and needy."

He laughed rather than take offense.

"And being a man, you did not resist," she continued.

"Nay, I did not. She taught me everything I needed to know to please her."

Juliana spoke without thinking. "But did not the League teach you that?"

His eyes widened. "They taught you about intimacy?"

She wanted to refuse to discuss her foolish outburst, but that would only make him more interested. All she did was laugh. "Wouldn't you simply love to imagine that?"

He narrowed his eyes, but when he said nothing more, she almost sighed her relief. Someone knocked on the door, and she quickly went to lift her bag.

He took it from her. "Let the servants do that."

And he was correct, of course.

As they left Ware, she could not stop wondering about the mysteries surrounding his childhood. He'd had but two years when his parents had died. No one would have recognized him a few years later. He should have been free to learn about the world, to be with people, even if only occasionally.

But the League had kept the three Hilliard boys isolated, alone. Reluctantly, she began to see that that might make a man like Paul long to see more of the world.

After a morning spent sloshing through mud and avoiding holes, they lined up in single file to cross a small wooden bridge. On the far side, she reigned in her horse until Timothy caught up to her.

He eyed her, his expression concerned. "Roger told me what happened in the night, and that you performed well."

"He had the situation well in hand. I did little."

"'Tis only the beginning, where danger is concerned. Men both for and against the king will have reason to want Paul dead. Satisfied am I that he has you at his side."

"At least *someone* feels that way," she murmured, shaking her head.

"Your pardon?" he asked, watching her too carefully.

"Nothing, sir."

They rode on side by side, letting the motion of the horses lull them both. She glanced at Timothy when at last he took a deep, satisfied breath of the country air.

"'Tis a good thing the weather seems clear today," he said, "because we will make camp this night. Our position will be far more precarious than within the walls of an inn."

"We will keep careful watch," she said firmly.

He nodded as if he expected nothing else.

She hesitated, then spoke her mind. "Timothy, Paul told me a story today, but I cannot believe it true."

"One never knows with Paul," he said, shaking his head.

She squinted into the sun as she glanced at him. "He said Robert ran away to see a girl."

He shrugged good-naturedly. "Boys will be boys."

"I received the distinct impression that Robert—and his brothers—had never seen a girl before that."

Timothy's smile faded to one of faint melancholy.

"You know I cannot discuss a Bladesman's past, Juliana."

"But . . . why would he have never seen a girl? It simply doesn't make sense. Unless he was never permitted to leave the fortress. And I do understand the threat of death they were under, but . . ."

She let her voice trail off.

Timothy sighed. "Paul did not discuss it with you?"

"Not the reasons, nay."

"He knows the League rules."

And she had not followed them, for she'd told Paul of her past, felt compelled to, as if she needed him to know the truth. Had she been trying to drive him away, make him wary of being associated with her? His reaction had been to take off his clothes, deliberately forcing *her* away.

It was all such a puzzle, the way they played games to distract each other. But she wouldn't forget, and would do all she could to discover the truth. She couldn't explain why she felt this way, wouldn't look at it too closely. But the need to uncover his secrets was like an itch she had to scratch.

They stopped for the midday meal at a village crossroads. Still mounted, Paul watched cows graze the village green nearby, while he awaited Timothy's preparations. Many men lingered outside the tavern on benches, eyeing them with unabashed interest.

To Juliana, Paul said, idly, loudly, "Another village tavern. Rather small and plain, is it not, my little duckling?"

She dismounted and went to him, leaning against his leg to look up at him. "It is, my love, but that cannot be helped. This is not Paris."

"Ah, Paris," he murmured, staring off into the distance. He could see that he'd aroused some interest as well as disdain. "Do you remember that romantic boat ride we took down the Seine? I do believe you danced for me that night, a pale Aphrodite in the moonlight."

He saw the way the men now looked with lascivious interest at Juliana, but it couldn't be helped. It had to be apparent what kind of woman she was from the beginning.

Timothy ducked as he emerged from the tavern doorway, then led them inside, leaving Joseph to care for the horses. Theobald stayed near Juliana, hand on the sword hilt at his waist. Most of the Bladesmen had to duck to enter, and Paul saw that even Juliana almost grazed the door lintel. Vegetables hung on strings along various beams, as well as a ham. A large table had been cleared for them in the rear, and they had to pass down a narrow aisle between several crude tables.

Paul tossed his cloak back from his shoulders, letting the villagers see his doublet embroidered with gold threads. He was bigger and broader than most of the men, and he knew his fair coloring stood out.

Soon they were seated, with the tavern's specialty of mutton pie with chunks of meat and vegetables steaming before them.

Paul didn't find it too difficult to make a nuisance of himself. He asked for wine they couldn't possibly have, patted the backside of every maidservant that went by, and laughed too loudly at Juliana's display of cool anger. He chatted with farmers and peddlers and met with success when he learned that the local lord's son was dining as well. The man had long since seen his first tournament, and he watched Paul with speculation.

Paul made a point of asking about the countryside, and how far it was to York, where he had vague memories from his youth. Timothy and old Roger exchanged obvious looks of discomfort at his chattiness, but it was all part of the charade.

Michael was overly obvious as he pushed Juliana against Paul's side as if to distract him. She smiled up at Paul, leaning her breasts against his arm in a way that was a bit *too* distracting. Slipping an arm about her, he drew her even tighter against him until she was forced to brace her hand on his thigh or fall across his chest.

He leaned down toward her face, and he saw the awareness in her eyes, the moment when she thought he would kiss her. Instead he nuzzled his face against her neck as she gave a belated giggle.

"Next time," he whispered.

Her fingernails dug into his thigh.

After pressing a kiss to her cheek, he brought her hand to his lips.

"Seems as if you need to persuade the wench," the lord's son said, laughing.

"She comes to my bed quite willingly." Paul grinned down at her before returning his attention to the self-important man. "I found her in Paris, where her protector had left her when he tired of her."

"I tired of *him*," Juliana corrected, her voice sweet with certainty.

"And after our first night in bed, I even believed you, my little duckling," Paul said, chuckling.

Several of the other men joined him, openly admiring Juliana. Paul had been right about the gown—it did amazing things to her breasts. Not that her breasts needed help . . .

"What were you doing in that foreign city, sir?" the lordling asked.

Timothy gave him an open frown, and the other Bladesmen glanced at each other, shifting uneasily. Paul pretended not to notice.

"I was raised here and there on the continent," he said brightly. "A varied childhood. And now I've come home."

"And where is home?"

"Ye're an inquisitive lad," Timothy said in an unfriendly voice.

"I meant no harm." The lordling raised both hands in appeasement.

Paul didn't hide the glare he aimed at Timothy, then concentrated on his mutton pie, stopping now and again to feed a particularly tasty piece to Juliana with his fingers. She giggled and leaned in to him. Her eyes knowing, she teased him by nipping his finger, then drawing the tip into her mouth.

Paul felt his breath catch at how suddenly she aroused him. Did she know what she did? How could she not? Her hand still rested on his thigh, her breasts pressed into his chest, and her long, black hair draped across his arm where it embraced her back.

He was almost glad they were not remaining in the village for the night. He wasn't sure what he might do to learn what else she knew about pleasuring men. Though he'd teased her that morn, he couldn't imagine the League training her in something so intimate. So that could only mean she'd had much practice with those full lips.

It had worked, Juliana thought, when at last they were away from the tavern and traveling north on roads that grew ever more uneven.

She glanced at Paul, but he was staring straight

ahead, his eyes focused in the distance, his expression unreadable.

She'd put her mouth on his fingers, and any attempt to tease her seemed to totally flee his mind, as if he could no longer even think.

She'd been warned that men could lose the very ability to reason because of sexual thoughts, but she hadn't imagined Paul to be susceptible. Yet he was. She could still remember the way his gaze had focused on her mouth, his thigh tightening beneath her hand.

It had proven most illuminating.

But she'd also noticed that the encounter had not left her unaffected. She'd felt strangely alert, her senses heightened, her lower stomach gripped with a strange trembling that had been far too pleasurable. Desire again, a very powerful force that could also work its will on her. She couldn't allow that. Knowledge was power, and she had that in abundance. It would keep her safe.

As the sun began its slow descent, Juliana unhooked her bow from the saddle and loosely strung an arrow. Her eyes scanned the fields, and when she spotted a rabbit, she stood in the saddle, knees bent to absorb the motion of the horse, and made her first kill.

Paul, who yet rode at her side, clapped approvingly. "She even provides the meal. What a valuable woman."

"I earn my keep," she answered lightly.

Joseph and Michael shared a smile as Theobald

fetched the carcass. Old Roger pointed out another rabbit to her, and soon she made another kill. After they established their encampment in a clearing beside a stream, some distance from the road, she offered to prepare the rabbits, but that, Timothy didn't allow.

"Not something a woman of your . . . a woman like you would lower herself to do," he said, correcting himself mid-sentence.

"A woman of my—what?" she called back, laughing, from where she stood directing the raising of Paul's pavilion. Now if Paul would have said the same thing, she'd have bristled. But then she knew what he thought of women.

Paul himself caught her from behind, his arm about her waist as he pressed her back against him. "A woman of your arrogant charms."

With her elbow, she struck him hard in the stomach, and he bent over with a "whoosh," hitting his chin on her shoulder.

She smoothly stepped away from him. "Oh, dear, I do believe I lost focus of my character momentarily. What a relief that no strangers witnessed it. 'Twill not happen again."

Michael laughed aloud, and even Theobald couldn't hide a begrudging smile.

Only Timothy did not smile, looking from her to Paul with bemusement.

After sunset, Juliana sat daintily upon a blanket-draped log, watching the men bustle about preparing supper. One could become used to such service, she thought wryly. Her two rabbits were spitted over the fire, which hissed with each droplet of grease. Theobald served her, looking mysterious with the open side of his face lit by fire, the mask dark with the night shadows.

As they all sat eating, Joseph assessed Paul. "Sir Paul, tell us of your adventures in Europe."

Juliana glanced at Timothy, but he did not interrupt, watching Paul along with all the others.

Paul, sitting beside her on the log, tossed a bone into the fire, and looked around at the Bladesmen, his face lit with amusement. "One tournament is like another, boys. How could such stories interest you?"

Michael eyed him. "I guess we want to know what could lure you from a duty you'd sworn yourself to."

Smiles died, and Juliana watched Paul's face, which remained pleasant as he softly said, "I swore no vow, Michael, not like you did."

Michael frowned and looked to Timothy, whose lined face showed weariness and regret. Juliana felt just as confused. Paul was a Bladesman—he'd been her teacher, had gone on dangerous assignments for the League. What did he mean? But evidently Paul wasn't going to explain.

"Going to Europe alone presented a new challenge

for me, one I relished," he continued, elbows on his thighs, hands linked as he stared into the fire. "I knew the languages, of course, having been well trained, but I felt a great need to prove myself, to earn my way."

Michael opened his mouth as if to protest something, but Juliana saw Timothy shake his head. Michael knew Paul's true identity, something not usually permitted with Bladesmen.

"You've much skill, lad," old Roger said with obvious admiration. "Surely you showed those Normans a thing or two."

More than one man grinned, then seemed to remember themselves and look a bit guilty.

"I couldn't show them everything I knew," Paul said, "not without having to answer for my unusual training. But . . . I could make things look like an accident."

Joseph chuckled. "A sound technique. So you won?"

"Every tournament I entered. The purses were plentiful, the ladies full of admiration, the men indignant but intrigued. I never lacked for sparring partners, or a bed at night."

She imagined his bed well warmed by these admiring women, but didn't say so.

"An arrogant count did not believe I came from England. He claimed no Englishman fought as I did, that I must be lying to him. I found myself imprisoned until I would offer up the truth."

All the men were interested, Timothy avidly so, as if he could not hear enough about his absent foster son. She felt sorry for him, knowing that Paul did not return his depth of feelings.

Michael kept his back turned, tending the fire and roasted rabbits, but even he seemed alert.

"So what happened?" Joseph demanded.

"Torture?" Michael asked dryly.

Paul grinned. "Nay, it did not come to that. When next they returned for me in my jail built into a cliff, I had escaped. I believe I paid a visit to the count's daughter that night, too."

Juliana rolled her eyes as the men laughed. She wasn't sure whether to believe him, but the story was a good one.

And then Michael seemed to tip backward off his log into the twilit darkness. She stiffened, about to speak, then saw Paul ram his elbow straight backward.

They were being attacked, as if out of the shadows. They'd lingered too long at their meal, enjoying the camaraderie, feeling themselves invincible.

No enemy came for her, the lone woman in the party, as all the Bladesmen turned to meet the attack out of the darkness. She had a dagger in each hand and circled the fire with urgency to reach the spot where Paul had disappeared. Little could be seen away from the fire, but she heard them now, grunts and then the cries of their furious attackers. She knew better than to rashly interfere when she couldn't see well, but she was not used to feeling helpless. Crouching, she slid over the log, looking away from the firelight, waiting for her eyes to adjust.

"Over here!" an unfamiliar voice cried from across the campsite.

Glancing over her shoulder, she saw Timothy rise up and take a stranger down.

Out of the darkness beyond the fire, she at last made out Paul's silhouette. He carried a dagger, even as he tossed a man over his shoulder and out into the darkness. But she knew his dilemma—how could they kill people who perhaps fought in defense of their king? Their mission placed them on the side of traitors, targets to all loyal people. She saw Paul's hesitation to strike a killing blow, giving his opponent a chance to lift his sword.

Using only his dagger, Paul parried away a sword thrust. And then he saw her. She gestured, hoping he would turn his opponent, where she could take him from behind, but perhaps it was too much to imagine he thought a Blades*woman* could help him. Dropping to a crouch, she prepared to dive forward and take the man's feet out from under him.

Unfamiliar hands grabbed her from behind, an arm around her waist, a hand over her mouth.

She rolled forward, pulling the man with her over her back. His momentum carried him into his compatriot, who went down in front of Paul as his knees buckled from the weight. She pounced on her attacker's back, even as Paul knocked his own opponent out with a blow. With her arm about the man's throat, she held tight as he thrashed and tried to buck her off him. As he lost consciousness, she released him.

Breathing heavily, Paul stood above her, giving her a nod before his gaze took in the rest of the scene. She turned to look with him, finding the Bladesmen one by one gathering near the fire. Some of her tension left her as everyone was accounted for.

It didn't take long to tie and blindfold the vanquished. There were eight of them, dressed in nondescript tunics and breeches that labeled them as neither farmer nor yeoman nor soldier. Some still lay unconscious; others stirred groggily.

"They'll remain with us tonight," Timothy said, shaking his head. "Before dawn, we'll leave them in a farmer's barn where they should eventually be discovered."

"So they can come for us again?" Joseph asked dryly. Using the back of his hand, he wiped blood off his chin.

Timothy shrugged. "We have little choice. I will not kill innocents. And from now on, we have guards on duty even during a meal. We'll be within the walls of York soon enough."

"But hardly safe," Paul said.

He was still looking at Juliana, and she wished she could read his impassive expression.

"To bed, Paul," Timothy said softly. "We cannot have our *guests* believing you fraternize with soldiers. Joseph and Michael, take first watch."

After lighting a candle in the fire, Paul led Juliana to their pavilion. Though it was gloomy within, she'd prepared her raised pallet already, and didn't need to see much.

"You performed well," Paul said.

There was a stiffness in his tone that irritated her, but she let it go, telling herself it could not be easy for such a man to be helped by a woman, even one he'd trained himself.

"I feel as if we should be out there with the other men," she said, sounding just as awkward as he did.

"'Tis not so easy to be pampered nobility."

At least he did not imply that her life had been any easier than his.

The attack should give her something else to think about, but in the way she'd been trained, she was already putting it behind her. If only she could forget her uneasiness at sharing lodgings with Paul. But this afternoon she'd teased him in the tavern, and certainly disturbed her own senses. And he'd almost kissed her—she would have had to let him. To her dismay, she'd almost wanted it to happen. No man had ever kissed her, and she'd heard so much about it.

But kisses would lead to more intimacy, as she well knew. She wasn't going to allow that.

And then he was at her back, beginning to untie her laces.

"Paul—"

"I am here, and this is easier for you. No more protesting. Or one of our very interested guards might hear you and assume I'm pressuring you. Who could blame me, after the way you brought my fingers to your mouth?"

She inhaled swiftly, then lowered her voice, saying over her shoulder, "You fed me by hand."

"And you kept pressing your breasts up against me."

She forced her breathing into even tones, remembered her character, remembered whom she was supposed to be. "That is what a concubine, anxious to stay in her master's favor, would do."

"And I could have kissed you in front of all of them, and you couldn't have stopped me."

"And then you'd have shown everyone that I am not experienced in a concubine's ways."

"Really?" he said, his voice far too interested.

They stood too close, his hands brushing her back. The last of her laces eased and she tried to move away from him, but he put his big hands on her shoulders. She could feel his breath against her neck as he leaned down to speak softly near her ear.

"Why don't I believe you?" he murmured. "When you put your mouth on me, you knew what you were doing."

He was right, but she couldn't tell him why. He would be too curious—he would assume too much.

"Let me show you what you did," he said.

She wanted to run; she wanted to stay. Though playing a concubine in public, in private she was playing the part of a woman in control, knowledgeable, unfazed by his blatant sexuality. And she'd done such a good job that he believed her.

He turned her about, giving her ample opportunity to resist. But . . .

She didn't want to. She'd been taught so much, things that didn't make sense, that mortified her, that she couldn't quite believe. And he was making her see everything she'd learned in a whole new way.

They could still see each other in the gloom of the tent. He slid his hands slowly down her arms, then captured one hand and lifted it, making a show of examining it.

"Rabbit grease," he whispered, then met her eyes.

She held her breath, knowing what he intended, but still unable to believe the melting, sinful feeling of watching him lick the tip of her finger, then suck it slowly into his mouth. Had she truly made him feel this way—in public? Surely she couldn't have affected *him,* a man of the world, who had women falling into his bed right and left.

Then he released her hand, slid an arm about her waist, cupped her face with his hand, and leaned down to kiss her. She knew what to do, what to expect, but even then, she barely withheld a moan of pleasure as his mouth covered hers. Parting her lips willingly, she engaged in the dance of sweet kisses, reveling in the sensation as he suckled her lower lip, pressed gentle kisses to the corner of her mouth. It was she who initiated more, who tasted his lips with her tongue. And when at last his tongue swept into her mouth, she gave a welcome groan of gladness.

Feverishly they kissed, locked in each other's embrace. She pressed harder against him, on fire, as if she needed his touch to ease her ardor. She plunged her hands into his hair, feeling its silky fullness as she molded his head and held him to her. Her body took over, arching against him, knowing instinctively what she wanted.

His hand dropped to her hip, curving around her backside, pulling her into him, up onto her toes, lifting and separating her thighs until she felt the bold pressure of his erection against her most sensitive flesh.

And then she knew why the League had seen to all

of her training—she knew where this would go, what would happen. She would have to be the one to stop it.

She broke the kiss and leaned back in his arms. "Nay, Paul."

Bladesmen were patrolling all around them, separated by mere canvas walls. They'd be overheard, and she knew no one would blame Paul for taking what she'd been openly offering as his concubine. But she would never be one of them again.

Her teacher had tried to warn her of a woman's needs, of how her body could overwhelm her mind—and Juliana had privately scoffed.

She felt humbled by this new knowledge of the powerful desire that could ignite between a man and a woman.

How could she feel so drawn to a man she couldn't understand, who wanted nothing to do with the society of men who'd saved her?

Paul's eyes were hooded, slumbering, even as he cupped her face in both hands. "Juliana—"

"I will not do anything to compromise our mission. This ends now."

Chapter 7

Paul stared down into Juliana's dark, earnest eyes. Her cheeks were soft in his hands, her mouth a wonder as he rubbed his thumb along her full lower lip. He'd lost himself in her, her passionate response, in the very taste of her. It was . . . overwhelming.

Slowly, he let his hands slide from her body. For just a moment, he could still feel the pressure of her breasts against his chest, the indentation between her thighs. And then they were apart, two people again.

"Aye, you are right to stop," he said, his voice husky, too revealing. He cleared his throat. What was wrong with him? He was never so uncontrolled, so lost in the wonder of a woman.

And Juliana, yet! A woman who'd once been under his protection.

"So we can return to our roles, to pretend this never happened," she said calmly.

"Aye, we'll do our best. But forget?" He looked at her mouth, and even now he wanted to take it with his own, to have the rest of her, regardless of the consequences. "Nay, that will not be so easy, fair Juliana."

With a sigh, he turned to look at the pallet they would share, keeping true to their cover story.

And now he was supposed to keep his hands off her?

He only had himself to blame.

Soon he was lying beside her, staring at the way the firelight flickered on the canvas ceiling of their pavilion. He could hear her breathing, knew she was still awake. He tried to listen to the conversation of the Bladesmen on duty, the insects buzzing, the howl of a dog somewhere in the distance.

Yet still he noticed Juliana's subtle movements.

"You are not sleeping," he said at last.

She stirred, and for a moment he thought she would pretend otherwise.

"Nay, I'm not."

The moment stretched out, and he wondered if she was thinking of the kiss, and unfulfilled desires. She well understood what they were missing. And he was still hard with wanting her. He had to think of something else.

"So how many missions have you undertaken for the League?"

"Several," she answered promptly, as if she were just as glad for the distraction.

"Deliberately vague."

"Following the dictates of the League."

"To the letter," he responded with faint sarcasm.

"Of course."

She sounded so proud of herself.

"I know you will not speak of the specifics," he said, "but did you meet with much danger?"

"Nay, I was but a minor player, exchanging messages, gathering information for future missions."

"So this is your first major assignment."

She sighed. "Aye, it is. And now you see why 'tis so important for me to do it well."

"And I would not stop you."

"Not on purpose."

"Juliana, I am stung by such a conclusion."

"I am not blaming you, Paul. I certainly share the blame, for we both have to behave so . . . intimately in public. 'Tis only natural that once we're alone again, 'tis difficult to forget what we've just been doing."

And this wasn't helping, he thought.

"Do you know Diana, the first Bladeswoman?" she asked.

"Aye, I was introduced when she trained at the fortress."

"I have only met her twice, but she is the sort of woman I wish to be. She is the reason the League gave me a chance to become a member."

Paul disagreed with that, but did not plan to say so.

"Were you able to have a conversation with her? I imagine she could share her experiences as a woman among men."

"I hope to someday. She is with child now, and has temporarily withdrawn from assignments."

"She seems to have combined a real life with the League. What about you, Juliana?"

"'Tis not so important to me."

He turned his head to look at her.

"I have never been as other women."

"You seem just like any woman," he said dryly.

"But how would you know, Paul?"

Her voice was quiet, even tinged with a chill. He'd said something wrong.

"You were not raised in the outside world, as I was," she continued. "I was never at ease there. I spent my childhood on the tiltyard, playing with all the little boys. 'Twas a shame we couldn't trade childhoods—we might have liked that better."

"You were so unhappy with your family?" he asked.

"Sometimes," she whispered.

He thought her voice sounded tight and sad with memories.

"My parents indulged me more than most would. I learned to throw a dagger and use a wooden sword along with the boys. I was permitted this as long as I spent part of each day at my studies, and learning women's duties. But as I grew older, the boys began to change toward me."

"Can you blame them?" he asked, hoping to lighten her mood.

"I did then. They either pulled away, since I was the daughter of their lord, or attempted to become too close." She sighed. "I think my parents expected me to realize the foolishness of what I was doing, but at last, they grew tired of waiting. My father forbade me the tiltyard, and confined my days to the women of the castle. He was grooming me for marriage because he had no son, and wanted to see me and my dowry well placed. His distant cousin would inherit the viscountcy—this was before the title was taken away from the family—and Father perhaps harbored a wish that this cousin and I would marry."

"And did you wish that?" he asked, imagining a chosen husband as another thing the League took away from her.

"Nay, I knew I did not matter to him as anything more than another offering of money and a body to grant him an heir. I wanted to strike him for the way he looked at me."

Paul smiled in the darkness, glad that she couldn't see and misread his amusement. "So you had no one you wanted for a husband."

"No one. I was yet young; I thought I would be able to

find a man who loved me for what I was. And then . . ."

When she didn't finish, he said, "Your father was taken away."

"I learned how powerless it is to be a woman," she said with bitterness. "My mother let herself expire in grief rather than find a way to help us."

She died for nothing—how could he tell Juliana that?

"My parents' last thoughts of me were of disappointment." Her voice trailed off.

"I do not believe that," he said firmly. "You were a loyal daughter who did as they asked, even when you did not want to."

She cleared her throat. "'Tis a nice fantasy, Paul, but you were not there. I would have supported my mother, even if I'd had to serve tables as a tavern wench. I vowed I would never be that helpless again."

Her ability to believe in herself amazed him. He knew many men without that strength. "But Juliana, you could have a chance for a normal life again. Do you not want that?"

"If I can combine it with my duties with the League, but I don't know that I can. And this comes first for me, Paul. This is my chance to repay the League for saving me."

Saving her? he thought, almost choking on his bitterness.

After a quiet moment, she asked, "Do you have a

place in the world, Paul? Besides your brother's home, of course."

"I inherited a manor and land from my mother's family."

"How wonderful!" she cried softly, obvious delight in her voice. "Where is it?"

"I've never been there."

"But . . . when you left the League, you did not go to see it?"

He shrugged, and that brought his shoulder in contact with hers. She pulled away.

"When I left, I could not claim my own name."

"But now that your brother is Keswick in the eyes of the world, surely you're curious."

"Eventually I will be. My brother's steward is overseeing it for me now. But I feel in no hurry to see it. I have no family there, I know none of the servants."

"But 'tis all yours, your own home."

He heard the wistfulness in her voice, knew that she must feel sad that her family lost everything they'd built through generations.

"'Tis a place for a man to marry, to have children. I won't be doing that. I discovered while I was away— and to my surprise—that home is where my brothers are," he said simply. And then regretted it. She had no family at all.

"Aye, you are sensible, Paul. You are a lucky man to

understand a family's importance. But why ever would you say you will never marry?"

"Because I will not. There's a world to explore, and I will never tire of that." His feelings about having a wife and family were more complicated than that, but he was not about to share them with Juliana.

"But—"

"Perhaps the League has deliberately made sure neither of us can ever have a normal life," he said, his voice impassive. "Did you ever think of that, Juliana?"

"Nay, Paul, that is not true."

"Believe as you wish."

She paused as if she might argue more, but then only said, "A good night to you."

He heard her roll onto her side, and he lay there, feeling the fool. He'd brought up painful memories for her, when he was only trying to make her see that she could be a normal woman away from the League. But she parried every question, had her own beliefs. She was unshakable in her loyalty, and although he admired that, he knew that someday soon, her entire world would be shaken by the truth. She would survive the pain—and she would be free of lies.

After four days of travel—and disabling another attack before it even began—they arrived in York, northern stronghold of the House of York, once winners in the many battles for the kingdom, but now on the losing side. Paul knew that beneath the beauty of the town built by the Romans at the confluence of the Ouse and the Floss, tensions simmered, old wounds festered. If King Henry were ever to be safe to build a strong future for England, he had to have the loyalty of all the people, to know that his last English enemies were vanquished.

And Paul accepted the fact that he had to play the self-absorbed fool to make it all happen. His work did not need to display strength or intelligence. The irony wasn't lost on him.

As they passed through the gates of the town, Paul glanced at Juliana. She rode with her back straight, her chin lifted regally, her cool eyes constantly assessing everything. She looked arrogant—and expensive, a woman sure of her power over the man who owned her.

Paul watched as Timothy called from his horse, asking townsmen for the finest inn, the best service. When Timothy generously tipped the boy who responded, the boy gladly guided the whole party to the Rooster and Hen. Paul demanded the best lodgings, insisting other guests be evicted—and paid them and the innkeeper for their trouble.

The good will of his money followed him into the tavern that evening. Tables were quickly cleared for the entire party. It certainly helped that Theobald took the lead, his good eye narrowed, his expression menacing. He remained apart from the other Bladesmen, projecting his separation as if the retinue were not unified.

A serving man bowed to Paul when he came to take their order, glancing nervously at Theobald. "Is he as fearsome as we heard, milord?"

"What did you hear, good man?" Paul asked.

"A traveler just days ago must have passed your party. Yon Theobald nearly cut 'im from his horse for simply lookin' at yer lady."

Paul twisted one of Juliana's dark curls about his finger. "Aye, Theobald was part of the bargain if I wanted her. And she was worth it."

Juliana grinned at him with the seductive promise she was so good at. And immediately he was back in the shadowy pavilion, kissing her as if he hadn't kissed a woman in his life. He'd felt as desperate as a boy, well remembering how it had felt when at last he'd met girls.

His dreams had been haunted by her kisses, and lying beside her hadn't helped. As the nights grew cooler the farther north they'd gone, he'd awakened more than once with their arms or legs touching, as if seeking warmth from each other. Instead of being as embarrassed as a maiden, Juliana had only laughed when she'd discovered what their bodies had done in the night.

Paul hadn't felt like laughing.

When the servant had taken their order and left, Paul

leaned back in the settle and put an arm around Juliana. The other Bladesmen were at the next table, talking in low tones, and watching the locals with deliberate intent. Theobald spoke to no one, letting his angry eyes graze the growing crowd.

Perhaps word of a free-spending stranger's arrival had already spread, for more than one man entering the tavern had seemed to be looking for someone in particular—and stopped looking upon seeing Paul's retinue.

Juliana leaned her head against his shoulder and spoke softly. "Theobald is making himself quite feared."

"The better to keep the unsavory away," he replied, his gaze roaming, never staying on one table for long. "I'll make sure another story about him circulates later."

Paul noticed that it was rather easy to peer down her bodice to the enticing valley between her breasts. He was allowed to look, of course—he was supposed to. When Juliana realized the focus of his gaze, he leered down at her.

"Lovely view."

"Hmm." Her tone was not exactly friendly, but her bold smile gave the right impression.

Yet her gaze never stopped wandering the crowd, and Paul thought he sensed a different wariness.

"Is something amiss?" he asked softly.

She hesitated, then glanced up at him, letting her

hand rest on his chest, right over his heart. He tried to keep his thoughts on the mission, on their conversation, so his heartbeat wouldn't speed up and make her curious.

"Timothy surely knows, and you might as well, too. I was raised in Yorkshire."

He knew that, of course. "Yorkshire is a large county."

"Aye, but there is still the chance I might be recognized. It has not been that many years since my departure. But that's the reason I'm keeping my real name. I disappeared from home after my mother's death, and I'm sure many will not be surprised that I had to put myself in the keeping of strange men."

Yet the League had put her in this situation, not caring how she might be hurt as long as their mission was successful. But it wasn't all the League—Juliana had bravely made her choice, knowing what could happen.

To lighten her mood, he said, "So now I'm strange."

She giggled. "You say such silly things, my love."

"Only to amuse you, my little duckling."

This time, she pinched his thigh.

As their meal was served, a small quartet of minstrels set up near the hearth and began to play. The music was lively at first, leading to toes tapping, and tankards being raised in toast to their talent. A pretty serving wench, who openly flirted with Paul every time she brought him an ale, did a lively dance before him, hands on her hips, jumping from foot to foot, letting herself be passed from man to man as everyone laughed.

Paul admired Juliana's show of jealousy throughout, her narrowed eyes, her cool disdain. She kept her hands on him, and he certainly could appreciate that. More than once he saw Timothy watching them, although to the casual eye it was in the guise of a guard.

Did Timothy regret giving Juliana this opportunity? Or hadn't her age and inexperience mattered, when she was what the League needed?

The lively music ended, and the serving girl curtsied to hearty applause. Paul did his part by not attempting to placate Juliana. The minstrels began a new song, slower, with a provocative beat.

Suddenly, she slid out from beneath his arm and off the settle. Moving out into the open area before the hearth, where the serving girl had danced, Juliana turned back to Paul and lifted her arms toward him, as if beckoning. His smile slowly died. Out of the corner of his eye, he saw a glowering Theobald with his hand on the hilt of his sword. The other Bladesmen looked with interest at Juliana, as if she only concerned them as their master's entertainment.

The music thrummed louder, the musicians encouraging her. Paul swallowed hard.

And then Juliana began to move.

Her hips circled in sinuous rhythm, her arms swayed,

her long, black hair swung as if with its own dance. For a moment, the crowd went silent with an awe Paul shared. She was majestic, she was smoldering with sin, and all the while she never broke her shared gaze with him. She cast a spell, weaving a magic he hadn't imagined possible. The Bladeswoman was gone, the temptress left in her place, dancing, swaying, undulating to the slow, erotic beat of the music. He could hear his blood pound in his ears.

Some distant part of him tried to imagine how Paul, the arrogant prince, should act. He forced a grin, as if he'd seen this before, but still enjoyed the show.

And then he thought of Juliana, and the stir she was causing among all the men. Most were slack-jawed in wonder, but some licked their lips, bodies tense, as if they might take their chances on overpowering Paul's retinue.

Paul quickly came to his feet, stalking Juliana. She came to a stop before him, her body dampened with perspiration, her eyes full of triumph and pride. She swept into a deep curtsy, raising her amused eyes to him.

"Time for bed," Paul said.

She laughed at him, even as he swept her up into his arms.

Chapter 8

Juliana wrapped her arms around Paul's neck, feeling giddy with triumph. She'd made a spectacle of herself, of course, but she'd brought Paul even more notice, the noble northern prince returned home at last.

But although Paul carried her with ease, his muscles felt tense, and now that he was away from the tavern, his smile had been replaced by a frown.

Feeling her first unease, Juliana looked about and saw that the Bladesmen were surrounding them, alert, gazes scanning the entrance hall and the staircase. None of them looked at her.

Well, she didn't expect open congratulations, but perhaps a smile or two.

"Paul?"

"Not now," he said, in a low voice.

It was then she became aware of raised voices behind her, shouts and calls, the slamming of tankards onto wooden tables.

Someone was coming down the stairs just as they

were starting up. Paul laughed drunkenly, reeled a bit with her in his arms as he backed up. She gave a cry of laughter, tightening her hold on him.

The man they let pass bobbed his head in thanks, stole a wide-eyed look at Juliana, saw all the men surrounding her, then hastened his pace away.

"Sir, perhaps I should take Mistress Juliana," Timothy said, his tone full of a disapproval that seemed used often.

"Nay, I am fine." Paul bumped Juliana's feet against the wall as he negotiated the stairs.

She winced dramatically, but said nothing. At last they were outside their door.

"I will see you in safely," Timothy loudly insisted.

He obviously played to an audience who might be overhearing.

"I need not your assistance."

Paul spoke with tight petulance, a grown man who was not happy being ordered about.

"Well you shall have it." To the waiting Bladesmen, Timothy said, "You have your orders."

Juliana watched them disperse, feeling foolish because she was still held in Paul's arms. Once inside, he released her and stepped away rather abruptly. Timothy looked out the window, then closed the shutters. Both men turned to her, Timothy frowning, and Paul assessing.

"Is something amiss?" she asked in bewilderment.

"That was . . . quite the dance," Timothy said slowly.

Paul silently turned to stoke the fire.

Juliana spread her hands wide. "The moment called for it. I was playing my part. I believe I was a success."

She thought Paul's shoulders shook a bit, but he didn't turn from the fire until Timothy called his name. Paul's face was impassive and polite when he faced them.

"Paul—" Timothy began, and then broke off, looking back and forth between them.

Paul waited patiently, and so did Juliana, but she felt confused by the undercurrents she sensed between the men. She didn't like feeling this way, as if she should understand what was happening. So she waited as patiently as Paul, pretending to be unperturbed.

Timothy sighed.

"I think I will ask Theobald if he wishes to work in some training this evening," Paul said mildly. "The night is dark, and if we work in the stables, no one should notice me."

Juliana withheld a startled laugh. "That is a ridiculous idea—and dangerous. Why would you risk . . ."

But she trailed off when she saw Timothy giving it real thought. What was going on?

"Theobald has first shift tonight," Timothy said at last. He ran a hand through his hair.

Juliana gave a heavy sigh. "Good. I would have had

to follow you to do my duty, Paul, and that would have raised suspicions. *All* of this"—she threw her hands wide—"would raise suspicions. I might have had to forbid you, as your personal guard." She wanted to demand to know why they were both acting this way, but was beginning to suspect she would only be showing her naiveté.

Timothy gave a last sigh. "You are correct, Juliana. I will leave you in peace. I only ask that next time . . . you give us some warning of what you plan."

"I will try, sir, but I cannot guarantee it. If the moment calls for such a risk . . ." She trailed off with a shrug.

Timothy let himself out the door.

Juliana saw a shadowy glimpse of a large man in the corridor, and knew it was Theobald. Then the door closed.

Paul was watching her, and she could not read his expression. She put her hands on her hips, arched a brow, and waited.

"That was . . ." he began.

"Quite the dance. So Timothy already said. He seems to regret my interpretation of the character. Think you I was wrong?"

"Nay, you made it seem as if I must have great wealth, to be able to afford to keep a woman with such gifts as yours."

"I imagine that was a compliment, but it makes me

feel like a commodity rather than a woman," she said dryly.

Paul's smile looked strained. "I rather enjoyed being fought over through dance."

She heaved a sigh and began to tug on her laces. She could see that water had been left for her use, and she desperately needed to cleanse away several days' worth of travel. She would have to send for a bath in the morning.

And still Paul watched her, saying nothing. She wanted to ask for his help with her laces, but it felt awkward tonight, too personal. There was an uncomfortable, growing feeling of tension that seemed more powerful than any night they'd previously spent together.

She decided to respect her feelings of warning and leave him be. Thankfully, there was a changing screen in their bedchamber, and she retreated behind it, bringing a basin of water and linens. When she emerged in her dressing gown, he was standing at the open window, looking out.

He glanced at her briefly. "I am not tired. I shall join you eventually."

She nodded and retreated to the bed. It was narrower than at the last inn, so she lay down near to the edge to leave him room. He remained a long time looking out the window, but at last he took his turn behind the changing screen. She found herself dozing. When she came awake with a start, the fire had diminished, leaving the chamber flickering with darker shadows.

And then she saw Paul. Without holding a weapon, he was moving through a series of sword skills, as if sparring with an opponent. His skin glistened with perspiration, and he suddenly pulled off his shirt, as if his exertion had overheated him. Juliana found herself barely breathing, watching him move in a dance of power, his muscles smooth, his skill a certainty that was as alluring as his body.

This went on for some time. She came up on her elbow, making it obvious she was awake, yet still he didn't stop, pivoting and parrying, blocking and advancing.

At last she slid from the bed and went to stand before him. He stopped immediately, his breathing harsh, his chest rising and falling. He looked down at her with blue eyes gleaming by firelight.

"Paul, you must come to bed. You will be exhausted on the morrow."

He moved away from her, taking a towel and wiping it down his face and chest.

"Why are you doing this?" she asked.

"You and I have had no chance to train as the others have," he said. "Our roles forbid it. Do you not feel restless, as if you could crawl out of your own skin?"

"I know exactly how you feel. But is this only about training?" she asked.

He paused, then met her gaze boldly. "I'm trying not to remember the way you danced tonight. I keep imagining you making such movements beneath me in that bed."

What could she say to that? Though she imagined the same thing, she would not ease her curiosity so recklessly.

"You know what you did to all those men who watched you."

And she did know—she'd been taught how men react to a provocative woman, but had never seen it happen before her very eyes. And the way Paul was looking at her made her feel too good, too daring.

"I know not what you want me to say," she whispered.

"There's nothing you can say. Timothy is worried I won't be able to control myself alone with you night after night, and that your dance made everything worse."

"How could he believe that when he knows you so well? He knows the kind of man you are."

"Every man has his limits." He lifted a hand, as if he'd touch her hair.

She froze, knowing she should step away, but unable to do so.

"I want you," he said hoarsely. "I cannot stop thinking of that kiss, and now this dance . . . You're haunting my very dreams, sweet Juliana."

She hesitated, more tempted than she cared to admit. He was partially nude, so beautiful. He could show her the things she'd only heard about. And she even knew ways to avoid making a child together.

But this was a temptation to something she'd soon regret. Such intimacy would interfere with their mission, might make things awkward between them. How could she vow to never have a relationship with someone in the League, and then be so quick to consider breaking it with the first man who kissed her?

And she could not forget that he hadn't even wanted a female guard, that he couldn't treat her as the others. That was a disappointment she should keep at the forefront of her thoughts.

"We all want things we cannot have," she answered, striving to sound calm.

He gave a crooked smile, then looked down at the linen in his hands. "Aye, I know you're right. And you want the gratitude and good will of the League."

She frowned. He made it sound as if she was only here for her own selfish reasons. "I want to do my work, the assignment I accepted. I want to keep the kingdom safe. I vowed to do my best."

"Aye, and that is true as well."

She went back to the bed, feeling angry and frustrated with his words—and how close she'd come to giving in to her new weakness for him.

As she lay in bed, eyes closed, listening to him wash, she reminded herself that anything they shared would be temporary, for enjoyment's sake, and not the honesty of marriage vows before God. She remembered Paul saying he would never marry, and although she didn't believe it was simply because of his longing for adventure, that only proved that he could not be trusted. He was a man who dallied with women he didn't plan to marry, and there was no reason for him to change his mind now. She was simply convenient, and treating him as a lover in public. He was confusing what was true and what wasn't.

And he was dragging her with him into the fantasy.

Paul awoke before dawn and lay still, listening to the church bells peal across the town, calling the humble to daily mass. But not Sir Paul, the dissolute. He had absolutely nothing to do this morn. That was surely a first for him, and he felt . . . uneasy.

Through his boyhood, there had always been assignments and studying and training. When he'd left the League, he'd traveled and competed and trained some more. But Timothy had decided that Paul's character was fond of tavern-drinking late into the night, and doing little in the morn.

He dozed until the sun came up, telling himself to enjoy the quiet. But he could hear the enticing sound of Juliana breathing. He thought she looked impossibly young and innocent for all the responsibilities the League had put on her shoulders. Several curls had come loose from her braid and slinked among the cushions. She didn't look like a woman knowledgeable about men; she looked as if she needed to be protected.

But she would be offended by that, he well knew.

She wanted to protect *him,* and perhaps she was not far off the mark, for she needed to protect him from himself, for thoughts of her were constant, especially of that kiss. She'd been as hungry as he was. Two of them in that condition were an explosive combination, alone night after night.

She stirred and frowned, as if she sensed what he was thinking. Her lashes fluttered, then her eyes slowly opened and looked right into his.

With a groan, she closed her eyes again.

He gave a soft laugh and dropped onto his back, stretching his arms over his head.

"You take up too much of the bed," she mumbled, flouncing onto her side away from him.

He was so tempted to slide in behind her, to cup her thighs with his, let her ass cradle his erection. Instead, he took several deep breaths.

Dimly, he heard the sound of steel clashing outside. He tossed back his blankets, slid over the top of her—his body touching her hips and shoulders a bit too much—and went to the window. Throwing back the shutters, he saw that the day was overcast and hazy, cool for summer.

And then he saw their fellow Bladesmen. They were training in the stable yard below, and although they were holding back their true skill, they were still drawing a crowd of grooms and kitchen boys.

Juliana came up beside him and leaned both elbows on the window ledge. "Ah," she murmured softly.

"Ah?"

"You are thinking how we're trapped here, pretending to sleep off a drinking binge, while they're permitted to train."

"It did cross my mind."

He left her at the window and went to the door. As he reached for the latch, he was surprised to find Juliana suddenly there, bracing her hand on the door. She listened a moment, eyes closed, while Paul folded his arms over his chest.

"I can hear Joseph's footsteps," she said at last, looking up at him. "You may open the door."

"You remembered whose turn it was to guard our door?"

"Nay."

"A guess?"

"A logical deduction from my memorization of his pacing."

Paul reached around her and opened the door to find Joseph pacing the corridor. The Bladesman came to a stop and eyed them both in surprise.

"An excellent deduction," Paul said to Juliana.

She smiled at Joseph and went back to the window, ignoring Paul's praise as if she knew she deserved it.

Joseph shook his head. "Sir Paul, Mistress Juliana, how may I serve you?"

"Could you have the maidservant bring us food to break our fast?"

"This early? Would Sir Paul be awake?"

Paul sighed. "You simply don't want to show your pretty face to the maidservants and be overwhelmed."

Joseph grinned and brought forth a wallet from a pack resting neatly on the floor. "I brought you something to tide you over."

"You are a good man, regardless of what anyone else says." Paul opened the wallet to see bread and cheese. "'Tis a start. We'll want something far more substantial in several hours."

He watched as Joseph peered past him into the bedchamber.

"Did you wish to join us?" Paul asked dryly.

Joseph smiled and shook his head. "Nay, I have a wife waiting at home for me."

"And why do you mention something so personal about yourself, Sir Joseph?" Paul asked, amused. "Is that allowed?"

"I only mention it because you do not have the inducement of a waiting wife to keep you on a proper path."

Looking both ways down the corridor, Paul lowered his voice. "Nay, I have a fierce Bladeswoman who believes in this mission with the only passion she lets show. All by herself, she makes certain she is untouched."

"Untouched" was perhaps misleading, but Joseph seemed relieved to hear it.

Paul closed the door, took the food to the window, and watched Juliana rip a piece from the brown bread.

"Your Bladesmen are all concerned with protecting your honor," he said casually.

She swallowed her bread even as she frowned. "What does that mean?"

"First Timothy and now Joseph. All seem to believe I have designs on your person."

Stiffening, she said, "If I were a man, they would not be questioning my competence this way."

"I do not believe 'tis your competence they question, but my ability to control my raging passions," he answered with faint sarcasm.

She turned back to the view from the window. "You are behaving adequately, for a mere man."

"I do believe I should take that as a form of praise."

"Only if you are desperate," she said wryly.

He smiled, enjoying her sense of humor. She made it easy to be with her, and the rest of the morning only emphasized that, regardless of the desire he could never quite forget. They spent several hours shoulder to shoulder at the window, watching the Bladesmen practice. They dissected each man's skill, then debated who had needed the most training after they'd been selected to join. As the morning wore on, they even began to create wild stories about how each man had come to the attention of the League.

"That is one story you'll never have to create about me," Paul said.

Juliana withheld the urge to press him about his past. She was watching him closely, and felt their easy camaraderie fading. And she regretted it. It had been a pleasant morn, and she'd learned much about the techniques he'd discovered in Europe, as he discussed them in relation to the moves of the Bladesmen. He was a good teacher, able to explain himself succinctly. He hadn't lost the skill of patience. More than once he'd glanced at the door, as if estimating when they could be free of the chamber, but otherwise, he hadn't betrayed any restlessness.

Unlike the previous evening, but she didn't think that

related to restlessness so much as forced confinement with a woman he couldn't bed.

At the midday meal in the tavern below, she watched Paul pretend to drink too much in competition with old Roger. They easily displayed a long friendship that hinted at shared secrets, perfect for Roger's cover as the man who might have led the young Prince Richard out of the Tower of London to freedom.

Juliana felt more than one stranger watching her, and she knew that her dance of the previous evening had brought her a bit too much attention. She was uncomfortable with it, far too used to blending in with her fellow Bladesmen, or being unseen when in disguise for a mission. But as the concubine Juliana, she had to be bold, flamboyant, sexual, and far too focused on her man.

After Paul pretended to over-imbibe at dinner, Juliana stood patiently at his side while he talked to the innkeeper about the best shops to frequent. Acting secretive, in the way of a drunkard, he spoke too loudly. He even slipped the innkeeper several coins to be informed if people were asking about him.

Then they went on an afternoon tour of York, with only Michael as their guard, after a particularly loud argument about why Paul refused to let Theobald come and scare the merchants. Paul freely ordered clothing at the tailor's, hats at the haberdasher's, while managing to only pay part of each bill.

Everywhere they went over the next few days, they slowly built up more and more debt, but merchants continued to believe in him by his very attitude and sense of wealth. Juliana watched with amazement as the hardened warrior played the merry ne'er-do-well with true skill.

They frequented York's entertainments, from cockfighting and bearbaiting to gambling over dice, where Paul had an amazing ability to lose much.

And his debts increased.

While they played the waiting game, Juliana felt her patience slowly unraveling like a worn tapestry. She followed Paul's example and tried to exercise within their bedchamber, preferably when he was asleep. If he was awake, he watched her closely, and it began to feel too sensual.

They spent their evenings exploring the town's taverns, where loose women constantly approached him to flirt.

In a quiet moment, as they were awaiting drinks from a suggestive serving girl, Juliana asked with exasperation, "Do women throw themselves at you *all* the time?"

"All the time." He grinned and cupped her face as he kissed the tip of her nose.

She was growing too used to his touches, for he employed them frequently.

"And I don't often resist," he continued with true wickedness. "I would make a poor woman a terrible husband."

"Then 'tis a good thing I am not looking for one," she countered with sweetness.

And then his creditors began to approach him. Paul paid some, put off others, all while acting affronted and arrogant. As the League had planned, he'd given himself the perfect vulnerability.

He received an invitation to hunt with Baron Summerscales; the local nobility were finally noticing him. Yet the earl of Suffolk, a known Yorkist, did not attend. It would have been a particular triumph to reach him, since his brother, the earl of Lincoln, one-time successor to the late King Richard, had been killed in battle by Henry's army just months before. No one tried to speak to Paul in secret, but he well played his exuberant character. And Juliana felt happy to be riding again, and even brought down a deer with her bow and arrow.

Late at night, she watched Paul pace, his movements restless.

"This endless waiting is a terrible thing," he groaned, collapsing onto a bench. "And I swear my mouth hurts from smiling so much. I begin to question the League's plan."

"'Twill work," she said with confidence. She sat at the table in the faint lamplight, sharpening her daggers.

"Since I left the League, never have I remained in one place for more than a sennight. Even as a child I grew restless easily. Can you imagine me staying in one place forever?"

She glanced at him impassively, wondering if again, he was hinting that she should not grow too attached to him. He didn't have to worry.

Someone knocked softly, and after exchanging a glance with Paul, she quickly hid her daggers on her person. They both went to the door, he on one side, she on the other.

"'Tis late!" Paul half shouted, half slurred his words. "Who is it?"

"Timothy. May I enter?"

They looked at each other in surprise, for he hadn't used a League knock. Paul opened the door and closed it behind his foster father. Juliana was growing used to the faint tension between the men, but that did not mean she didn't grieve its necessity for both their sakes.

Timothy held up a rolled parchment and grinned. "You've been sent a message, Paul. I think 'tis the contact we've been waiting for."

The two men read it standing shoulder to shoulder, while Juliana waited patiently.

Paul looked up at her, his handsome smile full of satisfaction. "Someone has bought up all my debts."

"How thoughtful of him," she said, returning his smile with growing excitement.

"He wants to meet with me to discuss the best way to settle my obligations. We are to travel to his manor just outside of York, cloaked to hide our identities. He says he'll be watching to ensure we comply."

"Threats," Timothy said. "A good sign. And he's permitting you only one guard."

"And I will be foolish enough to go along with that."

Juliana said, "But you will also bring your concubine, because you cannot bear to be without her."

Both men studied her, and she knew Paul wanted to refuse. She was not flattered that he thought to protect her. It only proved that he considered her a woman, not a Bladeswoman.

Before Paul could speak, Timothy said, "Of course you will attend, Juliana. 'Tis the reason you are part of this assignment."

She had no need to show Paul her triumph, but she felt it just the same.

Chapter 9

The next morning, Paul rode with Timothy and Juliana outside the gates of York, well cloaked as requested. The day was overcast with a scattering of rain, so at least they did not look out of place. His restlessness had fallen away and he'd slept deeply, satisfied that at last the mission seemed to be beginning in earnest.

He glanced at Juliana, her expression serene, even as her gaze watched constantly for attack. He knew she was glad to be a part of this mission, but the longer it went on, the more uneasy he became about her. His concern only upset her, but he could not help it. A part of him felt she'd been placed into his protection from the moment she'd been taken in by the League, and he'd failed once. He wouldn't do so again.

Yet she thought she was protecting *him*.

The manor house was small but elegant, made of local stone. The fields surrounding it were bursting with grain almost ready to be harvested, all against a backdrop of high, barren moors to the west. It was a peaceful country scene, but one that hid discontent.

A groom led their horses away, and the double front doors opened silently from within as if someone were waiting for them. They stepped into a great hall of several bays, each separated by its particular furniture—tables and benches for the dining area, cushioned chairs before the fire, cupboards and coffers and a massive table spread with parchment and account books. At the far end, two doors led into other chambers.

A man walked toward them from the hearth, dismissing with a nod the usher who'd opened the doors. He frowned at Timothy and Juliana. He was of middling height and stocky build, with unruly brown hair cut just below his chin.

"I said one guard," the man said brusquely.

"And I brought one guard," Paul answered cheerfully, throwing back his hood.

He knew his blond hair gleamed in the faint light from the window, and he saw the man studying it. Then those cold eyes looked to Juliana. She smiled with her usual sensuality, then sighed and looked about as if the hall held her attention more than the foolishness of men.

"If these two cannot be trusted, they could bring about your death," the man said coldly.

Paul frowned in confusion. "We are talking about paying a debt, are we not?" he asked with exasperation.

"Let us not overly dramatize this. And the woman . . . she does as I tell her. I am Sir Paul. And who are you?"

"My name is not important. But you may treat me with the respect I'm due and call me 'my lord.'"

Paul shook his head. "As you wish." He rolled his eyes at Juliana.

The man briefly studied Timothy before addressing Paul. "Before you decide to seek me out again, I will have you know that this is not my home. You will never look for me—I or my masters will contact you."

Paul spread his hands wide. "Whatever you say, *my lord*. Or shall I say 'my creditor'?"

The man said nothing.

Paul stepped forward as if distancing himself from Timothy and Juliana, but spoke loudly enough for them to hear. "What reason do you have for buying my debts? Surely 'tis none of your concern."

The man still studied Paul. "'Tis uncanny how much you resemble the Plantagenets."

"You are not the first to say so. Have not they all been killed?" Paul frowned as if he thought the man was making no sense. "What does my handsome face have to do with the money I owe? I had been paying it back, but if you need it all now, you'll have to be patient."

"There is a way for you to repay the debt," the man interrupted in a soft voice, "and earn more money than you can imagine spending."

Paul glanced back at Juliana, shaking his head as if to say, *What kind of fool is this man?*

"You have the demeanor and bearing we are looking for, and the mysterious background of a man who spent much time in Europe. In order to be free of your debt to me, we need you to imply you are other than you appear."

Paul blinked at him, still wearing a half smile of confusion. "Other than I appear?" he echoed. "You want people to believe I'm someone else?"

"Aye, that is it."

"And you want to cancel my debt—and pay me more beyond," he continued in disbelief.

"If you do as you're told."

"Sounds entertaining," he said, looking at Juliana to share his amusement.

She gave a pointed yawn and went to look out the window.

"'Twill not be simply entertaining, but an assignment you agree to complete," the man said coldly. "You will portray this man until we are finished with you."

Paul widened his eyes. "And how long would that be?"

"I know not. But during this time, you will want for nothing, not money, not entertainment, not women."

"I already happen to own the latter," he said, then dropped his voice to a whisper that boomed. "Not that I'm averse to having more."

"Paul!" Juliana cried.

He looked over his shoulder to see her stamping her foot.

"I am returning to York." She headed for the door.

He followed, catching her arm. "Duckling, this is business. I am almost finished."

"Nay, I'm leaving now!" She wrenched her arm free and glared at the stranger. "Send for my horse."

"Oh, very well," Paul said, scowling. Over his shoulder, he said, "I will think on your offer."

"You are making a grave error," the stranger said coldly. "I need your answer now, and you have no choice."

Paul turned to him, walking backward toward the door as he said, "I always have a choice, *my lord*. I will send a man here with my response."

"On the morrow."

"If I make a decision by then."

In the front courtyard, the horses were delivered promptly, but the threesome were almost near the walls of York before Timothy spoke.

"Well played, Paul. You showed him an ignorance of the situation, and an arrogance that they can use to their benefit. I imagine they will debate how ignorant you really are."

Paul nodded. "I do as you've assigned. Did you doubt me?"

"Whatever you think of me, I've never doubted your skill, or your ability to follow the path to which you've committed yourself."

"Gentlemen," Juliana interrupted.

They both looked at her.

"We know his next move will be to threaten you, Paul, as a warning."

"Or to threaten someone in my party," Paul countered. He glanced at Timothy. "He could even attempt to kill one of us."

"We'll be prepared," Juliana said with conviction.

The first strike was the killing of one of their packhorses the next morning. The livery owner delivered the news of a slit throat, and his utter inability to explain how it had happened.

Angry at the senseless killing, Paul wished he could go out to the manor himself and tell the coward to try his tactics on a Bladesman and see what happened. But he played his part, pretending it didn't matter. He and Juliana went out to amuse themselves on the town, but the merchants had been ordered to advance him no more credit. On his return to the inn, he discovered he would have to pay for the coming night, or take his entire party and be gone.

"Enough to frustrate Sir Paul the Dissolute," Timothy said, using Paul's name for his character.

The Bladesmen were all gathered together in Paul's chamber at mid-afternoon.

"So do I send a message of acceptance," Paul asked, "or go there myself in a flurry of indignation?"

"Send a message," Timothy answered. "Agree to his terms, but say that at one sign of danger to your person, you will leave. After all, they're deliberately keeping you in the dark until you're trapped with no hope of escape."

Paul scrawled the message of acceptance, then sent Joseph, with his pretty, unthreatening face, to deliver it. Although Joseph did not see the mysterious stranger at the manor, he received an immediate response, as if Paul's capitulation had been a foregone conclusion. He returned with the message by supper—and Paul's deadline to vacate the inn.

Paul read the message then looked around the chamber at the Bladesmen, all in various positions of standing or sitting. Like a queen, Juliana sat alone on the bed they would again share that night.

"We are to go to a tournament and festival at Castle Kilborn," Paul said.

"An apt name," Michael muttered to Theobald, whose half face remained impassive.

"Seat of the earl of Kilborn," Timothy mused, rubbing his chin. "I've never heard word of antipathy toward the king attributed to him, but one never knows. Our man with the Yorkists is in the household of Suffolk."

"But 'tis a tournament held at Kilborn's castle," Juliana said. "Perhaps 'tis merely a place that all the Yorkshire noblemen will be gathering for an innocent celebration. The traitors might simply be taking advantage to gather together and plot. They want to control England—and they want revenge for the death of the earl of Lincoln."

"Aye," Paul said, glancing back at the missive. "And it seems we will discover the truth soon, for we're to leave immediately."

"But 'tis after midday," old Roger sputtered. "We'll have to make camp. If we leave in the morn, we'd arrive by supper at the latest."

Paul shrugged. "They seem to want us by midday. And I imagine the innkeeper will not allow us to remain another night."

"Did they give you an identity to assume?" Juliana asked.

"I am to use Sir Paul as my name, giving no surname. They will contact me after I arrive."

Juliana stood up. "Then I will pack."

They were on the road north of York within the hour, a scurrier, Theobald, far in front, and another, Michael, lingering behind.

The peacefulness didn't last. Michael quietly approached the remaining five near suppertime and said they were being followed by a troop of ten men, who were taking pains to remain well back from the party of Bladesmen.

"An escort to be certain we do as we've been told?" Juliana asked.

"Or someone else, who's suspicious of Paul's identity," Timothy countered. "They might be loyal Englishmen, defending a threat to King Henry. Either way, we will not kill unless we have to."

"You constrain us much," Paul murmured. "But I understand the reason. Surely we cannot wait to be attacked. If Juliana and I remain in character, it will be ten against five, and there will more likely be deaths on their side."

"Then we should attack," Juliana said suddenly. "And all seven of us can fight, if we disguise ourselves."

"As what?" Paul asked, hiding his amusement at her eagerness.

"Highwaymen, of course. We will steal from them, but we won't need to kill them. And they'll never know their attackers."

"I like it!" old Roger piped up from behind.

Timothy studied the road ahead, and Paul did the same. It curled between farm fields, sectioned by waist-high stone walls. But not a mile in the distance, the road began a slight climb into woodland.

"We will attack from there," Timothy said.

Juliana nodded her satisfaction.

"Michael, return to your position and signal us as they approach."

Michael nodded and reined in his horse, disappearing into a wooded copse to the east. With Timothy ahead of them, and Roger and Joseph just behind, Paul and Juliana rode side by side.

"If Theobald does not return in time," Juliana said, "we will still prevail without him."

"You know you must keep to your character," Paul said in a low voice.

"Pardon me?" She frowned at him.

"You are my personal guard, but these men don't know it. You're a woman in their eyes."

"They will not know I'm a woman. Even you did not a fortnight ago." Then she regarded him closely. "Do you distract me from the tension of coming battle, Paul?"

"Perhaps I distract myself." He glanced over his shoulder, but could see nothing in the distance.

"I have been trained as you have been—I have been trained by *you*."

"Not for long enough."

"And whose fault was that?" She smiled as if to ease the sting.

"I have only one regret in life, Juliana, and leaving the League is not it."

"Surely you will not leave me with such a mystery. Do we not all have regrets, Paul? And yet you can name only one? What was it?"

It wasn't a secret. "Not being here to aid my brothers in avenging the murder of our parents."

"Ah," was all she said as she looked forward again. "So you owe a debt to the League, and here you are."

"If you know that, then you know the League aided my brother Adam. I thought League missions were secret from uninvolved Bladesmen."

"'Twas hardly a secret among us that your brother kidnapped the daughter of the marquess of Martindale. We at the fortress were gathered together, ready to stop Adam from ruining his life."

"Yet he was only doing what the League wouldn't— challenging the marquess to combat."

"You know that at first there was not enough proof that the marquess had your parents killed. And Adam was using an innocent woman to force the man into combat."

"From what I hear, she wanted to help."

"Not at first, when she didn't know what kind of man your brother was."

"She was instrumental in making her father admit the truth."

"Aye, she was—along with the League. Hence, a debt you feel you owe."

"Do you not wish *you* could avenge your parents?" Paul asked softly, watching her face.

She didn't look at him. Were her regrets not as great as his?

"I do not think about my parents in that way," she finally answered. "I cannot change the past, and I am happy in my present life. They would want that for me." She smiled as if to lighten their tense exchange. "Perhaps 'tis a male thing to want justice long after it can do any good."

He shook his head and sighed. She was only saying that because she thought her father's case hopeless.

When they reached the trees, they dismounted and disappeared within, leaving no tracks on the dirt road.

Juliana was in the lead, rummaging through the panniers on their newest packhorse until she found what she wanted. She held up a cloak with a look of satisfaction, removed a dagger from her boot, and began to slice the fabric into long strips.

Paul stood above her, hands on his hips, even as the other Bladesmen led their horses deeper between the trees.

Juliana grinned up at him, her teeth white in the gloom. "Scarves to hide our lower faces."

"Our?"

She stood up to remove the fur-lined cloak she wore. "I will need a tunic and breeches. Michael is not much bigger than I, but—" She frowned. "His clothing is in his saddlebags and he will not be here in time."

"Then I guess you'll have to remain hidden and let me protect you."

She narrowed her eyes fiercely, and he held up both hands.

"I am teasing you, little duckling. I would not keep you from your life's work of pretending to be a highwayman."

She blinked as if his answer had surprised her, then seemed to gather herself as she said crossly, "I am not your little duckling, nor your concubine at this moment. I am a Bladeswoman."

"You need not remind me," he said.

Again, she seemed taken aback by his words. When Joseph approached to take a piece of fabric, she asked to borrow some of his garments, and they went off together.

Roger pulled a coif loose from around his neck in preparation for pulling it up as a hood. Paul handed him a piece of fabric, and Roger narrowed his eyes as if studying him.

"Aye, old man?" Paul said lightly.

"So concerned with the girl are you, that you haven't realized you need to change, too."

With a nod of thanks and a curse under his breath, Paul moved through the trees to his own horse.

Chapter 10

Juliana dropped from a tree branch straight onto the rider's back. The startled horse reared, and she clung resolutely, even as her target tried to unsheathe the sword at his side.

She ripped his purse from his waist and cried, "Coins! Me purse thanks you!"

With her elbow, she hit him hard at the base of his skull, and he slumped forward, unconscious. Taking his sword, she jumped from the horse, landing and immediately rolling, coming up in time to see the horse galloping away with him. She whirled, facing the battle behind her, tucking the purse into her wide belt.

Michael had joined them in time, and the six of them had each taken out a man immediately. She saw one horse galloping by, its rider crying out as he was dragged behind, his foot caught in the stirrup. Another man raced past, holding his arm and riding low.

Paul fought another on the ground, sword clashing with sword. After kicking the man's legs out from under him, he was able to use the hilt to knock the man unconscious.

Juliana ran forward as one of their opponents moved behind Paul's back. Her dagger was in her hand without thought, and she threw it hard, catching the man in the shin. With a cry he went down.

Paul looked up, saw her, and grinned. "I would have taken care of him meself," he called.

"Believe what ye'd like!"

It was over by then, the last two men racing away without even engaging.

Theobald appeared between the trees, his coif pulled low to hide his unique mask. "I am too late," he said with gruff disappointment.

Juliana wanted to laugh, but she restrained herself. Several of the strangers were conscious and might detect her sex. The Bladesmen quickly stripped them of valuables. Juliana's man flinched as she went for his throat.

"I won't kill ye," she said in a deep, husky voice, ripping the pendant from around his neck. "Unless ye give me reason."

When the last man was tied to a horse, Paul slapped its haunches, and the startled animal broke into a gallop.

"Night is almost here," Timothy said calmly, removing his scarf and tucking it within his garments. "Let us find a better place to camp."

When they were mounted and riding, Juliana looked down at the pendant she'd stolen.

"Your target wore that?" Paul asked, riding up beside her.

She nodded. "These were not desperate men, nor were they simple soldiers. Did anything else we take mark them?"

He shook his head. "They could have been sent by anyone. But we'll see that they prove useful—their stolen possessions sold and the money given to benefit the needy."

About the fire that night, Juliana couldn't stop watching Paul. There was an air of suppressed excitement among the men, a joviality in response to a successful battle. They'd all acquitted themselves well, but what she was still remembering was how he hadn't protested her being dressed as a man for the attack. She'd thought he'd be more resistant, considering that from the beginning he hadn't wanted her guarding him.

This was their last night to be as themselves. They told stories of their missions, pretending they happened to "a friend." Timothy didn't protest, as if he sensed that the emotions of battle needed some outlet.

Restless, Juliana couldn't imagine feeling tired enough to sleep. Paul's gaze touched her now and again, and she shivered with it, not out of fear, but out of an excitement she was working hard to contain.

Thankfully, he seemed to want to distract himself from thoughts of the two of them, for he launched into a tale of crossing the British sea, and having to fight off pirates with his shipmates. He looked more . . . alive, more fulfilled with just that story, than he did helping to protect the king. He would leave again, for such a man could not be content with a simple life.

And then the men began to settle into their blankets, and she knew she had to join Paul in their pavilion. A strained silence hovered between them as he set the candle on a tree stump. He left again to allow her to prepare for bed, but he returned before she'd had time to don her dressing gown. Her night rail was far too sheer, clinging at her thighs and stomach and breasts. It was there that Paul stared, and instead of leaving, he closed the canvas flap behind him.

She wasn't going to play the virgin, to let him think he affected her. Arching a brow, she calmly reached for the dressing gown. Except for the clenching of a muscle in his jaw, she had no warning of what he meant to do until he was beside her, gripping her arm before she could don the extra layer of clothing.

She froze, staring up at him, keeping her face impassive. "Is something wrong?"

He searched her eyes as if looking for a truth he didn't understand. Then something inside him seemed to change. She sensed the way he drew himself back, even though he hadn't moved.

And a part of her was disappointed.

"I do not suppose," he began in a light, conversational tone, "you'd take pity on a man who's just looked upon such beauty, and kiss him?"

The mere suggestion made her swallow the last moisture left in her mouth. Immediately, the excuses began to bubble up in her mind: *He could teach me, no one would know, neither of us would insist on marriage* . . . She knew too much already, for she could picture every caress she'd learned to please a man, every sensitive place on her own body.

But dwelling on the forbidden would lead to disaster. She would not give their passion credence, not when she risked her very future with the League. She kept her own tone amused.

"You do not wish to merely kiss, Sir Paul. Let us not disguise the truth."

His gaze leisurely dropped down her body, and she felt her nipples harden, knew that he saw it, too. "You know what we could do together."

And she did, although not as literally as he meant. She was a knowledgeable woman in his eyes, and she wanted to stay that way, not become a virginal girl he needed to protect.

He lifted his hand and very gently cupped her breast. She inhaled swiftly, for even that touch set off a storm of pleasure that could easily rock her from her lofty perch of certainty. She hadn't imagined, hadn't suspected that the feelings could be even more than she'd been told. But this was why they'd prepared her, so she could stop it.

She put a hand on his arm. "Nay, Paul," she breathed.

She felt the hardness of his muscle, knew what he was capable of. For just a moment, he ignored her denial, and she had a flash of understanding that she really didn't know what kind of man he was.

Then he released her and stepped back, and though she felt regret that she would not experience the pleasure his hands could give her, she also felt satisfied—he was not a man who would seduce a resistant woman. It seemed a small thing, but it mattered.

They said nothing else as she donned her dressing gown and slid onto the pallet. Though it was a warm evening, she covered herself with a blanket. He blew out the candle, and the walls of their pavilion seemed to shimmer with the campfire outside.

Then, in his usual manner, Paul crawled right across the top of her. She held her breath, eyes squeezed shut, feeling buffeted by the sensations she'd been trying to deny herself.

With a sigh, he settled at her side. "If you'd allow me

to sleep on the outside, we would not go through this every night."

"I take my duties seriously—as my refusal to bed you so recently showed."

"'Tis a good thing you take your duties seriously, or I might be dead this night," he said.

"You would have heard the man coming." She kept her tone mild. "My blade merely reached him first."

"Hmm."

He said nothing else. She closed her eyes, forcing her muscles to relax, but having to use force didn't exactly relax her. She could hear Paul breathing. Although she remained at the edge of the pallet, she knew that they would touch each other in the night. In their sleep, they'd have some of what they wanted, and she could only hope her dreams wouldn't reflect the same.

Paul came awake as if from the most wonderful dream. He and Juliana had been lovers, and her naked body was entwined with his.

Then he realized that although she wasn't naked, they were definitely entwined. She lay with her head on his shoulder, her arm across his chest, her knee practically riding between his. He was so close he could see each eyelash where they fanned her cheeks. The temptation to pull her on top of him was almost overpowering. The only thing that stopped him was her rejection the previous night. Seducing her until she couldn't think would definitely not endear him to her.

But obviously, she was beginning to thaw toward him, he thought, almost groaning as he noticed her full breasts pressed into his chest, and the warmth between her open thighs against his hip.

She was not always this soft, seductive woman. He thought about how she'd fought the day before, how she'd saved his life. He'd had a small part in her training, in making her what she was. He'd tried to think of her as another student, then recently, as a very desirable woman. And now he realized he had a more personal concern—he could get her killed. He'd never thought of another Bladesman that way; they all understood the risks when they'd joined. But she'd had just seventeen years when she'd come to the League, full of despair and a tenuous hope that at last she had a place to belong. She'd do *anything* to belong—fighting at his side, saving his life, risking herself.

And he cared—too much.

He felt her stir, move, her body sliding against his sinuously. The hunger she aroused in him was perhaps more than he'd ever felt before—and that was a revelation he hadn't anticipated.

Her black hair slid across half her face as she lifted her head to blink at him in sleepy confusion.

He let his hand slide up the long, supple slope of her back. "Change your mind so soon?"

He expected her to hop off the pallet in outrage.

Instead she gave a slow smile, spread her hand flat on his chest, and whispered, "I imagine you wish so, if your straining breeches are any indication."

Then she rose from their pallet, leaving him speechless and frustrated and amused, a mingled condition in which he seldom found himself.

At mid morning, they crested a gentle hill, and Juliana almost gasped with wonder as Castle Kilborn loomed in the distance. The keep rose up many levels, protected by outer and inner curtain walls. High towers were set at intervals along both walls, and the main gatehouse towers were the most elaborate of all. The gates were open, for guests streamed back and forth between the castle and a huge field, which was dotted with colorful pavilions topped by streaming pennants representing all the contestants come to participate in the tournament. An area had been cleared for the joust, with stands of raised seating for spectators.

Theobald, who'd been scouting ahead all morning, waited for them, his good eye glowering. "Many people to guard against," he muttered.

Juliana could not help wondering if any of the Bladesmen would be known by some within. After all, she did not know of their lives, their positions. They could be knights; they could be noblemen.

But she knew that Timothy had chosen them with special care. None of them displayed any trepidation.

Paul threw back his short cloak, showing off a burgundy doublet. His sleeves had been slashed to reveal his white shirt. He wore striped hose and an elaborate codpiece that had made all the Bladesmen snicker as they broke their fast that morn.

But Paul had been unfazed, a peacock preening in the sun. His hat with its padded roll was tilted rakishly, so that his burnished hair, as light in color as the Plantagenets, would be revealed to all.

Juliana had taken special care with her own gown that morn, choosing a yellow silk embroidered with gold threads, so that she almost glittered in the sun. She left her dark hair flowing down her back, wearing a token headdress, a veil of sheer gauze that only skimmed her hair.

She met Paul's gaze. His nod to her was small and sure. Then his smile broadened into that of Sir Paul the Dissolute, and he raised his arm, setting their retinue in motion.

As the road wound down among the fields scattered with pavilions, they garnered a slowly building wave of attention. No one recognized Paul, of course, but by his arrogant bearing he proclaimed himself a man of importance.

Juliana felt the stares she inspired, some men openly interested, a few, more God-fearing perhaps, showing their disdain. She wondered how the gentlewomen would take her presence, and could only hope they would not interfere in her ability to remain at Paul's side.

As they approached the curtain walls, the battlements loomed above them, where guards looked down to monitor all they saw. The party passed through the gatehouse, and Juliana glanced up into the dark recesses, knowing a sharp portcullis would normally block their path. There were also secret openings where soldiers could rain death on them from above in an attack.

But if men watched in secret, assessing them, none attacked. They entered the outer ward first, which had been given over to a sprawling tiltyard. Men practiced their skills with sword and dagger and lance. Juliana absorbed the sight with great regret, knowing she would not be able to join them. She feared her battle readiness would be compromised if she didn't soon find a way to do some kind of training in secret.

The inner ward had several courtyards setting apart the stables, the soldiers' barracks, carpenter shop and smithy, and sheds for storage. Juliana spotted a wall enclosing a lady's garden, with the kitchen garden located behind. Half-timbered buildings lined the curtain wall, more lodgings for the earl's family and guests.

Grooms from the stables came to take their horses, and Paul blathered on about the best oat mix and the perfect currying. Juliana paid no attention, and she knew the grooms probably didn't either, though they appeared to focus respectfully on their lord's guest.

Steep stairs led up to the first floor of the castle, and the massive double doors were wide open. Inside the great hall, high windows had been cut out of the stone to light what had once been a grim fortress. Fireplaces taller than Juliana bracketed both ends of the hall. Lines of trestle tables had been set up for dinner, the most elaborate meal of the day. Servants were even now adding final touches to the top layer of tablecloths that would be taken away with each course.

"Good sir!" shouted a voice from somewhere to their right, barely heard above the cacophony of guests and servants and dogs.

The Bladesmen all turned together to find a table laden with stacks of parchment, and several harried men sorting through them. The man who'd called for their attention now gestured, and Paul walked toward him. He was short, thin, with a head of dark curls.

"Sir—my lord," the man began, looking at Paul's elaborate clothing as if he couldn't tell how to classify him, "my name is Bevis, and I am the usher for the great hall. I must register you for the tournament."

"God, no," Paul said. "I do not know if I even mean to remain. My party was attacked last night and we barely escaped with our lives. I will have to be greatly assured of my safety or I will be gone."

They'd all decided that a supposed attack would be a good way to speed up contact with the traitors who might believe they could lose Paul after all.

Bevis, eyes wide, bobbed his head. "I am sorry to hear that, sir, and I hope none of your party were hurt."

Paul only grumbled a response.

"May I have your name, sir, so that I may introduce you to the steward, Sir Reginald? He will reassure you as to the precautions we've taken to guard our guests, and see to your lodgings."

"I am Sir Paul, late of Flanders," he answered stiffly.

The two men seated at the table looked at each other. Flanders was well known as a country sympathetic to Yorkists who'd fled England.

"My thanks, Sir Paul," Bevis said, furiously writing on the parchment. "Please sign here to approve that I've numbered your party correctly."

He did so with a flourish. "I need to be introduced to the earl immediately."

"I will tell Sir Reginald. While you wait, please quench your thirst. Dinner will be served shortly."

Paul's nod was brusque as he turned away from the

usher. Juliana put her hand in his elbow, offering comfort to her patron.

With his hand on hers, he gave her a reassuring smile. "All will be well, my little duckling. I will keep you safe."

Several footboys appeared carrying platters of tankards brimming with ale. Paul and the Bladesmen each took one, but Juliana accepted a goblet of wine.

She noticed that other than servants, the women of the hall were all finely dressed, their hair covered in headdresses that varied from caps with veils hung behind to gable hoods. They regarded Juliana with the wariness of birds defending their nests, but she saw no open animosity, even received a faint smile or two. She imagined all would reserve judgment until they knew exactly who her patron was.

At dinner they were assigned seats above the salt, a mark of importance, though not even the steward had yet been introduced to them. However, at least they could now see their host, Lord Kilborn. He sat on a raised dais, white-haired, but with the leathery face of a man used to the outdoors. His wife, younger than he and bearing his child, sat beside him. There were surely two hundred guests crowded into the spacious great hall. Several elaborate courses were served, and although Paul ate with gusto, his demeanor was that of an impatient man. To the men seated near him, he told of being attacked.

And during it all, Juliana glanced at the earl's guests and wondered if she would eventually encounter someone who knew her. Her father's castle was less than a half-day's journey away. The king had yet to decide upon whom to bestow it. She didn't like to think about someone else holding her father's viscountcy, but the ache of it had long since left her.

Her parents had never been the kind to host tournaments or festivals of their own, but they'd attended the events of others, and Juliana thought she recognized a face or two. But how could anyone know her, when the last time she'd been seen, she was a girl dressed as a boy? There had been no official mourning for her parents; no one came to grieve, only gave whispered offers of condemnation and secret sympathy.

After dinner, as the trestle tables were being cleared, a short man with a serious, lordly bearing approached them. He bowed briskly, as if he didn't enjoy doing so, and then looked at Paul. "Sir Paul, I am Sir Reginald, steward of Castle Kilborn. Bevis told me of the unfortunate attack upon your party. Lord Kilborn expresses his regret, but hopes you do not leave us because of something out of his control."

"The highways leading to his estate are not in his

control?" Paul asked loudly, hands on his hips like a crowing rooster. "What else isn't in his control?"

Sir Reginald bowed his head again. "Lord Kilborn wishes you to know that his soldiers will scour the countryside for these thieves. Please be at ease, and enjoy the tournament."

Paul continued to bluster, and at last, Juliana touched his arm.

"My love, surely Lord Kilborn will see to our security."

He seemed to grit his teeth, then said to Sir Reginald, "We will spend the night, but I do not promise more. Tell Lord Kilborn that. Now see us to our lodgings, where we can tend our bruises. I will need a chamber for my companion and me, and a chamber on either side for my men to share."

"Soldiers are housed in the barracks, Sir Paul. I cannot—"

"I cannot be left unprotected," Paul interrupted, his expression urgent rather than arrogant. "Surely you understand that."

It was a test of words—did Sir Reginald know why Paul was there? Were he and his master involved in treason?

Sir Reginald spoke in a placating manner. "I understand that you fear being attacked again. I will see what I can do to accommodate you."

And then he was gone, moving through the crowds and disappearing down a corridor.

"His response revealed nothing," Juliana murmured.

Paul smiled down at her intimately, as if she'd just whispered words better suited to the bedchamber. He patted her hand, still tucked within his arm. "I agree."

Sir Reginald returned and gave Paul a brusque nod. "Your lodgings will not be as spacious as I could have granted had you only needed one chamber, but this will suit your needs. I've even been able to house you within the keep itself, rather than the outlying apartments."

She wondered if there was a darker reason for that. Did someone wish to keep Paul close, to better watch his movements?

Their bedchamber was small, but generously furnished with woven mats on the floor instead of rushes, coffers for their garments, several cushioned chairs before the hearth, a changing screen—thank God—and a bed, large enough that perhaps their shoulders wouldn't overlap. In the chamber on either side, servants were even now setting up several pallets for the comfort of soldiers rather than noble guests.

The baggage from their horses had already been brought up—"Searched?" Paul mouthed with amusement—and even now a maidservant began to unpack for them.

Juliana smiled at her. "I will finish that for Sir Paul."

The servant curtsied and left them. Although she would have liked to collapse back on the bed and rest, Juliana went to the window first. It overlooked one of the tiltyards, and off in the distance, beyond the castle walls, she could see the village of Kilborn, and the spire of its small church.

When Paul joined her, she smiled up at him. "You played your part well. I think word of your displeasure will spread to the right people."

"If not, I can be even louder at supper."

They became silent then, memorizing the layout of the grounds, landmarks in the countryside, anything that might be useful during their mission. Timothy stopped by to announce that he and the others would explore the grounds, while Juliana and Paul should examine the keep itself.

It was most important for a Bladesman to know every entrance, any vulnerabilities in defense, ways to escape if all traditional exits were blocked. So Juliana and Paul strolled the keep, every level, every corridor, occasionally pretending too much interest, or pretending they were lost. They made certain no one saw them enter the undercroft beneath the castle, for there could be no reason guests would enter storage rooms.

As they headed back toward their lodgings, they passed an open door and the chattering of women. They were surprised to hear someone call Paul's name.

They stepped inside what could only be the sewing and weaving chamber, for there were many servants and ladies busy at large tables and looms.

Lady Kilborn was the one who'd called for their attention, and even now she slowly, awkwardly rose from her chair, her stomach hampering her movements. She was a plump woman with deep dimples meant for laughter, and she regarded the two of them with interest, blushing a bit when she looked at Juliana.

"Sir Paul, I am so glad you brought your . . ." She gestured to Juliana as words failed her. Her blush deepened.

"My lady, I am Mistress Juliana, his concubine," she said, her voice warm and frank. "You do not need to feel awkward calling me what I am."

Paul squeezed Juliana's hand. "We are companions in every sense, my lady. Alas, if only we could marry."

He didn't elaborate, but that seemed to relieve some of the countess's confusion. To Juliana's regret, she found his explanation touching, as if he'd tried to ease her way with the judgmental people they'd encounter.

"Ah, how sad for you both," Lady Kilborn said. "Marriage is a wonderful comfort for two souls to share." She patted her stomach. "And good things come from it, of course."

Behind her, ladies twittered with laughter. More than one looked at Juliana as if she should fear such a result, but she kept her expression serene.

"Surely, you have manly things to attend to, Sir Paul," Lady Kilborn said. "Leave Mistress Juliana with us."

The thought of Paul wandering the castle without protection made Juliana squeeze Paul's hand harder than she intended to.

He smiled down at her. "She would enjoy that, my lady. She does not always need to be looking after me."

But that was her assignment, she thought. Yet she couldn't alienate these women. Through friendships with them, she might discover much about their husbands' loyalties.

"I will see you in our chamber before supper, Sir Paul," Juliana said, hoping he understood her hidden message: *Stay there until I return!*

As Juliana sat down among the women, she asked for something to sew, so she could be of help. They gave her a man's shirt, which needed embroidering at collar and cuff. At times such as this, she was glad her parents had insisted she learn the basic skills of a woman, however rebellious she'd acted about it. She was never going to be praised for amazing talent, but she could get by.

Conversation flowed about her, and she absorbed the noble titles of guests and where they were from, the size of their parties, and news from London. There was heightened interest when all discussed Paul's brother, newly revealed as the long lost earl of Keswick—not that anyone knew that Paul was related to him.

She tried not to think of Paul himself, although concern for him always simmered beneath her thoughts. What if someone had told Lady Kilborn to separate them with ill intent?

To the women, Juliana slowly revealed the background she'd carefully constructed for herself: daughter of an impoverished London gentleman, forced by her father into accepting a Frenchman's protection. It was scandalous, but might evoke some sympathy. Now her liaison with Paul seemed more the product of a love that could never be legalized due to her disgrace. Most of the women seemed sympathetic, while a few, obviously, felt she should have thrown herself into the Thames rather than submit to such degradation. They didn't understand what hopelessness felt like, she thought.

At last they released her, and she was able to hurry to her own bedchamber. As she passed through the corridors, she received much in the way of speculative stares and open lascivious interest, but she was growing used to it. She was now a concubine after all, and the character was becoming part of her. Plain Juliana, who could disappear even among men, had faded away. It was as if she were playing a part onstage, except that it had become her life every moment of the day. Even with Paul, she was playing a part, she thought, feeling a touch of regret.

At her door, she paused, hearing feminine voices. She stepped inside, only to see Paul towering over three women, who were calmly stripping him of his garments.

He looked over their heads at Juliana and grinned with charming helplessness.

Chapter 11

Paul felt a surge of satisfaction when Juliana opened the door. He'd been hoping she'd arrive, had imagined the look on her face at seeing the women preparing him, their guest, for a bath.

But all Juliana did was blink her eyes for a moment, then calmly said, "Please allow me to fulfill my duties by assisting Sir Paul."

The maidservants had only removed his mantle, boots, and doublet, and were working on loosening the laces at his neckline with nimble fingers, but they all ceased at once, to his disappointment. Juliana held open the door for them.

He could not allow her to triumph so easily. "Elizabeth, please remain and assist my companion."

"Aye, sir," the girl murmured, red hair escaping the coarse wimple that swathed her head and neck.

Elizabeth turned to the stack of linens and began to sort through them, while the other two maidservants filed out, nodding to Juliana.

Paul was hoping for a glare from Juliana's dark eyes behind Elizabeth's back, but all she did was lift one eyebrow, as if he were a little boy caught in a prank. She might feel she'd bested him, but what did she intend to do now that she'd told the maidservant it was her own duty to bathe him?

She walked right to him, so regal, so composed, and lifted her hands to unknot the laces of his shirt. He wondered how many other men she'd done this for, and the prick of jealousy surprised him. She'd made her choices, and perhaps she could allow herself to be intimate with him as well. The League would not be rent asunder should she have a moment of pleasure.

"So you cannot undress yourself now?" she murmured for his ears alone.

"They quite overpowered me with their willingness to serve."

She bit her lip, eyes narrowing as her fingernails worked on the knot, but he thought she was withholding a smile. He liked that she was taller than most women, that he didn't have to bend over so far to kiss her. That stray thought grew, until he was looking at her mouth and remembering.

At last the knot loosened, and she reached down to lift his shirt. And then she stopped, meeting his gaze.

A faint smile teased the corner of her mouth as she said, "Sir Paul, you have taken this too far. I know you're ashamed that you're not in fighting shape, but I'm sure Elizabeth has seen other men such as yourself."

And then she patted his stomach. Damnation, but he'd forgotten his slouching disguise. And she'd caught him out.

He sighed. "Elizabeth, my concubine is trying to pretend she's not jealous of all other women where I'm concerned. My thanks for your assistance, but I can see that Mistress Juliana would like privacy."

The maid departed.

Paul and Juliana stared at each other, not moving, and he knew it was a bit of a battle between them. He'd teased her, she'd paid him back.

And then she lifted up his shirt, and bemused, he took it from her hands to pull it over his head.

"It seems you are quite eager to be bathed, Sir Paul." She glanced at the bathing tub, already full of steaming water. "Since you insist, I will comply."

He opened his mouth, but nothing came out. What the devil was she doing? She began to untie all the points connecting his hose and codpiece to the waistband of his braies. One by one, everything slid down his body in loose folds. He wasn't breathing—couldn't breathe. As it was, the braies he wore certainly would not disguise his straining cock.

But she did not glance at it as she bent, lifting each of his feet to remove the discarded garments.

She turned her back to test the water, murmuring, "Perfect," even as he put a hand on the back of a chair to steady himself. *She* was perfect, and seeing her bent over, he wanted to toss up her skirts and show her how perfect they could be together.

While he stripped off his last undergarment, she busied herself at a low table setting out a cloth and soap. He stepped into the padded wooden tub, then sank down, sighing aloud as he leaned back. The water only came to his waist, and nothing was hidden, but as she bent over him, she acted as if she saw a naked man every day.

And then she put the cloth to his chest and he closed his eyes in bliss.

"Why are you doing this?" he asked on a groan of appreciation.

"Since you wanted a bath, my lord, you should have one."

She spoke in even, almost impassive tones, and he opened his eyes to watch her. She held his arm aloft while working the soap down his skin, her eyes downcast as she seemed to concentrate.

And washing took so very much concentration, he thought, holding back a grin.

"And since you saw fit to abandon me with those women," she continued casually, "to tease me in front of the maidservants, I thought it only right that you be paid back in kind."

"This is hardly a terrible punishment," he said, inhaling as she moved her ministrations from his other arm to his chest. Her strokes were slow and gentle, circling, moving ever lower down his torso.

He opened his eyes again to find her watching him.

Wearing a faint smile, she said, "Please sit up so I can work on your back."

Disappointed, aroused, he did as she asked, bracing his arms on the tub, head lowered. He anticipated each stroke of the cloth, appreciated her deft teasing as the cloth dipped once or twice below the water line. Then she used the sopping cloth to soak his hair, before lathering in the soap. He'd never imagined that massaging his scalp could be so sensual.

"Sit back please, so I may bathe your legs."

Leaning back against the tub, he watched her from beneath half-closed eyelids, wondering if he'd ever felt so good without being inside a woman's body. He wanted to be inside *this* woman's body, and hoped that these games they played might eventually lead him there.

She lathered his feet, then worked her way up one lower leg, and then the other. His breathing grew uneven, and it took more and more effort to appear relaxed. Soap clouded the water now, so she couldn't see what she was doing to him, but if she continued, she'd discover it.

Would she continue?

Slowly, carefully, she soaped her cloth again, and then bent over to begin on his thighs, going back and forth between them until she reached the water line not far from his groin.

She glanced up at him, her long hair half covering her face, her dark eyes watching him. "Should I continue?"

He stared at her, realizing that she would totally bathe him, but still didn't intend to make love to him.

"This is a cruel way to punish me, my little duckling," he said in a husky voice.

And then she smiled, a slow, seductive smile. She knew what she did to him, just how to arouse him. Somehow he would find a way to show her that bedding him would be a great adventure.

He reached over the edge of the tub, picked up a bucket—and tossed some of the warm water at her before dumping the rest over his soapy head. She gasped, hands splayed, wet hair clinging to her cheeks. Then he dragged her into the tub. She shrieked with laughter, before covering her mouth, eyes wide with shock.

"I think our masquerade calls for laughter in the bedchamber," he said, holding on to her while she squirmed and giggled and only made herself wetter.

Juliana could barely breathe, her face plastered into his wet chest as she worked desperately to subdue her laughter. He tried to dip her head under water, and she eluded him, twisting his arm in just the right way to make him release her.

"Nice trick," he said. "I wonder who taught you?"

When she didn't answer, he tried to dip her again, and at last she was forced to say, "You did."

Her gown and smock soaked up more and more water, clumped in wet heaps all over his lower body, thankfully keeping her from feeling his arousal. She knew she would have washed between his legs if he'd have dared her—she could weather the storm of temptation far better than he could. And she would have stopped after that, leaving him to suffer.

She didn't like to think that she enjoyed the thought of him suffering a bit too much. It wasn't his fault she was so attracted to him.

"I must get out," she finally said, propped up on his chest.

When she didn't, he said, "What is stopping you?"

"My garments are very heavy."

"Then let me take them off you."

She gave him a mock frown. "You would gladly accept such suffering?"

His grin was lazy. "Hopefully not for long."

At last she dragged herself out, her soaked skirts still

trailing across him. Together they tried to squeeze out the excess into the tub, and she kept stealing glances at his face. She'd never imagined that he would be able to find amusement so easily, that she could enjoy his company. He'd returned to the League so angry about the past, but he'd never allowed that anger to take over his life, to make him bitter.

There was a sharp knock on the door, with the subtle cadence of a Bladesman, deliberately alerting them.

Their gazes met, hers alarmed, his calm.

"We're in character," he reminded her.

"Nay, we were not." But she nodded and went to the door.

She paused until she heard him leave the bath, waited, then glanced behind her. He'd wrapped a towel around his waist, and she well understood why he paid particular attention to the folds at the front.

She opened the door and stood back, wanting to sink into the floor as all five Bladesmen entered.

Paul used his fingers to comb the wet hair from his face. "You did not see any maidservants lingering in the corridor, did you?"

Joseph, grinning, shook his head. "And why should we?"

Juliana strove to remain impassive, interested, unaffected. But old Roger hid a smirk behind twinkling eyes, Michael gave Paul a suspicious look, and Timothy exuded worry. Theobald merely went to the window and looked out as if this did not concern him.

Paul gave a heavy sigh. "The maids were trying to bathe me."

Joseph choked on laughter.

"We rid ourselves of them, but they were listening in. We put on a show."

"How difficult that must have been," Theobald mused from his place at the window.

Juliana's eyes widened. She didn't know if he was teasing or speaking the truth. She couldn't read too much into any of their reactions, told herself there was nothing she could do, that her part as a concubine naturally opened her up to speculation by her fellow Bladesmen.

But she felt ill inside at this blow to her dignity, to her place among them. And she hated herself for feeling this way.

She would *not* be so insecure.

Timothy sat down at the table. "Let us report on our findings."

Their discussion on the layout of the castle and wards was matter-of-fact, expected. Juliana gradually relaxed, except for the occasional chill that shook her. But it was a warm summer day; a little dampness would not hurt her. Paul paced as he reported for the two of them, wearing just the towel, and though she wanted to avoid even looking at him, she didn't.

When he reached the point in his narrative where she remained with the ladies in the sewing chamber, Timothy turned to look at her.

She related what she'd heard of the various guests, then with faint irony mentioned the gossip about Paul's brother.

"We Hilliards are famous," Paul said dryly.

"But at least *you're* lucky enough not to be infamous for stealing women, unlike your brother," Timothy answered with disapproval.

To Juliana's surprise, he was looking at Michael as he said this. Paul seemed to realize the same thing. Michael remained impassive, but she could see a flush on his pale redhead complexion.

"Michael, were you with my brother when he kidnapped his future wife to use against her father?" Paul demanded, his voice soft but firm.

Michael glanced at Timothy, then answered almost belligerently, "Aye."

Joseph, Roger, and Theobald all turned to stare. It was not League custom to discuss the missions of others. But then Juliana knew that Adam's only mission had been a personal one of vengeance.

"He and Robert were acting alone," Paul said. "Why would you go with them?"

"Because I am a knight of Keswick," Michael said with pride, "as was my father before me. I would never allow my lord to travel on so dangerous and important a journey without me."

In the tense silence, Juliana watched Paul. She knew his regret—that he hadn't helped his brothers avenge their parents. Yet here was another man who'd had the privilege of doing so, and he looked down upon Paul.

"You are my brother's knight?" Paul asked slowly. "And a Bladesman. Why do I not remember you?"

"I came to the League just after you'd left. It gave me great satisfaction to find your honorable brother and aid him."

"My honorable brother," Paul repeated, eyes narrowed. "But I am not like my brother, am I."

It wasn't spoken as a question, but Michael's stiff shoulders and tight mouth said he agreed.

Juliana thought Theobald and Joseph looked as if they'd have to step between a fight. To Timothy's credit, he still seemed relaxed, though grave.

Soberly, Paul said to Michael, "I envy you the privilege of riding at his side."

Michael blinked, his belligerence fading. "But you left your brothers; you left the League."

"I would not have done so had I known the name of the murderer. But I cannot change the past. And I still would have eventually left the League."

Michael studied him in confusion, but said nothing.

Timothy slapped his hands against his thighs as he rose, breaking the spell. "'Tis time to prepare for supper. Mistress Juliana, I will send for a fresh bath for you."

She didn't like to be singled out. "I can just use—"

"She accepts," Paul said.

To her surprise and consternation, Timothy winked at her.

"'Tis my duty as manservant," Michael said. "Allow me to send for the bath, Sir Timothy."

The Bladesmen all filed out, and before Paul could even loosen much of her damp lacing, a line of servants came, with empty buckets to haul away the cold dirty water, and then heated water that steamed as they poured it.

Juliana dipped her fingers in, closed her eyes, and sighed.

As Paul continued with the lacing at her back, he said, "You care too much what the Bladesmen think about how we conduct ourselves."

"I do not." But she knew she was angry with him— nay, angry with herself. "I know that success is the truest measure of my work."

"Good of you to convince yourself."

She tried to face him, but he held her in place.

"Hold still. This requires extreme concentration."

She bit her lip, upset that even a small amount of amusement could surface after this last tense hour.

"I can feel you shivering," he said.

"I am not."

"I should have insisted that you be allowed to change before we had our discussion."

"You are only saying that because you were wearing just a scrap of cloth."

"That did not bother me."

She looked over her shoulder and met his gaze. "And the state of my garments did not bother me. I do not wish to be treated differently, Paul. Understand that."

"Oh, I understand you well," he said softly.

She pressed her lips into a flat line of disapproval. He gave a last tug, the laces sagged, and she gladly stepped away from him.

"Get dressed behind the screen," she ordered. "I will be finished bathing before you're done."

"Is it not a woman's prerogative to enjoy a long bath?"

"I do not need such things. Now go."

He chuckled even as he took several garments out of the coffer and disappeared behind the changing screen. "Michael unpacked our things," he called. "I am certain he did not enjoy it."

She muttered an agreement, but she was focused on hurrying as she disrobed. The wet garments landed in a heap on the floor, and then she was in the bathing tub, almost shuddering as the heat warmed her muscles and bones.

"Do you need assistance?" he called.

She ignored him, washing hurriedly. Her hair was more difficult to manage. She didn't want to waste the bucket of rinsing water simply wetting her hair, so she awkwardly dipped her head where she could, and used the wet cloth, as she'd done for Paul.

"Your hair must be difficult."

"If you are spying on me, that will lead to a challenge," she said firmly.

"I would not dream of something so underhanded." He paused. "Nay, I would *dream* about it, but never would I do it."

She poured the last bucket of water over her head, hiding her laughter.

Chapter 12

Throughout supper, Juliana felt eyes regarding her—regarding both of them. It was important for people to speculate about Paul, of course. And he played Sir Paul the Dissolute as a charming man with grandiose gestures, poorly hiding a weak intellect. It would be amusing were it not so serious. They were waiting for the next contact from traitors against the Crown, men so desperate they would invent a lost, living prince.

But something else was bothering her, and she'd learned never to ignore her instincts. Gooseflesh rose along her arms, even as she finished eating the first course of lampreys spiced with ginger and cinnamon. There were hundreds of people in the hall; it was so crowded that she rubbed elbows with Paul and the man on the other side of her. Yet, still she felt that something was wrong.

It wasn't until she was eating from the cheese selection at the end of the meal that her gaze met that of a man two tables away from her. He was staring intently at her.

And then she recognized him, and her stomach did a little twist of both gladness and dismay. He was Alexander Clowes, a young man who'd fostered with her family throughout his childhood. He'd been her dearest friend, her staunchest defender—and now he thought her a strumpet, for she could see at once that he recognized her.

She didn't alert Paul; perhaps she was wrong.

The guests rose at last from the tables, and the servants began to dismantle them. Musicians warmed up in their gallery overlooking the hall.

And still Alex watched her—if it was Alex, of course.

His hair was as dark as Juliana's. Though his eyes must still be the green of forest leaves, his body had changed, maturing into a man of average height but with impressive shoulders. He'd always taken his training seriously, and she'd admired that about him, watching him on the tiltyard when her father had forbidden her own training.

Now Alex watched *her* openly, for any man could.

"I am going to leave you," Paul suddenly murmured into her ear.

She almost jumped in surprise.

"Fear not. No one shall aim a dagger at my heart in front of all these people."

"But where—"

"I go to join the men surrounding Kilborn. Concubines are not permitted. Can you occupy yourself?"

She nodded, feeling distracted, and Paul's attention sharpened on her for a moment, but he said nothing. Then he leaned down and pressed his lips to her cheek—focusing her attention back on him.

"Ah, a reaction," he murmured, his lips still touching her. "You soothe my battered pride." He chuckled, squeezed her hand, and left her.

It seemed only a moment had passed before Alex moved toward her with purpose. She was used to remaining calm in even the most dangerous of situations, and that skill did not desert her now. She would deal with whatever happened, bear his scorn with the grace of a longtime concubine. Drawing her character around her like a cloak, she smiled serenely at Alex when he came to a stop.

To her surprise, he bowed to her, even as she saw Theobald moving closer, hand on the dagger sheathed in his belt. Alex saw him, too, and hesitated, looking from one to the other. She shook her head at Theobald, and with a nod, he retreated.

Alex was waiting patiently. "Mistress Juliana," he said, as if trying the name on his tongue. "The others called you that, but I already knew."

"Aye, as I knew you, Alex. Or is it Sir Alexander now?"

He was a younger son, not in line for his father's title.

He grinned. "It is, but I do not wish you to call me that."

She began to relax. Though playing a proud concubine, she'd once been a gentlewoman. The character she was portraying should be embarrassed to be seen in such humbling circumstances by someone from long ago.

She was not fooling herself—she *was* embarrassed to have Alex think she'd not been able to provide for herself, had had to depend on a man's money and protection.

But it could not be helped. The mission was more important than her pride; it meant a peaceful future for the kingdom.

Alex was staring down at her as if bemused. "I had not imagined that you could grow lovelier."

Playing her part, she glanced as if to be certain Paul wasn't watching. And he wasn't; he was listening intently to the other men, looking a bit confused.

And then she smiled softly at Alex. "You are too kind."

"Where have you been?" he asked. "When I heard about your father, I came as soon as I could, but by the time I arrived, your mother had already died and you had disappeared. Juliana, I am so sorry."

He whispered the last words with such sympathy that for the first time in years, she felt her eyes sting with tears. Mortified at her lack of control, she blinked them away.

"You are kind, Alex, but I could not stay where I was no longer welcome."

"But your steward said they would have cared for you."

"I know—and they would have offended the king and risked their own livelihoods. I couldn't allow them to do that."

"Always thinking of others," he said, shaking his head.

She didn't know what to say, didn't think of herself like that.

Now it was his turn to glance at Paul, before saying, "We were told you'd gone to a nunnery."

She felt her face flame—she couldn't help it. But she met his gaze evenly. "And now you know the truth."

He stared at her, then looked down, his smile wry. "Part of me is relieved, if you must know."

"I do not have to know your feelings, Alex. You owe me nothing."

"But I want you to know that I . . . that I understand. I am relieved to find that you did not hide yourself away, spending your days kneeling in prayer. It may be blasphemous, but I am glad you have been in the world, and perhaps known some happiness."

She was Juliana the wise concubine as she said, "Happiness? You show your ignorance, Alex."

His smile faded. "Does he beat you?" he demanded

softly, his hands fisted, his body tense as if he'd attack Paul.

"Nay, please, nothing like that," she quickly said, reaching to touch his arm, then stopping herself.

He noticed and dropped his gaze awkwardly.

"But I am his toy, Alex. I do what he wishes. And in return I am safe and warm and well fed. I never expected happiness, but I am content."

"Content?" he echoed, his tone tinged with sorrow. "Is that how we dreamed of our lives when we were children, lying by the stream waiting for fish to nibble our hooks?"

She smiled at the image of such innocence; it seemed so long ago. Alex had been her one true friend, for the little girls hadn't understood her, and the boys were the children of her father's soldiers and servants, trained not to become too personal. They'd tolerated her on the tiltyard, with her little dagger and her wooden sword, because she was the viscount's daughter.

But Alex . . . Alex had befriended her. He'd come to them homesick at eight years of age, away from his parents for the first time, and been teased by the other little boys. Juliana had understood his pain of being an outsider, and they'd become playmates, and then friends, until his parents had taken him away for good when he was fifteen.

"Juliana?"

She realized Alex was studying her with concern. She fluttered her hand. "I am simply remembering. Pay me no heed. I had a much better childhood than most, and you improved it."

He blushed, and she wondered if he could still be so innocent.

"Alex, I need a favor."

He glanced at Paul once more, then said resolutely, "Anything."

She chuckled. "Nay, I do not want to be spirited away from Sir Paul. But . . . I told Lady Kilborn that I was the daughter of an impoverished gentleman who sold me against my will to a Frenchman before I met Sir Paul."

His expression softened with compassion.

"I no longer use my surname. I do not wish to hide our friendship, but . . . would you mind not mentioning my real family?"

"Of course, Juliana! I understand you not wanting to remember such pain."

"Yet I am of Yorkshire, and bound to meet others I know. If that happens, so be it. They'll think the truth, that I'm lying to cover a shameful past. I do not think anyone I know would deny me that small comfort."

"Your true parentage will be our secret," he said sincerely. "Does Sir Paul know?"

She shook her head. "Nay, he is a man who thinks appearances are as important as a person's worth."

"Then he has no depth to him, Juliana. You should—"

"Don't, Alex," she said sharply.

He stared at her.

"My life is private, my decisions my own. You would not want anyone to gainsay you, now would you?"

His smile was reluctant, but it appeared at last. "You always were a strong woman, Juliana."

She met his smile with one of her own. "And how are *you*?" she asked brightly.

"A subtle change of topic." He shook his head in amusement. "I am well. My older brother is now the baron."

"I did not hear that your father had died. You have my sympathy."

He smiled. "Thank you. But save your sympathy for my brother. He is married, with three unruly children and a shrew of a wife."

She laughed aloud, then saw several people look her way in curiosity. Tamping down her mirth, she said, "Did you not always say he deserved such a woman?"

"Aye, and he's paying for his years of bullying me. I almost feel sorry for him."

They both paused, and she asked the question she found herself surprisingly reluctant to vocalize. "And are you married, Alex?"

"Nay, I am not."

Was that another blush?

"Surely, there is a lady you are interested in."

He shrugged. "No one in particular. I am the younger brother of a baron, Juliana, and not supremely wealthy. There are better choices for young ladies."

"Then they're fools," Juliana said firmly.

This time, *his* laughter turned heads.

Paul had seen the man approach Juliana from the beginning. Since Paul had easily managed to appear stupid and distracted all at the same time, most of the men around him surely guessed he was jealous of this stranger making his concubine smile.

And he hadn't seen that kind of smile on Juliana in . . . well, perhaps never. When he'd first known her, she'd been a brave, eager young woman, still tense with hidden worry about her future. Now he'd been with her a fortnight, and he'd seen her sensual smile, her confident smile, but this stranger inspired a new softness in her, one that made his chest feel uncomfortable. It was easy to portray simmering jealousy when he suspected he felt a bit of it himself.

He shouldn't be jealous; Juliana was focused on the mission, and somehow, she must believe that this stranger could help her.

But that smile . . .

He tried to distract himself with consideration of Michael's revelation about being a Keswick knight. It made the man's anger toward Paul perfectly understandable.

Michael was loyal to Adam, and thought Paul ungrateful and perhaps even selfish. He could not change Michael's opinion of him—he would never explain the full truth—but at least now he understood and could even sympathize with the knight.

But Paul had a mission to perform, and it required getting to know his host and the other guests. Besides Lord Kilborn, there were a number of aristocrats present, from two dukes all the way down to several barons. Thrown into the mix were several dozen wealthy, influential knights of property. Most of the guests were from the north of England, so that did not narrow down his list of suspects.

But someone in this castle had brought Paul here for a reason; someone wanted to use him to throw the kingdom into an uproar, lure foreign invaders, and overthrow the king. Much as he could only wait to be contacted, he had the ability to study the guests and make his own deductions.

But he kept hearing Juliana laugh.

When at last he'd run out of simple things to say, and it was obvious Kilborn was growing tired of explaining things to him, he took his leave and began to move across the crowded hall.

Many couples danced to the musicians' lively tune. Men played dice against the wall, and he saw Joseph and Michael in that crowd. Theobald stood beside the great double doors, near to Juliana, his charge, arms folded across his chest, his expression impassive. The mask was like a wall between other people and him, and Paul suspected that was the way the man preferred it. Old Roger sat before the hearth with other men his age, appearing to drink far too much.

And then he saw the stranger lean toward Juliana as if he would touch her arm. And she was still smiling that soft smile at him, and it took everything in Paul not to jerk the man away from her.

Juliana saw him coming, and her expression turned sensual for his benefit, even as he knew it was part of a façade.

"Sir Paul, you finally returned to me," she said, tucking her hand in his elbow and briefly leaning her head against his arm.

Paul looked down at the stranger, whose height did not reach his chin. "Do I know you, sir? You and my companion seem already the best of friends."

Juliana gave a low chuckle. "And we were. Sir Paul, may I introduce Sir Alexander Clowes. We knew each other in childhood."

Sir Paul the Dissolute wasn't supposed to know about her life, but the real Paul understood her message. Clowes knew the truth of her background. But Juliana seemed so at ease that she must not fear that Clowes would reveal her.

Then they'd had a close friendship, Paul thought, feeling again that awkward pressure in his chest, that need to hold her against him as if he owned her.

And to everyone here, he *did* own her, he realized. He slid his arm about her waist. "Sir Alexander, 'tis good to meet a friend of Juliana's. We can exchange stories about her."

Juliana rolled her eyes. "Paul, you say such silly things. You need not know the boring details of my life."

Paul studied Clowes. "So you two did boring things together?"

"We were but children," Clowes said, "playing games of childhood." He reddened, glancing between Juliana and Paul as if he didn't know what to say.

Paul assumed the man worried about protecting her secrets, but perhaps that was not all. Had there been more between them?

"By games, do you mean helping her learn to use weapons?" Paul asked.

Clowes's mouth dropped open, and Juliana stared at Paul, projecting shock at first, then the bemusement of the real Juliana underneath.

"I never told you that," she breathed, fake fear quickening in her dark eyes.

"I know much about you, my little duckling," he said, giving her a reassuring squeeze. "And now here I have the chance to learn even more."

She gave a halfhearted smile, as if she still feared Paul's mention of her past. "You know I've always answered any of your questions."

"Aye, but 'tis not the same as meeting someone who's known you much longer than I have." He elbowed Clowes. "But you haven't known her that well, eh, Sir Alexander?"

Clowes shook his head. "She was but thirteen when I was sent home. 'Twas a friendship we shared, nothing more," he said firmly.

Trying to protect Juliana. Admirable, of course, but revealing.

"Glad I am to hear it," Paul said. "Juliana, let us find a tankard of ale and listen to the minstrels. A good evening to you, Sir Alexander."

When they retired to their bedchamber, Paul allowed Juliana to shut the door. He removed the belt at his waist, then glanced about, only to realize that Juliana had leaned back against the door to regard him.

"Looking forward to watching me disrobe?" he asked lightly.

She said nothing for a moment, her expression quizzical. "We had agreed to never mention my past. Why did you speak of it to Alex?"

"Alex, is it?" He smiled.

"We were children, so I would call him nothing else."

"Of course, of course." He walked slowly toward her. "But I cannot help my curiosity about you. I can hardly talk to 'Alex' about you if we're pretending."

"Why would you want to talk to him about me?" she demanded, putting a hand on his chest before he could get too close.

He had her boxed in near the door, and enjoyed the feeling of looking down on her, knowing she couldn't retreat.

Softly, he said, "How else can I get to know the little girl who played war games with the boys?"

Juliana's expression softened. "In truth, as I grew older, Alex was usually the only boy who would play with me. He fought the others on my behalf."

"Did he?" Paul crossed his arms over his chest and continued to study her. "Why would he do that?"

"Because the boys began to treat me differently, and he would no longer permit me to fight my own battles."

"Smart young man," Paul mused. "I imagine many a maturing boy would have liked to wrestle with you."

"I did not like how things were changing." She pushed past him and walked farther into the chamber. "I could understand, of course. I was the lord's daughter, and the boys were finally realizing they'd been crossing swords with someone they could marry."

"But not Alex."

She tilted her head as she watched him. "As I told

you, we did not think of each other like that. Do you find jealousy stirring in your breast, Sir Paul?"

"Sir Paul the Dissolute certainly does. He knows he doesn't have the brains to keep a woman such as you for long."

"A woman such as I doesn't require brains in her man—or so I told Alex," she added, beginning to smile.

"He must have been very curious about our relationship."

Though her smile didn't fade, it became tinged with melancholy. "He understood all too well. He thought I'd gone to a nunnery."

Paul wanted to wince, but knew she hated pity. "Would he have preferred that?"

"Strangely enough, nay. He said he was glad I wasn't shut away, that I was out in the world with a chance at happiness." She shook her head ruefully.

"Juliana the Concubine would not admit to that."

"Nay, she would not. She is in the profession of serving you—Sir Paul the Dissolute, that is."

"Serving me," he repeated, dragging the words out.

"I believe I already served you today," she said, picking up her night rail.

"You did not finish," he reminded her.

"I *offered* to finish bathing you," she said sweetly.

"And you know that's not my meaning."

He wished he could push aside the screen to watch

her. He heard the splash of water into a basin, and knew Michael must have been here to prepare for them. Michael was behaving appropriately for his character as manservant—Paul found it too easy to behave exactly as his own character would. Juliana was a woman he desired—an experienced woman, who'd already given herself to a man.

He pulled off his tunic and hose, dragging on a thin pair of breeches to sleep in. He opened the shutters to let in the night air, feeling overly warm—overly aroused. But he could be patient.

He'd been saying that to himself for days now, he thought ruefully.

Juliana heard the door softly open, and she snapped to alertness from a deep sleep. She pulled her dagger from beneath her pillow, knew Paul was doing the same.

Her fellow Bladesmen would have heard the footsteps in the corridor, were monitoring who came and went. They'd allowed this person to pass.

In the dimness of the chamber, she saw only one man, a dark silhouette. Instead of approaching the bed, he set something on the table, then pulled the cover off to reveal a lantern.

Quickly, she undid the laces at her neck, let the dressing gown and robe reveal her shoulder. She had to hide the fact that she'd worn a dressing gown to bed. Giving a little gasp, she half sat up. "Paul?" she cried, then realized that her thin garments had fallen so much they revealed the upper curve of her breast. She didn't cover herself.

"I am not here to hurt you," the man said in a quiet, impassive voice.

Paul scrambled over the top of her, standing in front of the bed as if he were partially shielding her. "I know you not, sir. Do you have the wrong lodgings?"

The man remained in front of the lamp, which kept his face in the shadows. "I do not, Sir Paul."

"You know my name, but I know not yours."

"My name is not important, and neither is yours. You will soon be pretending 'tis a false one, regardless."

Paul said nothing for a moment. "Speak freely, for my companion knows of the bargain I made that put us in too much danger."

"You made the bargain, Sir Paul." His voice took on a dangerous edge. "We agreed to cancel your debts and pay you more besides. And now I hear you are threatening to leave."

Sitting up, Juliana held the coverlet to her breasts, and kept her breathing loud and full of fright, as she looked back and forth between the two men in worried confusion.

"No threat, sir, but a statement of fact," Paul said. "I was promised there would be no danger to myself—and we were attacked on the road!"

"By highwaymen," the man said dismissively. "They are everywhere, and if your men could not handle them, 'tis not our fault."

"I am here, without a scratch upon my person," Paul insisted. "My men acquitted themselves well. But that is not the point. I thought I would be playing a part for you, an amusement, and now—"

"You are not so much the fool," the man interrupted impatiently. "You know 'tis no amusement we are about, not for what we are paying you."

"Then tell me!" Paul demanded.

"Keep your voice down!" the man commanded in a low, threatening voice. He moved toward the door, head bent as if listening.

Juliana squinted her eyes, trying to see his face, but he was too good at hiding it.

"You know the truth, Sir Paul," the man said with sarcasm. "You made yourself quite visible at every major town between here and London, spending money and showing your fine clothing, all while not saying your surname. 'From Flanders' I heard—as if many do not know what that means, or who might be backing you."

Paul said nothing.

"You know that your features resemble the boy king and his brother. You know that desperate men will take great chances to right the wrongs done to our country."

Juliana let herself gape at the man in confusion.

"You have offered yourself up, and we intend to use you. Change your mind, and suffer the consequences as you're tossed in debtor's prison—and that would be only if you were lucky. Right now, you live because we protect you. Go to prison, and you're on your own."

Paul remained stiff with tension at the center of the chamber. "What do you want me to do?"

"Wait. Make yourself visible, as you've been doing, but reveal nothing. Be a mystery—which means keep your mouth shut. We begin to question whether you can do that."

"I can do what I have to," he said heavily.

The man covered the lantern again, and the chamber went dark. "We will contact you soon," were his parting words.

Then the door shut behind him.

Chapter 13

Paul lit a candle from the embers of the near dead fire, and turned to face Juliana. Her hair was disheveled, her shoulder bare as if they'd just finished bed sport.

"You might want to fix your garments," he said. "We will not be alone long."

She slid from the bed, and he watched her retie the laces of her night rail, spied the fine lace trim that teased him so unmercifully before she closed the dressing gown and belted it at the waist.

"You wanted him to notice your pale flesh by lantern light," he said wryly.

"Of course. I could not allow him to realize I wore a dressing gown to bed with my patron."

"So then if we have to continue our disguises in bed, you'll wear just your night rail—or nothing at all. I might insist that my concubine be ready for my every whim."

She rolled her eyes. Then the Bladesmen used their

knock and invited themselves inside. Theobald went to the window, while the others arranged themselves in chairs or leaned against the wall.

Paul's amused expression faded. "Was our visitor accompanied by others?"

Timothy shook his head and stretched out his legs to cross them. "He was alone. Very bold of him."

"He was confident he held all the power," Juliana said.

Paul briefly explained what had happened. "At least we know they truly want to use me somehow."

"And that they picked up on your knowledge that you look the part," Joseph added thoughtfully. "You appear gullible, weak when it comes to money, but not quite so stupid."

Paul bowed his head. "You flatter me, sir."

"Too stupid, and you'd be too hard to control," Michael said grudgingly.

Paul knew that was almost a compliment. "So we wait," he said.

Timothy turned to Juliana. "Someone recognized you."

She nodded. "Sir Alexander Clowes. He fostered with my family in his youth, and we were friends."

"Will he cause problems?"

"Nay, he sees my place as tenuous at Paul's side, and he would not wish me ill. He agreed not to reveal my surname, thinking I would not wish to be shamed. As if being a concubine was such a prideful position," she added, giving a faint smile.

"Then continue as you've been doing," Timothy said, rising to his feet. "And the rest of us will continue to befriend the soldiers and servants."

The Bladesmen filed out, all taking a moment to wish Juliana a good sleep. Paul wondered if as the men grew more fond of her, the more they'd see him as the enemy from whom she needed protection.

"I think you surprise Timothy and the others," Juliana said quietly when they were alone.

Paul turned to her, eyebrows raised. "Why? Certainly, Timothy has known me my whole life."

"Not the last few years. Surely, he had cause to wonder how your bitterness toward the League had changed you. But you work well within the group."

"A Bladesman well trained," he said, not bothering to disguise his antipathy as he turned toward the bed.

She caught his shoulder. "Of course you were well trained," she said angrily. "You now have skills that have caused you to win tournaments, that have saved your life. Why are you so ungrateful that the League kept you safe from murderers as a child?"

Though Juliana had thought that bitterness hadn't warped his life, now she wasn't so certain. The shadows in the near dark chamber made him look like an angry stranger.

"If that's all it was, I *would* be grateful," he said coldly. "But your precious League voted to try something never done before, and my *foster father* didn't stop it."

"Then tell me, Paul. Make me see why you and I are on opposite sides of an insurmountable wall where the League is concerned. Show me why you disdain a man who tries to love you as a son."

His smile lacked amusement. "A father would have protected us. He gave us over to an experiment."

She could only study him in confusion.

"Instead of allowing us to be children, they trained us as Bladesmen from the start, hoping to make perfect weapons out of the three of us, a new army."

Uncertainty encroached at the edge of her mind. "That cannot be. You were only a child, how could you know that—"

"Our only toys were wooden swords and daggers, not balls or hoops. We studied constantly, everything from the techniques of the Holy Land to estate management, for when we would be in disguise within a household."

"But surely any knowledge is for the good."

"Knowledge, aye. Imprisonment—nay. We never left there to see the outside world, Juliana, never saw women, not once. A murderer took our parents, and the League took our childhood. Bladesmen came and went, but never us. The Council thought they were preparing us for assignments, but they didn't prepare us for life."

He stalked across the chamber, anger simmering almost visibly about him.

"But . . . 'twas to help people," Juliana said with quiet conviction. "The League is a noble cause."

"Aye, you sound like my brother, Adam. I resented his dedication, his inability to see how our lives had been corrupted without our permission. If our parents had been alive, would *they* have allowed it?" he demanded.

She bit her lip, knowing the truth.

"I don't think they would have, but then again, what do I know? I don't know anything about parents and children, or how to relate to them."

"But Timothy was—"

"My foster father? Aye, he was. But he had a home to return to, where they did not know his secret life. He tried to be with us as much as possible, but you can see how that would have been difficult. We were *different,* Juliana. And as we reached manhood, and they finally began to allow us some freedom, they realized that we were flawed as Bladesmen. We didn't know how to disguise ourselves among men, because we'd never been as other men. We hadn't grown up in the world, didn't understand its intricate rules. The experiment had failed."

"I would never think you didn't know about the world, Paul."

"Nay, not now. When they realized their mistake,

they worked rigorously with us to teach us everything from serving a lord to dancing with ladies—without real ladies to dance with, I might add."

She winced. "You surely did not appreciate that."

The image she had of him dancing with his brothers must have occurred to him, as well, for at last his pacing slowed, and a faint, mocking smile touched his mouth.

"I know you will find this terribly hard to believe," he continued, "but I did not understand courtship, how to appeal to ladies, the subtleties of compliments and slow seduction."

"Subtleties? And you think you're capable of that now?"

He didn't answer, but his lips twisted in a wry smile that seemed somehow sad. He had said something important, something revealing, but she didn't understand what it was, didn't know even how to question him.

"But you went on missions for the League, you saw how they helped people, helped the king."

"The people they chose to help, aye. But perhaps others were not so fortunate. And which king? We've had several these last few years. It makes one wonder if they helped one king against another."

He seemed to be studying her, looking deeply into her eyes, and it made her uncomfortable.

"Nay, they are not about politics, you know that," she said. "They help innocent people. Right now, with the king in danger, all Englishmen need help." Turning toward the bed, she said, "I do not claim they did right by you, Paul. But you had to be kept secret and safe, away from an unknown murderer."

"Making excuses for them, Juliana?" he asked softly.

"The League does not need that from me. They thought they could help more people by training you and your brothers."

"Aye, they thought that," he said impassively. "But that does not excuse the fact that they carelessly hurt the innocent to achieve their noble goals."

"They made a mistake," she insisted, as pain settled on the edge of her awareness. "You said they agreed the experiment failed."

"Aye, they said they would never do such a thing again."

Her relief was a bit too overwhelming, but she didn't want to think on that. "They're not perfect, Paul, and they now know that. But 'tis a terrible shame that you and your brothers suffered."

"If it makes you feel better, my brothers do not consider that they suffered. They are both still members of the League."

It did make her feel better. "That was honest, Paul. You did not need to make light of your own feelings by showing me that your brothers disagree."

"You should know the facts, all of them."

His voice sounded strangely full of purpose, but she didn't question him. She hesitated, then removed her dressing gown before climbing into bed. Although he blew out the candle, he didn't join her.

"Paul?"

"Sleep, Juliana. I find that memories, once resurrected, do not easily disappear."

She pulled up the coverlet and rested her head on the cushion. She fell asleep watching the faint dark shadow of him as he paced.

The next morning, mass was held in the courtyard, for the tower chapel could not hold all the guests. Paul knelt at Juliana's side and rather than piously bow his head, he found himself watching her as she prayed to God.

Did she pray that the League experiment was its only flaw? That her great and glorious League had learned its lesson and would never sin again?

Last night, the truth had been on his lips, burning to be told. But then she'd tried to defend the League, to see the good in them. He found himself feeling sorry for her rather than angry. It would crush her to know the truth of her father's innocence, and the League's part in his betrayal.

They broke their fast in the great hall, and Paul watched as afterward, all the men rose up to go out onto the tiltyard and to the lists, practicing for the opening of the tournament on the morrow. He'd already determined that Sir Paul the Dissolute would think himself above needing to practice. He listened to the excited voices, the boasts, the cheerful rivalries. Then he realized that Juliana was watching him from her place at his side. The other people they'd shared the table with had already gone, and the servants had begun to swarm out from the kitchens.

Softly, she said, "You would normally be with those men, preparing for the tournament."

"Aye. But if I practice, 'twill be obvious how 'unskilled' I'm to be. Rather, they should be curious."

She smiled. "Do you usually boast as they do?"

"There is no need," he said loftily, pushing to his feet. "I developed quite the reputation in Europe. All wanted to challenge me, and my presence signaled a tournament's success."

"All that, and you do not even boast," she said dryly.

He smiled down at her. "Shall we walk out in the ward? 'Tis a fine summer day."

She allowed him to take her hand and slip it into his elbow. From the corner of his eye, he saw Theobald leave his place at the door and follow them, watching Juliana's back as if he didn't trust Sir Paul the Dissolute. As they walked down the stairs to the courtyard below, people hurried back and forth, or lingered in groups to talk. A flock of geese was being driven toward the kitchens at the rear of the castle by a goose girl; they could hear the mooing of cows in a dairy shed, and the clang of metal on metal at the armory.

The walked through the open gates to the outer ward, and on the dirt grounds, dozens of men practiced every discipline, from sword fighting to jousting to grappling to throwing daggers. The few benches were filled with spectators, so they wandered slowly among the crowds.

People glanced at them, but no one approached, although occasionally, one of the women from the sewing chamber smiled at Juliana.

"Do you see the messengers?" Paul asked beneath his breath.

She nodded. "I've seen two leave since we've been outside. They could simply be carrying correspondence from the noblemen to their estates."

"They could. But I imagine Bladesmen will be following them to see."

They stopped beneath the shade of an apple tree, heavy with unripe fruit, and studied the sword fighting. Men used dull swords for tournaments, but bruises—and broken bones—could still result. Quietly, they talked about what they saw, mentioning skill, wincing over poor technique. She was very easy to talk to, something he'd found difficult with other women. Oh, he could charm and make small talk with ease, but true exchanges of conversation meant one had to be interested or familiar—and he'd never been either with women.

Off to the side, little boys mimicked their fathers and older brothers. They had wooden swords and they hacked each other unmercifully, laughing and jeering.

"My brothers and I occasionally enjoyed ourselves in a similar fashion," Paul commented.

"Only occasionally? I assume you practiced much."

"We did, but we had to treat it seriously. No games on the tiltyard. It was drilled into us that it would someday be life and death. But when we were alone, sometimes our practice became a wrestling match."

"And who won?"

"Adam, being the eldest." He smiled down at her. "There was much celebrating on my part the day I finally defeated him."

"Celebrating? Or crowing like a rooster?"

He chuckled.

On the fringe of the children stood one lone boy. Paul couldn't estimate his age, but he was old enough to be carrying a wooden sword. It hung from his hand, and he moved from foot to foot restlessly as he watched the others.

"He looks so sad," Juliana said.

Paul glanced at her. "Childhood can sometimes be sad. You know that too well."

The little boy, in scruffy breeches and a dirty tunic, lifted his toy sword halfheartedly, swinging it a bit, trying to thrust once, although he tripped on his feet.

Juliana suddenly tugged on Paul's arm. "Let's talk to him."

He frowned, but couldn't resist her without drawing attention. "Whatever for?"

"Do you have something else to do?"

As they came closer, the boy swung the sword without looking behind him, and hit Juliana in the hip. The boy turned about and then gaped, his face white.

Juliana smiled brightly. "'Twas an accident."

He dropped the sword and ran.

Paul watched the disappointment and concern sadden her expression. She was a woman, though she always tried to pretend she was just one of the men, and women felt close to children.

"I would follow him," she said with a sigh, "but that might frighten him worse."

"Allow me!" called a young woman. Petite and plump, she practically ran past them, holding her head-dress in place. "He is my brother!"

Paul saw the hope and relief in Juliana's eyes, but she said nothing for several minutes, until she shaded her eyes and pointed. "Look! She found him!"

The young woman had the little boy by the hand as they walked through the outer ward toward the inner. She was talking to him softly, while his head hung with shame. But she glanced at Paul and Juliana and smiled with encouragement before disappearing through the gatehouse.

"There," Paul said. "All is well."

Juliana hesitated as if she might disagree, then turned back to the tiltyard with a sigh. "Look at the way the man in green holds his sword. He will not last during the melee."

Juliana was trying hard to distract Paul from her mistake, but she knew it wasn't working. He kept giving her puzzled looks, and she realized she might have revealed a bit too much of her softer side by her concern for the little boy. But she hadn't been able to help it—and she was not about to apologize.

Just when she thought he'd forgotten her foolishness, the woman who'd found the little boy approached them alone. Juliana recognized her from the sewing chamber, but they had not spoken.

The woman smiled and said, "A good day to you. I am Lady Margaret Foxe."

Juliana returned her smile. "And to you, Lady Margaret. I am Mistress Juliana, and this is Sir Paul."

Lady Margaret ducked her head shyly at Paul's regard, but she kept peeking with curiosity at Juliana. Perhaps she was intrigued to be openly talking to a concubine.

"Is your brother well?" Paul asked.

Juliana glanced at him in surprise.

"He is," Lady Margaret said. "Our mother is quite exasperated with his shyness and sensitivity."

"Then we need not worry that we will be challenged by your father?" Paul asked dryly.

Lady Margaret giggled. "Nay, please do not. My father is quite preoccupied with himself at this tournament. He is the earl of Staincliff, and you would think that he was attending Parliament, so serious has he been."

Juliana shared a glance with Paul, wondering if her father had a darker purpose.

"He has no time for Edward," Lady Margaret continued, "and does not want to see that he struggles." She briefly covered her mouth. "Oh dear, I am speaking too freely."

Juliana smiled. "Nay, you are easing my conscience."

Sir Paul the Dissolute shook his head. "I will leave you ladies to discuss such feminine matters."

Lady Margaret blushed as Paul kissed Juliana's hand. Juliana watched him find Timothy, who'd just stepped off the tiltyard, covered in perspiration and dirt.

Urgently, Lady Margaret said, "Tell me I did not offend your—your—"

"My patron?" Juliana finished for her, smiling faintly. "You did not."

"Forgive me, you must think me a fool." Lady Margaret wrung her hands. "I have never—I know not what to say—"

"To a concubine?"

Lady Margaret winced and nodded.

"You are doing fine, my lady. I am simply a woman."

Well, perhaps not "simply."

"Yet, my lady, you should also think of yourself," Juliana cautioned. "Perhaps you do not wish to be seen speaking with me."

Lady Margaret's lips pursed mutinously. "That concerns me not, Mistress Juliana. People cannot be judged for the choices forced upon them."

Lady Margaret had of course heard Juliana's tale of a cruel father.

"There are many who believe I should not have submitted."

"Should you have killed yourself then? Is that not one of the worst crimes in God's eyes?"

Juliana grinned. "I like you, Lady Margaret."

She blushed and shrugged, then smiled herself. "And I like you, Mistress Juliana. Could I simply call you by your Christian name? I would so like it if I was just Margaret to you."

"Aye, Margaret, 'twould be my pleasure."

Margaret looked over her shoulder, then sighed. "I must go. My mother requested my presence. Shall I see you this afternoon at the festival?"

"The festival?"

"Aye, out on the tournament grounds and in the vil-

lage. There will be quite a celebration in anticipation
of the beginning of the tournament tomorrow. You will
enjoy it!"

"My thanks. I will see you there."

Margaret waved and hurried back toward the keep.

Paul stood stiffly at Timothy's side, while his foster
father drank thirstily from a wineskin. Paul glanced
behind him occasionally at Juliana, who spoke anima-
tedly with Lady Margaret.

"We met the daughter of the earl of Staincliff," he
said, gesturing with his head toward Juliana.

Timothy wiped his mouth on his bare forearm and
eyed the two women.

"She says her father is acting far too serious, for a
mere tournament. Perhaps he is one we're looking for."

"Perhaps." Timothy continued to watch the women.
"Juliana seems to be enjoying herself."

"As much as she can knowing all think her a prostitute. But aye, she knows how to behave in character. She
tells me constantly how well trained she is."

Timothy sighed. "She accepted this assignment,
Paul," he said softly.

"And you knew she would."

Timothy looked around to find no one close enough
to overhear them. "There are few Bladesmen who refuse
an assignment, even yourself."

"But I am one of the few who did refuse. She has difficulty understanding that."

"Does she know why you left us?"

Paul stiffened, but Timothy could not possibly suspect that Paul knew the connection between Juliana's father and the League. "The experiment, you mean?" Paul asked sarcastically. "Aye, and she's defending you and the League to the bitter end. She is too loyal. I only hope she's not hurt."

Timothy perused him for a moment. "As for someone hurting Juliana," he began, "the bathing tub incident concerns me."

Paul clenched his jaw. "It shouldn't. She and I know where we stand with each other."

"I am not berating you, Paul," Timothy said quietly. "I know you well, and—"

"Do you?" Paul asked. "I have been gone several years, and much as the League might have kept track of me, you know not whether I've changed, whether I've become a man who hurts women. And yet you put Juliana with me, alone, night after night."

Timothy faced him, his frown one of concern. "You're wrong. I know the man you grew to be. I trust you with my life, with Juliana's life, or I would never have suggested you for this mission."

Paul didn't know what to say, what to feel. He was full of anger at Timothy's part in the League's failings, but Timothy was not the only man making the decisions. Paul could not focus all his ire at his foster father.

"I trust you, Paul," Timothy repeated. "I think of you as my son, and as such, I hope you never have to make a decision someday that will cause you heartache. No one deserves that."

"I will make a better choice," Paul said coolly.

"I hope you do."

Chapter 14

With her arm in Paul's, Juliana walked through the last gatehouse and left the castle. She glanced at Paul, who took a deep, satisfied breath.

He saw her watching, and grinned. "'Tis overcrowded in the castle."

"But you've been to so many tournaments."

"And always I stayed at an inn, or in my own pavilion. Being surrounded by so many people in the castle felt confining."

"Then let us breathe the open air and enjoy ourselves. Although that does seem contradictory to our purpose here."

He drew her into his arms. "I *am* supposed to enjoy myself."

As always, her breath left her lungs at just the feel of the length of his tall body against hers.

"I have orders to act as if nothing is happening," he continued, "orders from both sides. Today I am Sir

Paul the Dissolute, and I am enjoying a festival with my concubine."

"You are taking advantage of this concubine," she murmured, patting his chest and trying unobtrusively to push away.

"I could kiss you, you know," he said slyly. "No one, not even you, would stop me."

"You know the Bladesmen are watching us," she said, growing curious. "Is there more meaning than a simple kiss?"

His smile faded as he looked down at her. She felt his hands stroke her back gently.

"Is there such a thing as a simple kiss with you, Juliana?" he whispered.

And then he leaned down and gently kissed her cheek, lingering too long. His mouth was moist and soft, his breath warm near her ear. A quiver moved through her, and she knew he must feel it. The tenderness of the gesture was as overwhelming as the sensuality.

Then with a pat on her backside, he released her. She was left with an unsettled feeling of confusion and yearning, as well as disappointment, the latter of which she regretted. Sooner or later, she would not be able to hide her eagerness for what he could teach her. But that would break the vow she'd sworn to herself.

Yet . . . she was beginning to question how being with Paul broke her vow. He had his own vow, that he would never return to the League, so if he were not a Bladesman . . .

But oh, he was her partner in a dangerous mission, where emotions might affect judgments. She had to remember that.

The earl of Kilborn treated his guests well. He'd had tents set up throughout a field of flowers, where tables overflowing with food awaited hungry guests.

For their further enjoyment, several football games commenced between the boys of the village and those of the castle. There were running races and stone-throwing competitions for the men, and the winners received prizes of horses and arms. Juliana saw the occasional Bladesman from her party competing, but none brought attention to themselves by winning. Theobald, on the other hand, never left her perimeter, his expression impassive, but menacing just because of the mask.

To Juliana's delight, she saw Alex hurling a stone in the final round, and he won a large fish for second place. He held it up to laughter and applause, then handed it off to a squire to be taken to the kitchen.

He waved at Juliana, and she waved back, beckoning him. As he approached, she saw him glance at Paul almost hesitantly, but Paul's smile did not fade. Yet she felt his occasional touches, a caress to her hip, the slide of his fingers as he brushed her hair back from her cheek. He made it hard to concentrate on her conversation with Alex, but she was determined not to show it.

"Well done," she said, smiling, when Alex approached.

He bowed elaborately. "Ah, if only you could still throw a rock as you did when we were children. You might win!"

"Who says I have lost the skill?" she inquired, tilting her head.

He laughed at first, then looked taken aback. "In truth?"

"I may look feminine," she said in a softer voice, "but I have not forgotten the arts of my youth."

"She likes to challenge me with a dagger," Paul said dryly, pinching her cheek as he spoke.

Alex's eyes widened. "That, I cannot believe."

"He is teasing," Juliana said, reaching behind her to push Paul's hand off her backside. Alex didn't seem to notice.

"So what skills did she favor?" Paul asked Alex.

She didn't know what purpose these questions served, but she could not challenge her patron.

"She was very good with a dagger, now that you mention it," Alex said, green eyes gleaming with mischief. "She could hit the center of a target with her arrow when others could barely find the target in the distance."

"By others, do you mean yourself?" Paul asked. "Was she your better?"

"If it gives you pleasure to think so, sir," she said sweetly before Alex could speak.

"Aye, she was my better in many ways," Alex answered anyway. "Her horsemanship was legendary."

"That, I have seen," Paul said, nodding. "Mounted, she can ride endlessly."

Alex did not seem to hear the subtle insinuation, but Juliana did. She swallowed heavily, tried not to look at Paul, then at last had no choice. He was watching her, his eyes a devilish blue, his mouth sensually amused.

Though her own mouth was still dry, she said, "But the feminine pursuits eluded me, Alex. Do tell Sir Paul that I was a failure with needle and harp."

Alex looked confused. "I am certain you grew out of that, Juliana."

"And she has no need to convince me of her femininity," Paul said huskily.

Juliana's simmering passion was replaced by confusion. He played the jealous lover well, but could he mean it as a true warning to Alex? Why would that be necessary?

Unless it was to keep Alex away from the danger of their mission. If so, she was surprised by Paul's thoughtfulness.

Alex took his leave with a bow and a grin.

"You chased him away with your questions," she said with a sigh, sitting down on an empty bench.

Paul sat beside her, long legs stretched out, his arm behind her on the back of the bench. "Did you want him to stay?"

She studied him, looking for the truth of his question. "Aye, I did," she said softly. "He is a reminder of another time in my life, when the world stretched before me."

"Do you not feel that with the adventures of the League?"

"Of course but . . . there was an innocence then, that has since been lost."

"Do you regret the loss?"

His fingers touched her earlobe, rubbing it until she shivered again.

"Or do the pleasures you share make up for it?"

His eyes were hooded, his touch gentle, his words too intimate. He was talking about lovemaking again, and she knew what he thought, because she'd led him there—that she was experienced. It gave her a certain power, took away the girlishness.

But it also exposed her to his seduction.

All she had to do to stop it was tell him the truth: that she was a virgin.

She knew she wouldn't do it. She wanted to be his equal, not an innocent.

And she *liked* the way he could make her feel.

It was as if she danced too near the coals of a fire, and

she thought she could keep herself from getting burned.

"You speak of pleasure," she whispered, then slowly smiled. "'Twas worth it."

He stared at her, then with a groan, he hung his head. "You are a temptress, Juliana."

"I need to be, do I not?"

She turned away from him, and the first thing she noticed was Margaret, standing near a colorful group of pavilions. An impressive pennant flew above the largest, and she recognized the coat of arms of Staincliff.

An older man had his arm around Margaret, and a hand on little Edward. The man had close-cropped gray hair, but beneath his embroidered tunic, he still stood tall and imposing.

"Think you that is the earl of Staincliff?" Juliana mused.

Paul looked up. "With Margaret? Aye, it seems so. And there is young Edward," he added.

Juliana felt Paul's curious regard but ignored it. Her interest in the boy would seem too . . . parental to him. "And here they come," she said, as Margaret took her brother's hand and marched toward them with determination.

Poor Edward looked anything but happy, and although Paul hid it well, she thought he might be uncomfortable. Perhaps these clues that Juliana was more than the object of his pursuit were too much for him.

Margaret smiled brightly. "A good afternoon, Juliana, Sir Paul."

Edward stared at his scuffed boots, his sandy brown curls damp with perspiration. Clutching his sister's hand, he slowly inched behind her.

"I would like to introduce my brother, Edward, Baron Foxe," Margaret said with determination. "Edward, this is Sir Paul and Mistress Juliana. Say good day to them."

He didn't lift his head; he didn't speak.

"Good day, Lord Foxe," Juliana said. It was obvious by his title that this little boy would inherit his father's earldom.

Edward mumbled something.

Margaret's smile didn't diminish, but she looked exasperated. "Your pardon, Edward? We could not hear you."

"Just Edward."

His voice was weak, but now Juliana heard him.

"A fine name, Edward," Paul said in a too-cheerful voice.

Juliana winced. The boy shrank back as far as he could without releasing his grip on his sister's hand.

Juliana and Margaret exchanged the look of women who don't know what a man could be thinking. Juliana realized it had been a long time since she'd shared this silent female communication. Perhaps the last had been with her mother. The thought made her feel melancholy, yet glad for the memory.

"Edward, how old are you?" she asked.

The mumbling started again, until Margaret leaned down and spoke in his ear.

"Six," he finally answered, without looking up.

Juliana wanted to put him out of his misery, let him drag his sister away, but Margaret seemed firm.

"I thought you had at least ten years," Juliana said in shock.

She had a quick impression of dark blue eyes as he gaped at her, then looked back down.

"I thought the same," Paul said. "You handle a sword well."

"Nay, I do not," he said, stamping a foot. Then he glared at Paul with damp eyes. "If the sword were real, I would have hurt a lady!"

He yanked hard and escaped his sister's grip, then ran as if the hounds were chasing him.

Margaret shrugged, then said in a matter-of-fact voice, "He will forget all about this by the morrow."

"Aye," Paul said. "Little boys find other things to occupy them."

Juliana glanced at him in surprise. Was he trying to make her feel better? She turned back to Margaret and the mission.

"Was that your father you were with?" Juliana asked, patting the bench beside her.

Margaret sat down, and Juliana slid closer to Paul until their thighs touched.

"Aye. He means well, but he's rather distracted at tournaments."

"Does he yet compete?" Paul asked.

"He ordered new armor just for this event. I have never seen so much decoration in my life." She shook her head. "Forgive me for saying so, Sir Paul, but you men are quite vain."

Margaret paused, her expression showing concern that she'd offended Paul.

"I tell him so all the time," Juliana confided, as if they shared a secret about men.

Margaret brightened. "Do you remember that shirt you embroidered in the sewing chamber? 'Twas for my father."

"Did he approve?" Juliana asked, squinting as if she awaited an unfavorable verdict.

"I admired the handiwork, and he must have as well, for he said nothing ill."

Juliana wasn't quite certain that was a compliment.

Paul stood up. "I do believe the final footrace is upon us. One of my men is competing. I shall go watch him."

"We'll follow at our own pace," Juliana said, then

shared a quiet laugh with Margaret as Paul strode ahead of them.

She felt a warm ease in Margaret's presence; it was unfamiliar, uncanny, and pleasant, all at the same time. Yet why should she be at ease? They had nothing in common—Juliana didn't even like the feminine arts, knew only the basics of running a household. Now, estate management, the account books—those she understood.

But she didn't know how to oversee the brewer's latest ale, or what vegetables one planted first in a kitchen garden after winter. She was helpless as a woman, and it had never bothered her in the least—until playing Juliana the Concubine.

But Margaret liked to gossip, and that could prove useful, so Juliana encouraged it. Margaret had amusing insights into people and a commonsense approach to life. She knew her worth as a bride, but did not overly concern herself with it. Together, they strolled the tournament grounds, Juliana subtly guiding them so that she could keep Paul in her sights. Being away from him allowed her to see who was watching him—and there were plenty, Margaret's father included.

And always the messengers continued to arrive and depart on hurried, unknown missions.

Chapter 15

To Paul's surprise, several wellborn men were paying particular attention to him throughout the afternoon since Lord Kilborn's introduction. He did his best to seem cheerful, yet not the greatest thinker. He bragged a bit about his preparation for the tournament, knowing he'd look more the fool when he didn't perform well.

But always he kept an eye on Juliana. Oh, he knew that Theobald guarded her well, but he found that she was usually in his thoughts—not a good thing when one is trying hard to infiltrate a group of traitors. He told himself that it was because he was so frustrated by desire for her, but he was beginning to wonder if that was entirely true.

And when at last he was alone, and looked for her, she was watching him, waiting, and answered his beckoning. He watched her walk toward him, glad he didn't have to hide his admiration.

She took his arm and leaned into him, whispering, "Any intriguing news?"

He dropped a kiss on the top of her head. "None, but the introductions will be helpful. There seems to be interest in me, which is good. And you?"

"I talked with more of the ladies, met some children. I had assumed before arriving here that I would be something of an outcast, but Margaret is making far too much effort to include me. 'Twas . . . interesting—oh, not for the mission, of course. You don't need to feign interest."

"I am hardly feigning. Tell me."

They strolled near the stands set up along the lists, where the jousting would begin on the morrow. Children ran, people hurried by, but it seemed as if they were alone with their conversation amidst the din of revelry.

Juliana took a deep breath, glancing at him as if to say, "You asked for this."

"'Tis Margaret I worry about. Being the daughter of an earl, she is prepared to soon make a good marriage. Yet should she be seen so much in my company?"

"You are worried for her reputation?"

She nodded. "Even though she seems not to be. And her parents have not forbidden her."

"She did say that her father paid Edward little mind. Mayhap her parents are the same with her."

"Mayhap."

But she still seemed troubled.

"Do you worry that your friendship will disappoint her?" he asked softly.

She stared up at him with wide eyes. "How could I—" Then she paused, her brow furrowed.

"You told me you felt you were a disappointment to your parents. I still believe you were being too harsh on yourself, but regardless, being a daughter and being a friend are two different things."

She smiled without much mirth. "Aye, I disappointed them. Yet I miss them, too. And Margaret makes me consider that perhaps I missed the closeness of other women more than I realized."

Paul felt almost guilty that he had family, and had left them, when she so obviously missed hers.

"Being with women is not easy, of course," she continued, her expression wry. "We do not have so very much in common." Then she hesitated, and spoke in a softer voice. "And there is a small part of me that does not want to appear too feminine, too weak before our fellow Bladesmen." She glanced at him out of the corner of her eye, as if to gauge his reaction. "You should understand how the Bladesmen might see me, since you were obviously upset when you discovered a woman would be guarding you."

He stared at her in surprise. "You think my anger had to do with the fact that you're a woman?"

"Of course it did," she said dismissively. "I saw your

reaction when Timothy brought me forward."

"My reaction had to do with the League, not you. I hated having to behave so incompetently, or having to rely on other people to protect me, when I was proud of what I'd accomplished on my own."

She watched his face as if looking for any hint that he was not telling the truth. And because she was a solitary woman in a very male League, he did not take offense.

Juliana barely kept herself from gaping like a fool. He hadn't objected because she was a woman? She'd been looking down on him for, lo, these many weeks, for a groundless reason?

"You seem surprised," he said dryly. "You did not think much of me, did you?"

"Well, did you give me a reason to? I could not fathom why you distrusted the League, who'd saved my very life—and yours," she added pointedly. "But believe me, I do not discount your pain."

He arched a brow, but said nothing.

And she had much to think on. She felt relieved in one sense, because now she knew he valued her work, even though she was a woman. Yet this further accentuated the softness she'd been feeling for him, and that could not be good, when one was battling both his desire—and her own. It was one more crack in the wall that held her back from giving in to passion, giving in to what he could teach her.

"I am pleased that you're enjoying meeting other women," he said, reaching out to scoop up two tarts from a nearby tray. "Even from the moment I first met you, I was worried that you would be too isolated living with the League."

"If you felt isolated, why did you find it so easy to leave all you knew and travel to Europe, where you knew no one?"

"I am a man," he said, as if that answered everything.

"So you think a man bears isolation better than a woman."

"I did not say—"

"But you're glad I'm making friends, behaving as other women. And a woman's purpose, according to society, is to marry. You do not think it can be isolating to leave all you've ever known, marry a man and put yourself into his household, where you're a stranger?"

"And bear his children, and be a part of a family. It does not sound isolating to me—but then I wouldn't know," he finished wryly.

She sighed. "Aye, you wouldn't know."

And he didn't want to know, she realized.

That evening, when the trestle tables were folded away and the minstrels began to play, Paul found himself a popular man. He liked to dance and made it his mission that evening to meet the ladies of the castle. He had to achieve the notice of the men somehow.

But of course, he reserved the first dance for his concubine. The dance was lively, couples intertwining, linking arms to pass the ladies around, and then having the chance to lift Juliana high into the air before passing her to the next man. She moved with such grace, and the memories of her dance in a tavern before a dozen gaping men still aroused Paul every time he thought of it. She had a special way of meeting his gaze that was at once intimate and erotic, and yet full of amusement.

When he danced with the next woman, and the next, he warned himself that he was used to different women every night, in every city—that he would grow bored with Juliana's constant companionship now that he had so many women to pick from. But strangely, he didn't find himself drawn to any of the others. Surely, it was because he was aroused by the chase, by the hopeful triumph of having Juliana at last in his bed—naked, not clothed up to her chin.

And watching her dance with other men was not as easy as he'd imagined. More than once he thought Theobald should have intruded on too familiar a touch, but always Juliana controlled a man's free hand, her expression pleasant, but without the glimpses she gave to him of the fiery woman underneath.

And then she danced with Alex.

Paul was drinking a tankard of ale, standing alone near one of the hearths as he watched them. Alex wasn't all that much taller than Juliana, and that kept their heads too close together. The song was slower, and partners did not change, enabling them to carry on a disjointed conversation.

Paul felt someone approach from behind, turned alertly, only to find Theobald standing next to him, hands clasped behind his back.

"A good evening to you, Theobald," Paul said, surprised.

"Sir Paul."

"Are you enjoying the tournament?"

Theobald eyed him impassively. "I am a soldier, sir. I do not need to *enjoy* such things."

"But you like to win."

"Aye," he admitted at last.

" 'Tis not easy to pretend we are not better than most here."

"As you will discover on the morrow, Sir Paul."

"But what if I face you?"

"Then I will win, will I not?"

Paul chuckled. "Only if we meet toward the middle of the competition. I intend to win a few before I go down with my ineptitude."

Theobald said nothing, turning down an ale when Paul offered.

"Is your home near here?" Paul asked, needing a distraction.

"We do not discuss our backgrounds."

"I thought that a rather innocuous question. But very well. Tell me how you came to wear the mask."

Again, Theobald did not speak immediately, and Paul thought he might have gone too far.

"Not many men question me about such a thing," Theobald finally admitted.

"You intimidate them."

"The mask intimidates them," he said impassively.

"Nay, 'tis the man beneath it. You do not make it easy for another to talk to you."

Theobald said nothing.

Paul smiled. "And you make my point for me."

Frowning, Theobald sighed. "An opponent's sword laid open my face and destroyed the eye. It healed poorly."

Paul withheld a wince. "You were lucky to have lived."

"I saw it that way. Upon seeing my face, others did not."

Paul wondered if he had a wife who had been horrified by the disfiguration.

"So you took to wearing the mask."

"'Twas simpler. Yet sometimes it makes it easier

to do what we do. People don't want to see me. Yon Joseph"—he pointed to their fellow Bladesman, who was surrounded by several eager women—"always stands out."

Paul put a hand on Theobald's shoulder. "You find a good outcome to something that would crush another. And you're talkative," he added, suddenly suspicious. "Why is that?"

"Some of us believe you might take poorly Juliana dancing with other men."

"I have no claim on her," he said indignantly. "We are partners as much as you and I."

"My good eye is still working," Theobald said with faint sarcasm.

Paul crossed his arms over his chest. "I am glad you see she is easy to look upon. Tell our fellow soldiers not to be concerned."

"Hmph," was all Theobald said.

Juliana found it was easy to talk to Alex. He danced effortlessly, yet still showed interest in conversation—instead of staring down her gown, as so many other men felt free to do, including Paul.

As she whirled in Alex's arms, she let herself imagine marrying someone like him. She'd never thought to marry at all, but Paul had made her realize that she could not live in isolation at the League fortress forever.

People had lives to go to, and she had to build one for herself. Her only relatives—cousins—had refused to take her in, and she would not go to them now. Hence, she had to find her own household. And that meant a husband.

Alex was convenient in so many ways. He knew she lacked a dowry, not to mention a woman's skills, that she preferred the pastimes of men—and he didn't judge her for it. Even now, he showed interest by seeking her out. Was that enough to begin a relationship?

Yet . . . a man like Alex could never know of the time she spent with the League. He would always believe he wasn't the first man in her bed, and someday that might make him bitter. She knew that other Bladesmen kept their secrets from their spouses—but they were men, able to travel as much as they wished. How would she explain needing to leave every year for two or three weeks, perhaps returning with injuries? She could not always say she was attacked on the road. And a husband would not allow her to travel alone anyway; he'd send guards, if he didn't insist on going himself. She would have to escape them all, and lose his trust in the process.

Here, among normal husbands and wives and families, she accepted with a finality that she could never be like them. And giving up the League? Nay, it gave her a purpose that being a wife and mother could not do.

And as she looked into Alex's smiling face when he

brought her a goblet of wine, she also had to accept that he did not draw her gaze the way Paul did. She glanced at Paul, to see him conversing with Theobald, of all people. He briefly met her eyes and nodded, his smile knowing.

There was a heat in the attraction between Paul and her, a temptation and a longing to be wicked, regardless of possible complications. Did she want to keep resisting?

Tearing her gaze away from Paul, she saw that Alex had not missed the exchange. He regarded her solemnly for a moment, sympathetically. She blushed, which no concubine should even remember how to do.

And then she saw Margaret, standing alone and watching the festivities with happiness.

"Alex, allow me to introduce you to someone," Juliana said.

She saw the way his face lit up when Margaret curtsied to him, and Margaret's momentary shyness and blushing.

Alex would never look that way at Juliana, a concubine in his eyes. And it was just as well.

A brief message awaited them when they returned to their bedchamber that night, and Paul felt a surge of satisfaction as he looked at the parchment, then dropped it on the table.

"What does it say?" Juliana asked.

"They shall be coming for me after midnight tonight, and I'm to be prepared."

"After the way men stared at you today, I cannot be surprised," she said.

"Ah, but did you see the way they stared at you?" he reached for her, but she eluded him.

"Not the men who are important to this mission."

"But what about Alex?"

"What about Alex?" she asked in surprise.

He arched a brow and said nothing. When she laughed, he felt something ease inside him.

"Which of you is jealous?" she asked, her voice still trembling with amusement. "Sir Paul the Bladesman or Sir Paul the Dissolute?"

He caught hold of her and drew her against him. "Both of us," he said hoarsely, and then he kissed her.

To his surprise, she wrapped her arms about his neck and pressed against him. He lost his reason as he lost himself in her mouth, mating with her tongue, sharing her breath. He felt her hands trace his shoulders, sink into his hair. Her moans aroused him as much as each intimate roll of her hips.

And then she crawled up his body and wrapped her legs around his hips. He held her thighs in his hands, but he needn't have feared she wouldn't be able to hold herself up.

"My God," he said hoarsely, after lifting his mouth briefly from hers.

"I needed to be closer, to feel . . ." Her voice trailed off as she pressed kisses along his jaw.

He slid his hands along the backs of her thighs, around her hips, cupping them. Pulling her hard against him, he rubbed his erection deep into the warm center of her.

With a gasp, she let her head drop back. Her eyes were closed, her expression one of concentration and passion. It was so beautiful, he could barely keep from losing himself without even being inside of her.

"The bed—" he began harshly.

"Nay, I will not sleep with you."

He froze, shuddering, as she squirmed against him, her head still back.

"Not tonight," she amended.

He bent and pressed his mouth to her throat, slowly following the elegant lines down toward the hollow. "Tomorrow?"

"We will be taking our time."

In two steps, he had her up against the wall, so he was able to free his hands. Still, she rocked against him, her heels against his ass, her thighs cupping his hips. She knew just what she did to him, what felt good. He was kissing her shoulders now, releasing the laces at the back of her neck, sliding the neckline wider so that he could press kisses ever lower, down to the rising of her breasts, and between. The sounds she made were strangled, full of pleasure, hushed so that no one would hear but the two of them.

Think, he told himself. "Why—why do we have to take our time?"

Chapter 16

Juliana clutched Paul's head to her chest, silently pleading with him not to stop. His hips pressed hard into hers, exciting her in a way that her teacher had tried to express, but had been impossible for Juliana to understand . . . until now.

She wanted to move, to squirm, to incite her passion until it reached the peak of bliss.

But he was talking to her, and she couldn't remember what he'd said.

This was what they'd warned her of, this loss of control, loss of reason. She'd been prepared, so she'd know what to do. But the urge was so powerful, so overwhelming. She wanted what only he could give her, *had* to have it.

Her consciousness swam briefly to the surface in time, trying to remember what he'd been saying. But he tugged once more on her neckline, and her breasts spilled free right before his eyes.

He stared at them, and she saw that her nipples were tight, aching points. Her uneven breathing made her breasts quiver. She should be embarrassed, she should stop, but—

She found her voice. "We have to . . . take our time because . . . I don't know if I'll . . . want to lie with you."

His narrowed eyes met hers, as he hoarsely said, "Am I to persuade you?"

"Believe me, you've already . . ." And then words faded away as he licked one nipple, his tongue flat and rough and wet. The sound she made was choked and hoarse, and didn't sound at all like herself. The pleasure was . . . wondrous, unbelievable.

"Should I persuade you more?" He spoke against her breast, and without waiting for her response, he took her nipple deep into his mouth, suckling while rubbing against her with his erection.

Such a twin assault was her undoing. He sent her beyond herself, beyond rational thought, into a state of pleasure that shuddered through her in waves that crested over and over again.

When she came to herself, he was breathing hard against her neck, and slowly lifted his head to meet her gaze. His deep blue eyes seemed to burn into her.

"Have I persuaded you?"

She realized she was languorous in his arms, unable to even hold herself up; he did it all for her, his hands beneath her buttocks, his fingers dangerously close to the center of her.

She cleared her throat, tried to let her legs drop, but he wouldn't allow it.

"Much as you acquitted yourself well," she began, then felt a spasm when he rocked into her again. "We cannot—cannot finish this. I still have much to think about, and our mission tonight has reached a turning point. The Bladesmen must know what is about to happen."

"Let me show *you* what's about to happen."

When he tried to kiss her other breast, she pulled up her loose garments and held them to her. "Nay, Paul, we must stop. Put me down."

A long, slow shudder moved through him, and then he straightened and released her. Her legs slid down his body, accentuating the ripples of pleasure that still moved through her.

Gasping, she clutched him for a moment. And then he stepped back. He was still aroused, still so ready, that she knew he ached with it, but she also knew that it would subside, that he could control himself.

"This went farther than I meant it to," she said, "and for that, I apologize."

"Never apologize," he said, cupping her face briefly, his low laugh full of strain. "That felt too good to be wrong."

She, too, touched his face, felt the day's growth of beard, the warmth of male flesh. "But I couldn't stop myself from kissing you."

He closed his eyes, his expression briefly hard with concentration. And then he looked at her again. "That is a good thing."

"We have to bring our men together and tell them about the message. Are you . . . prepared?"

His smile was pained. "Give me a moment. I do believe Michael thoughtfully left me a pitcher of ale."

He went to the table and poured himself a tankard, then sat down heavily in a chair.

Juliana turned her back, and with trembling fingers, began to retie the laces at her neck. This was the only way to control the passion building between them. To acknowledge it, experience it, dole it out bit by bit. She would consider her future, and make a decision when this assignment was over. She could not expect a future with Paul—he was too independent, a man who yearned for his freedom—but he would be able to continue awakening her passion.

The League had seen to her sexual knowledge to protect her, and she was going to prove them right—she'd be in control, and make the right decisions for her.

By the time the Bladesmen arrived, Paul had mastered his passion, mostly by avoiding looking at Juliana, and trying not to think about her expression when she'd found bliss. When the chamber was crowded with men, he tried to think of her as just another member of the League. Her eyes were back to their cool awareness, her movements the clipped, purposeful strides of Juliana the Bladeswoman rather than Juliana the Concubine.

He pictured her in a man's tunic and breeches, her favorite garments. Otherwise he would see her face alive with ecstasy, feel her shudders as she found a woman's ultimate pleasure, with so little effort on his part. She was so sensitive, so receptive . . . again, he forcibly wiped such thoughts from his mind.

The Bladesmen were adept at reading faces, at reading movements of the body. He refused to betray his thoughts—betray Juliana.

Paul showed the message to Timothy and the others, and they briefly discussed how they would follow him through the castle so that he would not be alone.

They all knew that the traitors would most likely forbid Juliana from accompanying him, although he knew she would try her best to be included. She took her duties seriously as the guardian of his body—and she had his body at her beck and call.

At last the Bladesmen retreated, and he and Juliana were alone again. From opposite sides of the room they regarded each other, and the air between them could have burst into flames.

"We need to try to sleep," she said calmly, and went to the coffer where she kept her clothing. "We know not what time they will come for you."

Sleep? he thought, exhaling slowly. He was supposed to lie beside her and relax enough to sleep? It would take everything inside him not to pull her beneath him and finish what they'd started.

But she was counting on his ability to control himself, to play by her rules. And he could do that.

She disappeared behind the changing screen, and he sat down, remaining clothed so he would be prepared for the night's work. Methodically, he checked every weapon hidden on his body, the ones he would allow them to find, and the others so skillfully made a part of his garments that they were undetectable.

She emerged all wrapped up in her dressing gown. There were candles lit about the chamber, and one by one she blew them out until she reached the bed. He was still sitting on the edge, and he looked up at her.

"I'll sleep on the outside," he said.

Unable to help himself, he slowly looked down her body, at her breasts covered in two layers of silk, down the length of the sheer gown to her toes peeking out from beneath.

He put his hands to the tie at her waist, and she covered them with her own.

"I will not lie with you, Paul," she said softly.

"I know. But you'll lie beside me, and you can no longer wear a dressing gown to bed."

He loosened the belt and let the dressing gown part. He held his breath at the sight of the silk molding to her breasts, outlining the hard peaks. Panels of lace decorated the bodice, stopping just before her nipples would have been revealed.

He gently pushed the dressing gown from her shoulders, and it pooled onto the floor.

"You are so beautiful," he said, his husky voice full of regret.

She smiled. "You merely praise me for a purpose."

He looked up at her, searching her face. "Nay, never think that."

She briefly cupped his cheek, and the warmth of her hand was almost as arousing as her near nudity. And then she knelt beside him and slid under the bedcovers beyond him. He lay on top of the coverlet, linked his hands behind his head and stared at the dark ceiling.

Normally he would have slept; he'd always had the ability to completely relax before a mission and get needed rest. But after that rousing kiss, he knew neither of them would sleep, but both would pretend to.

When the door opened at last, there was no announcing knock. He felt Juliana's brief clasp of his arm, and then he sat up.

Two men entered, one bearing a shuttered lantern, which let out only a faint light.

The lantern carrier intoned soberly, "Sir Paul, you will come with us."

As he rose, he heard Juliana's cry of distress.

"Paul?" she began, her voice changing from sleepy to indignant. "Does this have to do with the missive you received?"

"Go back to sleep," he ordered.

"Nay, I cannot. I do not wish to remain here alone. Let me come with you."

He could hear her movements as she sat up, although he never took his eyes off the strangers.

"She will remain here," the second man said.

"I accompany Sir Paul everywhere," she said indignantly, lacing her tone with cool intelligence.

She was trying to let them know that she was more aware than Paul was of what was going on. But it didn't work.

"Remain here and tell no one," the lantern carrier said, "or it will mean your deaths."

Juliana sputtered, but her protest faded into mutinous indignation. As Paul followed the men to the door, he gave her one last look. In the gloom of the fire, he could see the angry thinness of her lips, and the way she crossed her arms over her chest. But she would remain behind and allow the other Bladesmen to follow him.

The lantern carrier walked in front, then Paul, then the second stranger. They went down to the first level using the circular staircases built into the corner walls.

And then the man behind put his hand on Paul's shoulder. "You will be blindfolded now."

Paul tensed, yet the man didn't release him. "You said nothing about that. And why should it matter?"

"We meet in a place of great secrecy," the lantern carrier said. "You can understand our concern."

Paul allowed the blindfold, and the search of his body for weapons, then concentrated on the path they walked, even though his escorts retraced their steps once or twice to confuse him. He wasn't confused.

Gradually, the air grew colder, its scent dank and stale. He thought they were in the undercroft, but perhaps there were deeper places cut into the rock below, as some dungeons he'd seen. His ears strained for unusual sounds; he was constantly alert for tension in the man who held him by the arm. Paul deliberately stumbled now and again.

At last he could feel a change, as if the space around him was now expansive. The man pulled him to a stop, and Paul could hear the murmuring voices of other men, and then the silence as he was noticed. A door shut behind him.

To his surprise, they pulled off the blindfold. He was in a small chamber hewn in rock walls, with no windows, only torches in brackets on the walls. Four men sat behind a table looking at him.

And these men he recognized. They didn't bother to hide their faces, as proof they didn't need to fear him. The noblest was the earl of Redesdale, from Northumberland, on the Scottish border. The men of this county were hardy cattle stealers, used to constant warfare with their northern neighbors, and the earl looked a descendent of such stock, broad and barrel-chested, with an unshaven face of gray stubble and matching cold, gray eyes.

Viscount Gerard of County Durham regarded Paul steadily, but his hands moved with restlessness, linking and unlinking. He was thin to the point of emaciation, as if he were either ill or the deeds they were about to do tormented him.

The third man, Lord Byrd, reminded Paul of a fat pigeon waiting for an easy meal. Dark eyes beady in his fleshy face, he constantly turned his gaze from Paul to Redesdale and back, leaving Paul no doubt that Redesdale was in command. The last man seated, Sir Hugh Burton, was Redesdale's captain of the guard. He was the youngest, in his thirties perhaps, strong and tall and well trained, as Paul had seen on the tiltyard just that morn. The first man who'd approached Paul outside Yorkshire wasn't in attendance, suggesting that the conspiracy was even wider than this, or that he'd been well paid to risk himself.

The man who'd alerted Paul the previous evening was probably one of the two men behind him, if height and build were the only judge. They retreated, and he glanced behind himself, feigning nervousness as they took up positions on either side of the door.

The lord of the house, the earl of Kilborn, was not in attendance—did that mean he was innocent of the traitors' plot? Could Staincliff, Lady Margaret's father, be innocent, too?

Paul faced the men arrayed against him like accusers. "You have me here. What do you want of me?"

"Exactly what you hoped for when you traveled so conspicuously up from London," Redesdale said, his expression serious but with a hint of a smirk. "You want to be used. We want to use you."

"And in exchange, your debt will be canceled," Gerard said, "and you'll be well compensated—and you'll live."

Paul shuffled from foot to foot, but he kept his chin lifted belligerently. "Aye, so your man already said." He glanced behind him, but neither guard betrayed even the slightest interest. "But much depends on what you require of me."

Byrd chuckled, his jowls quivering. "Lucky for you,

we require little. Already we have word that King Henry is looking into your background. He perceives a threat. That was well done on your part."

Paul nodded stiffly, knowing the League had manufactured the rumor.

"With your coloring and demeanor, many will wonder at your identity," Redesdale continued. "Although there are several young men with more claim to the throne, like the missing Warwick, the son of the duke of Clarence, we have agreed that you will impersonate Prince Richard himself, younger brother of our boy king who so briefly reigned."

"Your Grace." Byrd laughingly bowed his head. "You will someday be King Richard IV, with our backing. The riches of the monarchy will be yours to share—as long as you do what we say."

Paul licked his lips. "What am I supposed to do? Do I openly claim such a thing?"

"Not yet," Gerard said, glancing nervously at his compatriots as his restless fingers picked up their pace. "First you will copy in your hand a letter to our fellow Yorkists staking your claim to the throne. We will use that to prove to our foreign allies that our plan will work."

"We have brave men in Ireland," Redesdale said, "the earl of Kildare and Lord Desmond, who will gladly supply Irish support in arms and armies. My connections in Scotland guarantee that they will march at our sides when we go to meet Henry's army."

"War?" Paul said faintly.

Byrd's round face stilled. "We take back what is not Henry's to have. 'Tis the birthright of the Yorkists, and Henry stole it from King Richard."

Paul said nothing, for Sir Paul the Dissolute would not care about the politics of the situation.

"Fear not that we will allow you to lead our army," Redesdale said with open sarcasm. "We would not want to risk our noble prince."

Byrd laughed with Redesdale, Hugh Burton smirked, but nervous Gerard only looked down at his twisting fingers.

Paul rubbed his hands down his face in his own nervous gesture. "What if I copy this letter for you, and you use it against me?"

"Why would we risk our exposure in such a way?" Redesdale asked calmly. "We'd lose our heads at your side."

But Paul well knew there was no proof that put these men as his backers—if revealed, the letter would look like it had been from him only, and his word would mean little against Henry's noblemen. It would insure his complicity with their plan.

"You brought your own guards," said Burton, the captain of his master's guard, "but they will not be enough. I will make certain others are at your back."

Paul nodded, swallowed, then tried to sound faltering and bold at the same time. "My man Roger, the elderly guard. He once worked in the Tower of London itself. I thought . . ."

He trailed off as the four men glanced at one another with amusement.

"You thought what, Sir Paul?" Byrd coaxed, leaning back to cross his hands over his large belly.

Paul lifted his chin. "He could be the man who spirited me—Prince Richard—away from the Tower in his youth."

"Always thinking, are you not?" Byrd said brightly. "We shall remember your idea if it is needed."

"What do I do now?" Paul asked, spreading his hands wide.

"Nothing," Redesdale said, his expression sobering. "Now that we have you to inspire our armies, we will begin to spread word among our northern colleagues and our foreign allies. You may behave as you've done before, making yourself seen and speculated about. If all goes well, besides riches, we offer you a girl of quite noble background as wife. I saw you with Lady Margaret; she would do well at your side as a future queen. Her father would not need much persuasion, once he sees how things are changing for the better."

So Margaret's father was not involved? Paul wondered. But he could not be certain if Redesdale's comments were cryptic or truthful.

Byrd pushed two pieces of parchment toward an empty chair, offering quill and ink. Paul sat down and began to copy the words about his flight from London under his uncle, King Richard's, protection after an unknown enemy had killed his brother, Edward. He remained in hiding much of his life, both in England and in Flanders, with his aunt, the dowager duchess of Burgundy. Now he returned to lead his people to retake the throne, which was legally and morally his.

Along with all the riches and power that went with it, Paul thought sarcastically.

When he was finished, he stood up. "I will await your next missive."

"And you will not speak of this outside this chamber," the earl of Redesdale said. "If we cannot trust your discretion, the consequences to you will be grave." He pulled the newly penned parchment toward him, sealing Paul's complicity. He lifted another sheaf of papers toward Paul, who took them. "These are details of your childhood, Your Grace. Memorize them and destroy them. If you are found with them, the proof will only lead toward yourself. And this letter will be mysteriously recovered as well."

Paul nodded, licking his lips as if they were dry. Again, they blindfolded him, removing it at the head of the corridor leading to his lodgings. Saying nothing, the two guards departed, leaving Paul to rejoin Juliana. He gave a subtle signal of his return at Timothy's door, but knew the Bladesmen would not risk coming to him too soon.

Juliana was pacing when he arrived. If she felt any relief at his safe reappearance, she didn't show it, only remained impassive.

"Was it as we expected?" she asked in a low voice.

He nodded. "They had me copy a letter staking my claim to the throne to convince reluctant Yorkists."

"And the Scots and Irish," she added.

He smiled. "Aye, and them, too. They even offered me a noble bride at the end of it all."

Arching a brow she asked, "Should I be jealous?"

"Only if you consider Lady Margaret your competition."

Her lips thinned. "Her father is part of it?"

"I know not. They implied that I'd shown interest, and that they can make certain I receive her."

"You've shown interest in Lady Margaret?" she asked, faintly smiling.

"I must not be receiving enough feminine attention," he said sadly.

"You've had enough feminine attention for one night." Her voice was dry, her tone light. "Now, who else was present?"

They discussed each man in detail, knowing that sometime before morning, he would repeat the same thing to their fellow Bladesmen. Then they went over the written history of Richard, and he memorized the few details he didn't already know before burning the papers.

Throughout their conversation, Paul felt a low hum of attraction, of desire, and if he let his mind dwell on it, he would again remember her look of ecstasy. When Juliana went to bed, he watched her for a long time, still feeling stunned by her earlier amorous behavior.

But he put it aside for later, dwelling on the secrets he knew about her past instead. In the meeting he'd overheard years before, the League had maintained that they had good reason to put an innocent man in jail for treason—surely they knew who the real traitor was, whose place Gresham had taken. If Paul could discover that, he could clear Gresham's name and restore Juliana's birthright, giving her some kind of peace.

And the best way to begin was with information that the League itself had. As far as they would know, it would help *this* mission. Perhaps the crimes were even connected. He would ask for an accounting of suspected and proven traitors, year by year over the last ten years, which included the year of Gresham's death.

At least he would be accomplishing something while he strolled around the tournament on display.

So by the faint light of a dying fire, he composed a missive to the secretary of the Council of Elders, the keeper of all archives. At first, he was rusty with the League codes, and it took him a bit of practice—and mistakes carefully burnt—before he succeeded in writing a letter that seemed only about an inquiry into family in the area—with the real message hidden deep within.

When he was finished, he hid the missive, knowing he would see it on its way in the morn.

Chapter 17

To Juliana's surprise and worry, she was alone when she awoke before dawn. She moved swiftly to the door and heard voices in the corridor. Not able to open it—she was barely decent—she went to fetch her dressing gown, only to hear the door open. She turned, reaching beneath her pillow for her dagger, but it was Paul.

He was fully dressed for mass, and she was in her night rail. They froze and stared at each other. His gaze down her body was almost as potent as a physical caress.

She swallowed. "Where did you go?"

"To give a missive to Joseph for delivery to the League."

Frowning, she said, "We did not discuss this."

"'Twas the report of my meeting. I couldn't fall asleep, so I wrote everything down." He smiled and spoke softly. "I almost didn't remember one of the codes."

"I do not believe that," she said, walking slowly toward him.

He looked down her body with appreciation. "Even the gray light of dawn makes you look wondrous in that night rail."

"And now you've seen me without some of it."

"Not enough."

When he came toward her, she held up a hand. "We have mass, and then you joust this day. Are you prepared? You insisted on not practicing, to leave them all wondering about your skill."

"But I've watched them. If I wanted to, I could defeat them all to win your favor."

"You do not have to defeat anyone for that," she murmured. She stood on tiptoes and pressed a kiss to his cheek. "Mass," she whispered, then, laughing, disappeared behind the screen.

But during mass, when Juliana needed to be praying to God for aid in this mission, she kept thinking about Paul. It bothered her that he hadn't consulted her about his missive to the League. They'd been together every single moment for over a fortnight; he'd probably never spent so much time in one person's company in years. Perhaps he was getting anxious to finish this mission, to have his promised freedom.

But as they walked toward the great hall, and he put an arm around her to whisper something meaningless in her ear, she knew he wanted *her* more than his freedom, she thought, feeling a delicious shudder curl her toes.

"Did he use the method of delivery in the stables?" she asked softly as they took their seats at the trestle table.

Paul frowned. "Your pardon?"

"Joseph's delivery of the missive."

"Oh." His expression lightened even as he looked away to hand her a napkin. "Probably, if he did not want to leave the castle. There are Bladesmen here we know not of."

"Aye, you have the right of it."

Any number of men could be watching—and she should be used to it by now. Since Paul had informed her of the names of the traitors, she had surreptitiously been watching their piously bent heads during mass, and their cheerfulness on this morn of the jousting competition. But she also noticed the earl of Redesdale and Lord Byrd watching Paul and her more than once. That made sense, for the traitors were trusting in his secrecy; they thought he was wrapped up in their spider web, unable to escape without implicating himself. Men with too much confidence made mistakes.

She laughed as if Paul had just said something amusing, letting her hair slide about her shoulders sensuously—who had ever thought that hair could be such a weapon?

The meal was a short one, as the men returned to their lodgings to prepare for the first round of jousting. Juliana silently helped Paul don his armor, and he told her he'd never had a better squire.

Out in the fields surrounding the castle, she gave him a kiss worthy of sending her hero off to battle. He laughed and gave her backside a push as if sending off a child.

She glared at him, murmuring, "We should quarrel now and again. Do I look like I could slice you apart with my eyes?"

"I'm shivering with fear, glad I am to be facing an unknown opponent instead of you."

"I'd knock you from the saddle," she said sweetly.

He saluted as he left. She saw Joseph and Timothy fall into place beside Paul as he went to see the order of competition. Over her shoulder, she spied Theobald openly following in her wake, her guardian.

"Juliana!"

She turned to see Margaret hurrying toward her, waving cheerfully. The other woman wore a dress as pale blue as the morning sky, her blond hair a sunny crown of curls beneath a fluttering veil.

"I am full of excitement," Margaret said, taking her and beginning to pull.

"Where are we going?" Juliana asked, smiling.

"To the stands, of course. The ladies who have men competing are all sitting together."

"And who is your man in this competition?" she asked.

Margaret's blush lit up her whole face. "Well . . . I am not sure. I—I sincerely hope a knight asks for my favor, but . . . well . . . I cannot be certain. But we must be positive!"

"Could that knight's name begin with an A?"

Margaret tugged on her hand and kept walking. "I hope to be surprised."

The ladies looked like a flock of colorful birds in the several tiers of stands erected next to the lists. As Margaret marched up the steps to the first tier, an older woman with a regal but craggy face beneath a towering headdress rose to stop her.

"Lady Margaret," she said politely, "these seats are for ladies only."

Margaret glanced back at Juliana in confusion, then said, "My lady, no gentleman follows me."

Lady Redesdale imperiously lifted her brows, then glanced pointedly at Juliana. Margaret inhaled with sudden understanding.

Juliana kept her shoulders back, her chin up, looking proud and unashamed. Most of these ladies knew that Juliana the Concubine had been forced to become what she was, and so far they'd been polite but distant. Apparently, they drew the line about acting as friends before several hundred guests at the tournament.

"My lady," Margaret began.

"Nay," Juliana interrupted, then spoke softly. "Your place is here, Margaret. I don't wish you to shame your family on my account. Your friendship is too important to me."

Margaret leaned down from the top step, clasping both Juliana's hands in hers. "But that's the point! Our friendship—"

"Is between us, and I know it will remain strong. I do not wish to sit with such women anyway."

"Then I will not—"

"Nay, a certain gentleman will be looking for you. Stay there, on display, as pretty as you are."

"You keep interrupting me, Juliana," Margaret said, her shoulders slumping. "You leave me no choice."

"Good. I will meet you afterward. And let us pray that Paul and Alex do not meet!" She pulled her hands away, curtsied grandly to the countess, then walked toward another group of stands filled with villagers and guests.

She was rapidly learning her place in the world, and coming to peace with it. She would never be like those women, although her lineage was as fine as any of theirs—not that they'd agree if they knew her family name. But in her heart, she knew the truth. She would be different, a woman outside the society she was raised in, living her own life.

She didn't have to give up everything about being a woman, she thought, glimpsing Paul's vibrant tunic of gold and blue over the armor that emphasized his broad, muscular body. He carried his helm under one arm, and rode his horse with easy grace, while Timothy and Joseph followed behind with several lances propped on their shoulders.

Pavilions had been erected near the lists for the use of the competitors, and they rode in that direction. Another man swung easily into his saddle, and as he turned, Juliana recognized Alex. She felt a momentary thrill to be seeing the culmination of her friend's childhood promise. And then she slowly began to smile as he walked his horse toward the ladies' stands. Several ladies waved and giggled, but Margaret only wore a serene smile and remained calm. He paused before her, and although Juliana could not hear what he said, she saw Margaret blush and nod, then remove a scarf from her sleeve. He maneuvered his horse close, and insisted she lean over the rail to tie her favor about his upper arm.

Several ladies applauded as he rode away, and Margaret looked about as if searching for someone. She spied Juliana, they waved at each other, and then suddenly Margaret started pointing.

Juliana lifted both hands in confusion.

A man's voice said, "Juliana, are you ignoring me?"

Laughter spread around her as she turned to find Paul mounted on his horse at the edge of the stands. He looked so handsome, so confident, his eyes soft with intimacy as he watched her.

"I await your favor."

"How chivalrous of you, Sir Paul," she said, her voice husky and low.

Though she knew she put on a show, it was also a private display just for him, as she reached into the low neckline of her gown and slowly pulled forth a bright green scarf.

There were whistles and shouts of encouragement, but Juliana barely heard them. Paul reached for her favor, but she leaned over the rail and tied it on herself, giving him a display of cleavage.

She didn't care what others thought of her—Paul was showing her that she was very much a woman, and giving her the opportunity to experience the true pleasures of her femininity. She would lie with him on her own terms, knowing it could only be temporary, but rewarding all on its own.

Paul kissed her hand, then rode away, and she waited, breath held, until she saw that Alex was jousting first, but not against Paul. She sagged back on her bench in relief. It took Alex two passes to knock his opponent from his horse, and she watched Margaret applaud wildly.

Several matches later, it was Paul's turn. An uneasy murmuring moved through the crowd at the announcement of Paul's name. Did the guests already wonder at his true identity?

It was not difficult to remain relaxed. She had no fear he would allow himself to lose so early in the day. But her heart picked up its beat as he thundered down the lists, staying on his own side of the rail, while his opponent remained on the other. Bent low over his horse, Paul guided his lance into his opponent's armor, just twisting his wrist so that it skidded harmlessly off the steel, rather than unhorse his opponent. Paul absorbed a blow to his own shield, reeling backward in a dramatic fashion, but keeping his seat.

At their respective ends, the two men each took another lance from their servants, and Timothy spoke urgently to Paul, as if giving him instructions. Again, the opponents galloped at each other, and this time Paul missed the man's shield altogether, while partially coming out of his saddle as the other man's lance splintered against him.

The crowd gasped, then cheered, shaking their heads and laughing at the display of mediocre talent. Juliana wondered how difficult it must be for Paul to pretend that he could not have taken this man clean off his horse with one lance.

This time, he managed to make it look almost accidental as he knocked his opponent to the ground.

Timothy and Joseph joined her cheering as if in great relief.

"Juliana!"

It was Margaret again, and Juliana leaned over the rail to wave to her friend. Margaret beckoned for her, and Juliana stepped over men's boots and ladies' shoes until she reached the stairs.

To her surprise, Margaret clasped her hands and swung the two of them briefly in a circle. "Was that not exciting?"

"Alex was certainly a strong competitor. I'm not so certain about Paul, but then I do not know the fine points of the rules."

"He is moving on to the next round, and that is all that's important."

"Speaking of Alex . . ." Juliana began.

Margaret's blush rivaled a red rose. "'Twas very kind of him to honor me."

"You think him merely kind?" Juliana teased. "I think he was selfishly claiming before all his right to court you."

Margaret clapped her hands on her cheeks. "Do

you really think—nay, I will not assume that, only to become disappointed."

"Alex is too honorable to disappoint a woman once he's shown her favor."

"You say you knew him in childhood, but that is a long time ago."

"Are you saying I am elderly?"

Margaret laughed. "Certainly not, especially when one considers the way you offered your favor to Sir Paul."

Embarrassed, Juliana looked away. "He likes my attention," she said lamely.

"Attention? That was . . . an interesting way of showing it. Very romantic."

Carnal, Juliana thought, but did not say aloud.

"Should I have done something more with my scarf?" Margaret asked.

"Nay! We are in two very different situations." Juliana looked about to make certain they were not overheard. "Do not say such things to others, or people will think I am a bad influence upon you."

Margaret's smile faded. "But you are not, Juliana. It was ungracious of the ladies to forbid you from sitting with me."

"I paid them no heed, and neither should you."

"Lady Kilborn spoke to Lady Redesdale in your defense. She said she imagined there were many women at the tournament in your predicament, and that we should not be so quick to judge."

"The countess is kindness itself," Juliana murmured, impressed that the younger woman had stood up to someone so formidable.

And then she remembered that Lady Redesdale's husband was a traitor. Juliana well knew how it felt to be caught up in the scandal and crime. She pitied Lady Redesdale, whose world was about to change for the worse.

"Is there space for me to sit with you?" Margaret asked.

They spent the next several hours cheering for each contest. Both Paul and Alex won again, and would participate in the continuation of the joust the next day.

To Juliana's surprise, she caught sight of Paul and Michael standing awkwardly together afterward. They seemed to be talking; she couldn't tell about what, but it was brief, as Michael soon walked away. The Bladesman had never made any secret of his disapproval of the choices Paul had made. Juliana could only hope that they could somehow find common ground—and not just for the roles they were playing.

And then she realized that boys were playing football in the field beside Paul—and young Edward was once again standing on the edges.

Juliana saw Paul glance at Edward, then look away.

"Has Edward forgiven me?" Juliana asked.

Margaret smiled. "For being in the way of his sword? You know he doesn't blame you for his foolish mistake. He's simply getting old enough to notice that he's more awkward than the other boys."

Edward's ball was at his feet, rough leather casing sewn together over a bladder. With a running head start, he attempted to kick the ball, and it went sideways instead of forward. When he saw Paul watching, Edward grabbed his toy and ran away.

Paul glanced at Juliana, an eyebrow raised. Surely he didn't think she blamed herself for this as well. Or did he expect her to play the mother and run to the little boy?

"I'll go to Edward," Margaret said with a sigh.

After Margaret had gone, Paul walked back to Juliana. She gave him a bright smile, but he only studied her. A horse went thundering down the lists behind her to wild cheers. Neither of them winced at the shattering of lance against shield.

Why did she care so much what he thought of her or her attachment to children?

She thought he would walk away, leery of her womanly feelings. Instead, he gently cupped her face in his hands and leaned down to kiss her. This was no kiss meant for display, for a masquerade. She felt a sweet, sad yearning.

She had fallen in love with him, and the realization of that frightened her even as she felt relief at admitting it. There was no rational decision to make when she felt like this, only decisions of the heart. And she was going to be hurt by him, in a way no man had ever done before, but she couldn't stop herself.

Her worries about her position with the League fell away as she looked into his beautiful blue eyes. Thoughts of a lonely future without him were as dust to her. It was the now that mattered, this moment, and what they meant to each other.

And all she could think about was the coming night.

Chapter 18

Paul watched Juliana across the great hall that night, trying to ignore the more intense way some people were watching *him*. The rumors were circulating, leading to awe in some eyes, disbelief in others. The traitorous lords were doing their subtle work.

And it was taking too long. He wanted to be done; he wanted to have Juliana to himself, with no mission, no Bladesmen. He wanted to persuade her to lie with him, to let him show her true lovemaking, unlike the men she'd lain with before. He wanted to worship her, just like . . .

Just like Alexander Clowes was worshiping Lady Margaret with his gaze. At least he wasn't watching Juliana, Paul thought wryly.

But Juliana was watching the two lovebirds she'd introduced, and she was smiling.

Did she want that for herself, a courtship? Perhaps even a marriage and family, if her awkward relationship with little Edward meant anything. She lost the chance to be wooed while still safe within her family. The League had taken it all away. She had no dowry, so she thought she could never marry.

"Surely, you've already shown that you're obsessed with your courtesan."

Paul turned to see Michael standing beside him, hands on hips, his freckled face impassive.

"Another Bladesman to distract me from my work?" Paul asked. "Last time, 'twas Theobald's turn."

He eyed Michael, who looked almost uncomfortable. Paul had been surprised that afternoon when Michael had approached him after the joust and expressed reluctant admiration for Paul's ability to fake mediocrity. Only another man so skilled would truly understand the difficulties.

In the loud hall, full of singing minstrels and cheering soldiers gambling at dice, no one was close enough to pay attention to their words. Paul rubbed his hands together. "If you must be here, I need answers."

"Answers?" Michael repeated suspiciously.

"Tell me about your journey with my brother down the length of England with his kidnapped bride."

"She wasn't his bride then," Michael said, then winced, as if he regretted the words.

"Ah, eager to talk are you. I'm eager to hear. So you and my brothers breezed into her father's well-guarded castle and simply stole her away."

Michael rocked on his heels as he looked at the floor, and for a moment, Paul thought he'd retreat into silence.

"We used a wagon," Michael said, crossing his arms over his chest. "Tossed her in a sack and buried her beneath the straw before anyone saw what we'd done."

Paul chuckled, feeling a tightness in his chest begin to loosen. "Tell me more."

Juliana approached Paul, walking slowly because she hated to interrupt. He and Michael were laughing together—laughing *together*!—and she couldn't have been more shocked. There'd been such antipathy between them: Paul, because he envied Michael's journey with his brothers to avenge his parents; and Michael, because he felt Paul had abandoned his duty to the League.

Finally she was close enough to hear their conversation.

"And then you became separated in London?" Paul asked, his voice full of disbelief. "And Florrie went to confront her murderous father alone?"

"Adam found her in time, of course," Michael said, shaking his head.

"Aye, Adam mentioned how difficult it was for his wife to hear the extent of her father's sins. She's a brave woman."

"And then there was Timothy's assistance."

Juliana expected Paul to change the subject, but he only nodded.

"Adam mentioned it. What did he do?"

"He caught up with us part way, and when he was supposed to bring back Lady Florence, he let us depart, going against the League."

Paul made no sarcastic comment, only sighed and said, "Glad I am that he took the right stand."

Both men suddenly noticed her, and Michael nodded. "I'll leave you in capable hands, Sir Paul."

"She *is* my closest guard," Paul said.

Juliana and Paul looked at each other, and when he reached out a hand, she took it but didn't walk into his embrace. She suddenly didn't know how to tell him what she'd decided, what she wanted. It seemed too brazen, and she couldn't play the concubine for something so important. She was restless and eager and uncertain.

"Paul, you jousted today, getting the exercise you so badly needed. I've had none. Come with me, for I need your help."

His gaze was curious, but he didn't question her, only followed her up to their bedchamber. Though she was distracted, she still did her duty, careful at every open door they passed, every corridor that intersected with theirs.

But at last they were alone.

And Paul watched her, waiting.

She felt foolish now, uncertain, but she presented him with her back. "Can you unlace me? I need to don a shirt and breeches. You might want to remove that fancy doublet for something more practical."

When she went behind the screen, he called, "What are we doing?"

She peered out and grinned. "Sword fighting."

When she emerged, he eyed her with interest. "We have little room to maneuver."

"Then it will be a challenge." She removed her sword from beneath the bed, drew it forth from its sheath, and grinned fiercely as it shone in the lamplight.

He lifted his sword and began to circle, as she did the same. He thrust, she parried, twisting so that their swords locked and they faced each other close across the blades. Part of the challenge was that these were no blunted swords, but lethal weapons.

"We could train in the nude, as the Greeks did," he said, his smile wicked.

"Patience," she said.

His smile faded into surprise.

This time she attacked, driving him backward, letting her sword just near him, trusting that he would counter the move. He put a table between them, and a chair crashed to the floor.

"Sure of yourself," he said.

"And of you."

"That will surely impress the League."

She frowned even as they both slashed. He drove low, forcing her to jump his blade. She felt alive, her muscles moving in the rhythm she'd almost forgotten. Feeling once again capable and talented, she drove him backward.

He tripped over the chair and crashed into the table on his back. Lying across him, she held her blade to his throat and laughed.

They heard the squeak of the door latch, and only had a moment to toss their swords behind them to the floor. She put her hands on his face and kissed him fiercely.

"What is the meaning of this?"

A Kilborn soldier stood in the doorway, gaping at them. Juliana looked up from her place across Paul's chest, her heart pounding, her breathing coming in gasps.

"What does it look like?" Paul demanded.

"I—I—forgive me, Sir Paul." The man backed out of the chamber and closed the door behind him.

They stared at each other.

"That could have been a Bladesman," he said tightly, staring at her mouth.

She licked her lips, and felt a groan reverberate through his body. "We both know they wouldn't have entered like that."

"What happens now?"

Wearing a slow smile, she tugged at the laces at his

neck and bared his skin to her hungry gaze. She suckled beneath his ear, tasting the saltiness, feeling his life's blood pump just beneath her mouth.

His breathing was harsh, his erection straining beneath her belly.

"Juliana, if we do not stop—"

"I don't intend to stop. I've decided."

She expected him to toss her onto the bed, to pounce on her.

Instead he pushed her up by the shoulders so he could search her face. His hesitation surprised her, but didn't stop her. She stood up, and knowing how much it pleased a man, began to disrobe for him.

He came up on his elbows to stare at her, the table rocking precariously beneath him. She pulled the tunic over her head, let him look at the way the thin shirt outlined her breasts. Her boots and breeches came next, and she made certain he could glimpse her cleavage as she bent over.

With a man, it was so easy, she'd been told. Give him a visual feast, and he could be manipulated, and she could remain in control.

But she didn't feel in control of her wild emotions— and she didn't want to manipulate him.

Giving him her back, she pulled the shirt up over her head. She was naked, and she could hear his groan of approval.

"Juliana, my God," he whispered hoarsely.

Turning slowly, she arched, let him see her breasts in profile as she released her hair from its leather tie. The curls cascaded about her, hiding her breasts, then revealing them.

She spread her legs as if bracing herself during high seas. For his blue eyes were full of storms as he rose up, breathing hard, tugging on his garments.

She stopped him and put her hands on his body. "Let me."

He closed his eyes briefly as she pulled off his shirt. She let her hands run down the muscles of his chest as she'd always wanted to, learning them, caressing his nipples until he shuddered. Again he reached for her, tried to push her back toward the bed, and again she eluded him.

She loosened the laces of his breeches, then reached her hand inside to clasp the hard, hot length of him. He sucked in his breath, his head dropping back as he shuddered.

"This isn't working," she said, feeling like she couldn't explore as she wanted to.

His eyes slammed open and he gaped at her.

She gave a low, sensual laugh. "Think you I mean to stop? Nay, think again."

And she pulled his breeches and braies down to his knees. His erection seemed to aim right at her, and as she admired what she'd only heard about, she tried to imagine what it must be like for a naive virgin on her wedding night when confronted with *that*.

She dropped to her knees, bending to remove his boots. When he was entirely naked, she sank back on her heels and looked up at him, feeling so aroused, yet also experiencing a sweet, soft yearning to please this man.

She came back up on her knees with purpose.

"Juliana, nay, do not, I won't last." His voice was guttural, desperate.

She pushed his hands away. "I'll make certain you last until I am well pleasured."

And then she took him into her mouth. He reacted in every way she'd heard of, but she hadn't imagined how she herself would feel, performing something that had once seemed so foreign to her. Her need to please him went beyond awkwardness. She wanted to give him all of herself, wanted him to remember this night when they were far apart, both alone in their beds because of their own choices. The thought made her ache, but she banished it from her mind.

With her mouth and tongue she played him, watched the subtle signs that she went too far, and retreated. He quivered beneath her touch, legs spread as he braced himself against her.

"Enough!" he finally said harshly, and lifted her clear off the floor.

He laid her on the bed with more gentleness than she'd imagined him capable of in his aroused state. Her hair draped across the cushions, even as she arched and lifted her arms above her head to let him see everything he would have. She expected him to take her with the single-mindedness of men, and she was ready for him, aroused and eager to have him inside her at last.

He slowly crawled over her, and she gladly spread her legs.

With a strained laugh, he said, "Nay, do not rush me."

He bent over her and pressed a kiss in the valley between her breasts. His hair touched her with its own caress, and she inhaled, startled. He took his time, lingering over her skin, tasting her without putting his mouth where she truly wanted it. She squirmed and wriggled, beyond content, needing to feel his tongue, his attention. If their desire weren't mutual, his power over her would have frightened her.

But she didn't feel fear, only a mindless ache of desperate pleasure.

He chuckled, eluding her breasts even as she practically put them in his mouth.

"You're rushing me, and that will only make me avoid what you want."

With a moan, she sank back, trembling, and it took all her control to lie still as he had his way with her. At last she understood how a woman's defenses, her very thoughts, could be swept away from her, unresisting. Paul licked her slowly, working his way to the peaks of her breasts, until she was panting, barely holding herself back from moaning too loudly. At last he took her nipple into his mouth, tasting, licking, teasing, doing the same to the other.

She was no longer Juliana the Concubine, but simply Juliana. Though she'd known what to expect, she felt overwhelmed, overcome, so grateful to be sharing this with him.

And when at last he settled between her thighs, she lifted her hips, whispering, "Yes, yes, yes."

Still he held back, his penis at her entrance, teasing her, drawing out each moment. Beneath him, she knew at last she was a woman, not just a warrior, and that by denying the feminine part of herself, she'd only been living half a life.

And then he entered her, thrusting deep. The pain was negligible; her gasp because he stretched her, filled her, made her know that she would experience all.

But braced with his hands on either side of her shoulders, he froze and stared down at her.

She was a virgin after all.

Chapter 19

Paul was so surprised he almost pulled out of Juliana. Yet she gripped him with her lithe thighs, pulled him down until their bodies were touching along their entire torsos. He was buried in the heat of her, felt her breasts like hot brands in his skin.

He shook his head, trying to clear it. "Juliana—"

"Do not stop—please."

It was the desperation of that final word that at last sank into his brain. The deed was done and could not be changed. She'd let him think—

But then she started tilting her hips, bringing his cock in deeper, and letting it slide out. He shuddered, and the last of his control was gone. She hadn't wanted to be treated as a virgin, so he didn't, thrusting into her over and over, feeling like he went deeper and deeper, losing himself in their shared moans. He kissed her openmouthed, his tongue mating with hers as they mated below.

He felt her every shudder, knew when her pleasure

was cresting by the urgent way she held his hips, guided him against her. It took everything in him to remain on the edge of his own need, waiting for her. When at last she cried out, he used his mouth to silence her, and sought his own release.

At last he braced himself on his elbows, their perspiring bodies still flattened together, his breathing barely in control.

Lifting his head, he stared down at her. "Juliana, you lied to me."

Her smile was catlike and contented as she undulated her body beneath his, so warm and slippery that they slid sensuously against each other. He was hard again inside her, his mind leaving him, his need for her overtaking everything else.

But he flung himself to the side of her and covered his face with his forearm as he tried to regulate his breathing.

"That was . . . that was . . ." she began, but could find no words, only laughed softly as if to herself.

He felt her roll onto her side and drape herself along him, tormenting him.

"That was sex," he said, his voice harsh with denial of his body's demanding needs, "and you'd never had it before."

"I never lied," she insisted, trailing her fingers through his chest hair and following the path lower.

He tensed. "You led me to believe—"

"You believed what you wished to believe, and that was fine with me. I didn't want you to think of me as a helpless virgin."

Though he gritted his teeth, how could he deny her logic?

"And as you can tell, I knew of everything that was going to happen between us."

"How the hell did you know that? Surely the League didn't—" He broke off, aghast, halting her curious exploration.

"It did not happen as you seem to believe. After you left, a new recruit thought I was not in the League for the same reason as he, that I must want to . . . be with men."

"What happened?" Paul asked flatly, already telling himself to remain calm.

"He tried to take advantage of my ignorance."

Gritting his teeth, he stared at her, feeling hot with remorse. He kept his voice quiet, controlled, as he said, "Just tell me, Juliana, if you can bear it."

"When I fought him off, he realized my innocence, and apologized."

Paul snorted. "Knew he'd be thrown out on his ass— at best—for daring to hurt one under the League's protection. What is his name?"

"I will not tell you," she said primly.

Although she was anything but prim as she continued to stroke his chest. She was soothing him, distracting him, and he took her hand in his again, not wanting distractions.

"How can you defend him, Juliana?" he demanded. "He tried to—"

"He misunderstood, and in his regret, he arranged for my . . . unusual education."

"You were educated in lovemaking," he said slowly, with disbelief.

She grinned mischievously. "Aye!"

"By whom?" he demanded.

"Not a Bladesman, if that is what you're thinking. They took me blindfolded to an elderly woman somewhere outside the League fortress. She taught me what to expect, what to do. I even know methods of preventing conception, and carry the necessary herbs. You need not fear there will be a child from this night."

He stared at her, speechless. A child?

"The League wanted me to understand the dangers, be able to control any situation."

"And any man." He thought about the wonders her mouth had performed, and knew he would have done anything she wanted.

She laughed. "You sound upset."

"You may feel in control, knowing what to expect,

but Juliana, it means you can use such methods in persuasion."

"I have not done that, Paul, and I do not intend to."

"You allowed me to believe you were experienced. What about the next man?"

Her smile faded, and she searched his eyes with her own. He'd said something wrong, but wasn't quite sure what.

She shook her head. "I did not treat you as just any man, Paul. This was my first time, and it meant a great deal to me."

She rolled away from him and reached for her night rail on a chair nearby.

Paul's guilt almost threatened to choke him. "If I'd stayed with the League, acted as your protector, none of this would have happened. You wouldn't have lost your innocence about the motives of men so soon." But then again, when one's father was betrayed, she'd already lost so much.

He almost told her all of it then, but she put a hand on his chest and smiled.

"Paul, I do not blame you for what another man did. And although I could never make the same choice you did in leaving the League, I understand now why you felt you had to make it. I could have run from the League after being attacked, but it was my choice to remain, for I believed in their mission above all else."

He nodded, not understanding his conflicting feelings of sadness and yearning. He didn't want to think about it, stopped her before she could don her nightclothes.

"So you received many lessons?" he asked, reaching to cup her breast.

She sighed with pleasure even as she grinned. "Aye, many."

"I need a lesson."

"I noticed."

Faking outrage, he rolled her onto her back. And then she rolled him onto his back, sat on his stomach and held his arms above his head. He groaned.

She looked over her shoulder at his groin. "I was told men need time to recover. I see that is not the case."

"I am a man among boys." He had a momentary thought that he didn't want her ever having other men, but it was not his place to control her. "But I could do with a lesson in intimacy."

"That, I can grant."

Their lovemaking was wild and exuberant. He was amazed at how different sex was with a woman who had a lithe, muscular body and knew how to use it.

And it was good that he didn't have to worry about a child, Juliana's child—but for some strange reason, he had to keep telling himself that.

* * *

The next day, Paul did not have to work hard to find a way to speak privately to Alex, to learn more about Juliana. They were facing each other in the first round of jousting, and Paul let himself be defeated—on the fourth pass. He didn't want to make it seem too easy.

Alex apologized after they'd dismounted.

Paul laughed. "Never apologize. You defeated me, and I congratulate you."

"I simply never thought I would be able to defeat someone like you." Alex only met his gaze briefly, seeming uncomfortable.

"Someone like me?" Paul echoed, wondering what Paul suspected.

"There are whispers . . . oh, you would think them ridiculous."

"Maybe I would be flattered."

"Nay, I cannot even repeat them. They could be dangerous." Soberly, he met his gaze. "Take care of yourself—and Juliana. There are people here who might wish you harm."

Paul nodded.

Side by side, they walked their horses back to the immense temporary stables that had been set up in a field.

"Alex, I would like to know more about my Juliana, but she does not speak much of the past."

Alex's expression was now wary. Paul thought with

exasperation that he'd never met a man less capable of hiding his emotions.

"She must have her reasons for her silence," Alex said.

"I know about the charges against her father."

His eyes widened. "She trusted you with that?"

"Aye, she did. But her father died before he could be found guilty. She says the king took her father's lands and wealth, but that was several years ago. She claims nothing from her past, not even mementoes of her childhood, and that is not right to me. Perhaps she'd like to visit."

"She wouldn't want to do that." Alex sighed. "I was too late to reach her before she . . . disappeared, but her people told me that those final weeks of hardship, trying to find a place to live, watching her mother die, were certainly some of the worst moments in her life. I cannot believe she would wish to return and experience those memories—and regret what is no longer hers."

Paul nodded. "You are right. I did not see it that way. You have my thanks."

"I—I do not wish to see her hurt," Alex said in a low voice.

Was there a subtle threat hidden there? Paul wondered with amused respect. "And I do not plan to hurt her."

* * *

Juliana found herself watching Paul from afar more than before. Yesterday he'd been speaking with Michael, and today it was Alex.

Margaret stood at her side next to the spectators' stands, wringing her hands. "You do not think Sir Paul is angry with Alex, do you?"

"Nay, he is not a man who places much emphasis on pageants such as this."

Although she placated Margaret, she could not quell her own feelings of uneasiness—and she didn't know why. She'd given Paul her body; surely that meant she trusted him.

But . . . what did he have to speak to Alex about that seemed so serious?

She was not going to question him about every conversation he had, especially since he seemed so sweet and amusing when at last they were alone together.

"Do you know what I saw, Juliana?" he asked, amazement in his blue eyes. "I was seated next to Lady Kilborn, and her stomach moved."

Juliana blinked at him. "She *is* with child, Paul."

"I did not realize a child was so active."

"Have you never seen a pregnant woman before?"

"Only from a distance. But this time, one of Lady Kilborn's ladies-in-waiting put her hand on the countess's belly and felt the child move herself."

"Tell me you didn't ask—"

"Nay, I did not. But I wanted to."

He was a hardened warrior in so many ways—and an innocent in others. Again, she felt doubt and disapproval about the League's treatment of him. It felt . . . disloyal, but she loved Paul, and she grieved for his losses.

Two more days passed, and Paul heard nothing from the traitors, who continued to attend events with their wives, cheering on their retainers, as if they weren't trying to destroy England's hard-won peace. What were they doing in private that they didn't feel they could confide in Paul?

They left gifts in his bedchamber, including a jeweled pendant. Although meant as a man's heavy necklace, it still looked perfect between Juliana's naked breasts.

After a rousing night of play, Paul was practically whistling as he sent Juliana ahead to break her fast. He ducked down the corridor to the garderobe, needing to relieve himself. He'd only just stepped inside the small chamber, beginning to unfasten his clothing as he stood near the privy seat, when the whistle of metal on metal alerted him, and he ducked.

He had the brief impression of a large burly man, cloth tied over the lower half of his face, stumbling forward as the empty swing of his sword left him off-balance. If Paul hadn't seen the man, he might have ended up headfirst in the privy hole—or perhaps just his decapitated head would have disappeared within.

With his elbow, Paul struck a blow to the man's sword arm, and the weapon clanged to the ground. Paul's fist sent the man reeling against the far wall, where he dropped like a sack of wheat.

He felt like one, too, as Paul carried him back to Timothy's chamber and left him tied within.

Down in the great hall, Paul found Juliana sitting with all of their Bladesmen for once, holding court like a queen. She tore a piece of white bread from the loaf and laughed at something Joseph said.

Timothy glanced at Paul as he took a seat on the bench. "You seem out of breath, Sir Paul."

"I was attacked in the garderobe."

Juliana inhaled sharply, and the Bladesmen stared at him.

"There was nothing you could have done, Juliana," Paul said, taking cheese from her plate. "Unless you plan to follow me every time I take a piss."

"What happened?" she demanded in a low voice.

He briefly told them. "I showed him the error of his ways—but not too forcefully, since he might be defending the king. I didn't recognize him. Timothy, I left him in your bedchamber. I imagine you can have him taken somewhere safe."

Paul found himself returning Timothy's smile before he looked away.

A small voice behind Paul said, "You—you were attacked?"

Paul twisted about to see young Edward Foxe standing behind him, holding his ball under one arm, his little mouth agape. Paul glanced at Juliana, but her expression betrayed nothing.

"'Twas not so terrible, Edward," Paul said, offering a smile.

"But . . . you were not competing then. Why would he do that?"

"I know not, but I do not think he was a nice man."

"He's tied up?" Edward asked, looking about as if evil men lurked in the few shadows of a summer morn.

"And I will turn him over to the proper authorities, I promise."

Edward nodded, but he kept glancing back at Paul once or twice as he walked away.

"You seem to have made a friend," Juliana said.

Was she envious that the boy was reaching out to him?

But Paul had to put aside Juliana's problems and his uneasiness with them. He had the mission to think about, and now he had a way to press the traitors. He cornered Sir Hugh before the archery competition, and although the man was furious at Paul for risking exposure, he backed down when Paul told him about the attack. Sir Hugh promised he would speak to the earl.

Juliana reclined naked in bed, waiting for Paul, who'd been called to a meeting with the traitors. These last few nights in his arms had given her so much joy that it was painfully sweet. Though they were all in danger, she almost wished the mission could never end.

But reality would come, and she would have to accept it.

Paul returned after midnight, and his frustrated expression faded when he saw her.

He would have fallen upon her, but she held up a hand. "Not so fast, Sir Eagerness. What did our traitors have to say?"

He opened his mouth as if to complain—and then grinned.

"We have dates—we have allies. Although the Irish took a beating at the king's hands just two months ago, they're sending more men."

She sat up and clenched both fists before her. "At last."

"Aye. Even now they make plans for the invasion of the Scots and the Irish, a coordinated insurrection against the king. 'Tis solid proof, once the king sends scurriers to confirm this. They'll capture the Scotsmen crossing the border to invade."

"We'll have even more proof soon," she said.

"They questioned my preparation for the role, of course, insisting that their allies would interrogate me. They say they haven't heard from every Englishman who will join them, but I imagine they've heard from enough, considering the way rumors seem to be spreading. A woman actually curtsied to me today."

Juliana grinned. "Probably just a mark of respect. I've been spreading the word of your talents in the bedchamber."

Laughing, he tossed a fur cloak onto a chair. "Another gift from my *masters*, although I begin to feel like their strumpet."

"Now you know how I feel."

"I think it is to pacify me, because I have a feeling there is something they're not saying."

"Then we remain patient." Juliana took the fur cloak and spread it out upon the bed, reclining upon it, one knee raised to entice him.

Paul pulled off his shirt so fast, she heard a seam rip. When he was naked, obviously ready to have his way with her, she stopped him with a hand on his chest. She could feel his racing heart, felt the faint quiver of his muscles as he held himself above her.

"I wish you to finish what you tried last night, when I was too eager to have you inside me," she murmured, smiling as she lay back on the cushions, feeling very much the concubine.

"You're no longer eager for me?" he teased, but already he took her knees in his hands and spread her thighs.

Juliana gasped, then laughed as he pulled her to the edge of the bed. But her laughter disappeared, as he met her gaze with dark blue eyes, and bent to press a kiss on her inner thigh, just above her knee. With kisses and caresses with his lips and tongue, it seemed to take forever for him to make his way up her legs. She was quivering and covering her mouth with both hands to hold back her moans, her eyes wide as she stared at him.

Then he licked her, a long, slow sweep of his tongue at the center of her that made her convulse with the exquisite pleasure of it. He parted her thighs further, lowered his head even more, tasting her, entering her, then following the long, moist line of her cleft until he once again reached the hooded bud that seemed to throb for him. He drew it into his mouth, suckling, licking, tormenting her until her orgasm was a hot, shuddering slide into oblivion.

Before she could even recover, he lifted her thighs and entered her where he stood, his deep thrusts setting off another explosion of pleasure inside her. It seemed to go on and on, wracking her with sensation. She reached for him, and held him to her as he found his own release.

Several minutes passed before he could lift his head. "That will impress the League," he said.

She hit him in the shoulder. But then she soothed the place she'd hit, and gathered him to her when he joined her beneath the coverlet. These quiet moments were the best, when their hearts beat against each other, and she didn't have to think about a future without him.

But within her was still a growing feeling that he was keeping something from her.

Chapter 20

Lady Kilborn surprised the guests the following morn by asking if the ladies would like to participate in their own archery competition, giving the men a morning of rest. There were several dozen eager entries, and another half dozen who allowed themselves to be persuaded. Juliana let herself be among the latter.

She pretended to need Timothy as her coach, and they walked the field where targets had been placed against bales of hay. The stands were gradually filling, and she knew Paul was there, with Margaret and Alex at his side.

"Timothy," Juliana said in a soft voice.

He must have heard the change in her tone, because as he worked on testing the tautness of her bow, he kept his voice to a murmur. "Aye?"

"Is there something more going on with the traitors than I know about?"

He met her gaze at once, frowning. "Nay, you know

everything. I have already sent off this new information about invasion to the League, and hence to the king."

She smiled. "I thought so. 'Twas . . . nothing. I should not have worried that you would still consider me too young for such a mission."

"You are well prepared, Juliana, and you have proven yourself."

He handed her the bow, and as she turned away, she noticed that Timothy's gaze sought out Paul in the crowd, and his frown didn't lessen.

Although she let herself take third place among the women, Juliana did not feel triumphant, because Timothy had not truly reassured her.

Timothy had thought things were better between Paul and him. But Juliana's concern now became *his* concern. *Was* Paul up to something? Juliana seemed to believe it was about the mission, but Timothy knew that wasn't so. He let his suspicions fester for the morning, watching the parade of mummers arrive for a performance that night. Acrobats tumbled over each other and balanced chairs on their noses, and Paul seemed to enjoy all of it at Juliana's side.

Then Timothy saw Paul talking to her cousin, a spinster approaching her elderly years. Timothy had known she might attend, but had not wanted to alert Juliana needlessly. The woman and her sister had rejected Viscountess Gresham's desperate plea for a place to shelter Juliana.

Timothy knew that Paul had also been speaking with Alex—all of his behavior had to somehow be connected.

"They're *here*?" Juliana demanded quietly of Paul.

They sat at a trestle table in the great hall during the midday meal, while outside, the course was being set for the horse racing competition.

"How did you learn of my cousins?" she asked, when Paul remained silent in commiseration—or pity.

"Alex."

"You are quite friendly with him of late," she said dryly.

"Because he is *your* friend. And in the spirit of friendship, he thought it might be best if I broke the news."

"I do not wish to see them." She pushed away her trencher of roasted beef, surprised that she almost felt nauseous.

"And you do not have to. They have not seen you since your girlhood. They won't recognize you."

Though Juliana could not blame her mother's death on these women, she wanted to. If only her mother had felt safe, had known she had a place to bring Juliana, perhaps she wouldn't have died.

She searched Paul's face. "You will not think me cowardly if I avoid them?"

"Cowardly?" He cupped her cheek and leaned in to kiss her forehead. "I think it wise, for once your infamous temper is unleashed . . ."

She bit her lip, but couldn't hold back a smile. "Infamous temper? I have never heard myself described so."

" 'Tis only those who know you well, know the truth."

Part of her was annoyed that he felt the need to take care of her—but the part of her that loved him was torn. It was getting more and more difficult to remind herself that this time with him was temporary, when he did sweet things like this.

She was tempted to ask what he meant to do when this was done, now that they'd found each other. She suspected he would return to France, and leave behind his memories of the League and the anguish they'd caused.

There was another part of her that hoped he might have changed his mind, that he might be falling in love with her as well—but his secretive manner told her that couldn't be true. And regardless, she could never be with a man who kept secrets.

This even more firmly convinced her she could never wed—she could never keep secrets either.

But she would not meekly stand by.

Through the day, Paul sensed Juliana's retreat from him, saw the close way she regarded him. It was getting more difficult to keep the truth from her. And now she knew what the League had done to him, what they were capable of. It was time for an end to his secrets.

He knew her better now, knew she would not be devastated that her beloved League had made another grave error.

That night, he watched her bathe, reveling in their intimacy, almost deciding to forgo any discussion. But he saw her sidelong glance of speculation as she donned her dressing gown, and with a sigh, he resigned himself to what had to be done.

"I've been keeping something from you," he said.

She frowned, studying him. "I know. Surely 'tis about the mission."

"Nay, I would never compromise you in such a way. You don't know that by now?" he smiled at her then, openly showing his enjoyment of her scantily clad state.

She stared at him, her eyes going soft, dazed. Then she blinked and looked away. "Do not try to befuddle me. It cannot be done."

"And I would never try," he said solemnly, though his lips twitched with amusement.

"Do not make me pull every detail from you one at a time." She threw up one hand. "Tell me, Paul. I deserve to know the truth."

He stared at her, his smile fading, worried about how she would take a truth that would turn her life upside down.

"You're frightening me," she whispered, her hand gripping the dressing gown at her neck.

She stood alone at the center of the room, and he wanted to go to her. Such soft feelings only confused him, so he straightened in his chair and began to speak.

"Juliana, I discovered a terrible secret about your past—although I didn't know it was about you until recently. 'Twas the final reason I left the League, for I could not bear to be a part of a society that believed only the final outcome mattered, not how one achieved it."

Though he could see she shivered, she spoke firmly. "Just tell me, Paul, so that your behavior at last makes sense."

"You know that your father was innocent of treason—the League knew it, too."

"Only because I told them. And there was nothing anyone could do, because it was too late for my father."

"'Twas all a League plot from the beginning, Juliana," he said with compassion. "I had a habit of eavesdropping on the secret meetings of the Council of Elders. Soon after you arrived, I heard them discussing it. To be honest, they felt badly about what had happened, but could not change it. Your father was blamed for treason to mask the real target of the investigation, allowing the traitor to believe himself safe."

Her face looked white, as if chilled by a deep winter

storm. "You're saying . . . the League knew my father was innocent?"

"They did," he said gravely. "All I know is that the mission was a success, except for what was done to your father. I do not believe they meant for him to die."

"'Twas an accident," she whispered. "Another prisoner, jealous of Father's fine garments."

"I overheard that the League had destroyed a man's reputation and family to protect the king. And it had worked."

She lifted her chin. "The king was saved."

"Aye, he was. But that cannot be the only consideration. You know that. The League cannot become the sort of organization that cares only about the outcome, not the methods used to bring it about. That will only encourage corruption."

Her nod seemed absentminded, and he knew she was still sorting it all out in her mind. She'd not yet seen that the League had brought her in out of guilt, and part of him hoped she didn't see that at all.

But as if she read his mind, she gave a great sigh.

"'Tis why they took me in." She nodded as if to herself.

Why did she not rail with anger and grief? She was so calm—too calm.

"Whatever their original motives, Juliana, you proved a valuable Bladeswoman."

"I know."

But did she?

She looked at him with impassive eyes. "Why are you telling me this now, Paul?"

"Because justice needs to be done. You deserve to know all of the truth, to have your father's reputation restored."

She frowned. "But Paul, that might reveal the existence of the League. All of their future good deeds would be in jeopardy."

"How can you care about them, after what they've done?" he asked in disbelief. "They let your father die!"

"They didn't kill him. I don't know what their plan for him was, but none of it mattered after his death."

"It mattered for *you,* for your mother."

She flinched, and he almost regretted his harsh words.

"Nothing can change the past, Paul."

"But the truth can shed light on it."

"The truth might hurt many people. I can't even blame them for keeping it from me, because in my youth, I had nothing but the League, and would have been damaged by such a revelation."

"And you're not damaged now?" he demanded in shock.

"I am . . . sad and stunned. But the League meant to

safeguard England by protecting the king. They didn't mean for my father to die."

"But they meant to ruin his reputation."

She continued speaking as if she hadn't heard. "They took me in when I had nowhere to go." And then she lifted her dark, sad eyes to him. "Leave it alone, Paul."

"I cannot. Think of the marriage you could have made, the happiness the League cost you."

"Paul, I'm happy, do you not see?" She approached him and touched his shoulder. "Please, I do not wish you to do this."

He rose to his feet and paced away from her. "I have to know the truth, Juliana. *You* need to know the truth, though you may not think so now. I do not plan to reveal the League to all the world. But perhaps the entire organization needs to know what was done in its name, so they're not free to ruin another family again. As of now, no one but the council knows, because of the secrecy surrounding every mission."

And Timothy, he thought, but he could not say the words aloud, a weakness that ate at him.

Chapter 21

Juliana felt numb as she stared at Paul's back.

She did not have all that many joyful memories, but there were definitely times of happiness, when her father tolerated her differences out of love, and encouraged her mother to go along. Until it seemed obvious that Juliana would not willingly put aside her fascination with weapons and training. And then her father had reluctantly, but firmly, agreed with the countess's insistence that Juliana's place was with the women of the castle.

Juliana inhaled deeply, feeling the old sorrow, but also a faint relief. She'd been right all along—her father had been innocent. But the humiliation of scandal, and then her father's death, had certainly contributed to her mother's. Juliana felt bereft, torn, her belief in the League shaken—but not destroyed.

Paul was the one who'd shown her that the League was comprised of fallible men who made the same human errors they all did—believing too strongly in the mission, when innocent people would be hurt. Her father might have been cleared if he'd lived, as part of the League's plan. She didn't know.

But Paul stirring it all up was distracting her from the mission at hand—another attempt to save another king. Who would suffer this time? Or could she make sure no one but the traitors suffered at all?

And their families, she thought stoically. Their innocent families would suffer, just as she had. And it didn't matter that their husbands and fathers were guilty, and hers wasn't.

Paul's determination to unmask the League's mistakes saddened her. His discovery of the League's involvement in her father's treason was too much for him, had driven him away from the only home he'd ever known.

Had driven him away from her, then and now, she thought sadly. It was far too ironic.

Paul stopped pacing to look at Juliana. She'd gone to the hearth to comb out and dry her hair. He took a moment to take in the beauty of her, to ease his troubled mind. He didn't understand her ability to put aside what the League had done—didn't want to understand it. She was wrong.

She glanced up at him. "Tell me you've used these silent moments to rethink your plan, Paul. Too much time has passed, and the League is very good at concealing what it must. Let this go."

"I have one more missive I await, from the League itself," he said stubbornly.

"You contacted them?" she demanded.

"I did not tell them my true purpose, nor that you were involved. For our current mission, I asked for a list of traitors spanning years—including the year of your father's accusation and death."

Her expression softened, even as she rose to her feet and reached to touch his face. "Paul, I would never think you would betray me in such a way. I know you well, and you know me. But you are wrong about this. I need you to let this go."

He covered her hand with his own and held it to his cheek a moment. "I cannot, Juliana," he said in a husky voice. "I need you to trust me."

She searched his face. "I do not know that I can, when you refuse to listen to me."

He moved away so that her hand dropped from him.

Once they were abed, she remained on her side and fell asleep quickly, while he lay there and held her long into the night and felt alone, as alone as if he'd already lost her.

Timothy was at their door as they prepared for mass. He smiled at Juliana, and Paul thought that some of her wariness eased.

"Paul, might I speak to you in private?" Timothy asked pleasantly.

Juliana nodded. "If you are not at mass, I will see you both in the great hall."

When she'd gone, Paul crossed his arms over his chest and waited, studying his foster father.

Timothy removed a small folded piece of parchment hidden within his belt. "Late yesterday a missive from the League arrived with the answers to your questions about the traitors."

Paul hid his tension, cursing his luck that Timothy would be the one to receive it. "I assume you read it. Have our present traitors been suspected before?"

"Only Redesdale, but nothing conclusive. But then that's not why you sent the missive."

Timothy's tone betrayed no anger, but Paul knew that it meant little.

"The years you requested information on included the year Juliana's father was imprisoned." Timothy sighed. "It saddens me that you didn't think you could come to me with questions."

"I did. You said the League secrecy overrode all else."

"Paul—"

"And I knew where your allegiance lay—to the League and the king, not to three brothers who needed you, or a lone young woman whose family was destroyed."

Timothy briefly closed his eyes, then said, "I cannot apologize any more than I have."

It was Paul's turn to sigh. "I know. But after I told her what the League had done, you didn't see her face."

"The poor girl," Timothy said softly.

"She doesn't know of your involvement."

The other man narrowed his eyes. "Why would you keep that from her? I was a part of the Council deliberations, involved in the decisions."

Paul rubbed both hands through his hair. "I couldn't tell her. Perhaps because the problems are between you and me." But he knew it was more than that.

Timothy seemed to accept his explanation. "Then read the missive." He held it out.

Paul stared at it in surprise, had thought Timothy meant to confiscate it. He read the encoded letter, then inhaled sharply at the details. "The Duke of Chellaston was the traitor the League was attempting to capture when Juliana's father was accused."

His foster father nodded. "Chellaston died within a year of Gresham, quite unexpectedly."

"Unexpectedly," Paul echoed with sarcasm. Someone had obviously ordered his death as punishment.

"Chellaston and his sons are cousins to King Henry."

"But if he was attempting treason against Edward, long dead, why would Henry care? Why has it not been revealed?"

"Because Chellaston's son, the current duke, is a powerful supporter of Henry—and very proud of his family's dedication and loyalty to England. He would be humiliated if his father's secrets were made public. Henry will not sanction the revelation, needing the duke's support at this crucial time." Timothy sat down heavily in the cushioned chair near the hearth. "Gresham's death was an accident, but the plan had been to exonerate him and return him to his family. When the king discovered how royal the traitor was—and that Gresham was dead anyway—His Majesty ordered us to maintain secrecy."

"The League didn't care about Juliana?"

"We made certain she was safe and protected." He briefly closed his eyes as if in pain. "I live with the sorrow of these decisions every day. But Paul, Gresham was a Bladesman."

Startled, Paul sank down on the opposite chair. "A Bladesman? Juliana never knew . . ."

"Why would she? He volunteered to risk himself and his reputation. He died for his beliefs. He would not have wanted us to put avenging him over the successful outcome of the mission he believed in so much."

"But Juliana—"

"Does she want you to go forward with your revelations?"

"Nay," he said. "She is as loyal to the League as her father."

"Stop now, Paul," Timothy said, leaning forward with urgency. "This obsession is risking your safety. You aren't concentrating fully on this assignment."

Before Paul could become defensive, Timothy finished in a pained voice.

"You could be killed, Paul, and I cannot lose you again."

Paul felt confused as he realized that his long-held animosity toward his foster father was beginning to fade. But showing the League its mistakes was still important to him. "Will you tell the League what I'm doing?"

"Never, though I understand why you question. But you are as a son to me, Paul."

Paul stared at him, then looked away. "I will discuss my decision with Juliana."

After Timothy had gone, Paul sat alone in the bedchamber, trying to make sense of everything. Then Juliana arrived, closed the door and leaned back against it, watching him. He beckoned, and when she approached, he tried to pull her onto his lap, but she resisted.

"What did Timothy want?" she asked.

Calmly, he told her about the missive, and everything Timothy had revealed.

"My father, a Bladesman," she breathed, her voice full of wonder and pride. "It explains so much."

He nodded, saying nothing.

She met his eyes. "Now that you know the name of the true traitor—and you see how much would be lost if you revealed it—will you keep the secret my father died for, Paul?"

"For now, Juliana. I cannot promise what my final decision will be." Timothy had been right—he might become too distracted during this mission, and that could bring harm to Juliana. He couldn't bear that.

But he saw the way she stiffened.

"Enough, Paul," she said angrily. "I do not want to hear another word about you pursuing the truth for which my father paid with his life to keep protected. It has nothing to do with you!"

He opened his mouth, and realized he couldn't disagree. Why was this so important to him, that he'd even go against Juliana?

"You've made certain I know that what we have is temporary," she continued, her voice cold. "I understood from the beginning and accepted it. We've taken pleasure in each other, and that's all we're meant to have. But now your curiosity is threatening what my father worked for—and I won't have it!"

He stared in surprise and admiration at her fury, at her snapping black eyes and the way she tossed back her hair when it got in her way. She was right—they were lovers, nothing more. It was what he wanted, wasn't it?

Yet he was hurting her, and the pain was like a blade into his own chest. He couldn't change his mind and do what she wanted. She was wrong—and he was right.

She glared at him. "You aren't happy, Paul, and you're looking for something to make you feel right again. I won't be with you and watch you suffer—and let you make me suffer. 'Tis finished between us."

Finished? He'd thought their relationship had to end at some point, but the finality of it suddenly seemed wrong. He frowned. "I'm trying to help you."

"Are you? I don't think so." She straightened. "'Tis time to show yourself in the great hall. You missed mass, and I saw many guarded looks sent my way. I cannot break my fast alone."

He stood up and followed her from the bedchamber. She was her usual careful Bladeswoman self, peering around corners. Just as they passed a corridor, Paul felt a breeze behind him, and had his sword unsheathed, parrying the blade aimed at his back.

Chapter 22

Juliana heard the slide of metal as Paul unsheathed his sword behind her. In that instant time seemed to stand still. She knew another Bladesman would be coming up from behind Paul's attacker.

Other men were running from the opposite way, and she only had this one moment to make a decision.

She threw a dagger, slicing the nearest torch in half, and it guttered out on the floor. The next torch was much farther down the corridor, leaving Paul and his attacker fighting in the shadows, and disguising her own participation. She backed up against the wall, before the next two attackers could register who she was. They ran toward Paul's back with blades raised.

She tossed another dagger, and it hit the first man in the thigh, as she'd planned. He went down hard, falling in front of his partner, who tumbled right over the top of him. She took the opportunity and used her next dagger on the second man, laying open his arm.

Glancing briefly at Paul, she saw that two men were

taking turns attacking him in the narrow corridor. And he was doing his best not to kill them, or they'd already have been dead. Beyond Paul, another battle raged, but in the murky light, she could not see which Bladesman was involved.

Juliana's two opponents were moaning and dragging on each other, trying to get away. She let them go. Still clutching her bloody dagger, she looked for an opening to assist Paul. One of his attackers was already on the ground, and Paul took out another by allowing the man to thrust toward him. Paul gripped his sword arm with one hand, yanking him off balance and using his hilt to render the man unconscious.

He was breathing hard when his gaze found Juliana. She gave him a brisk nod, and they both turned to the last battle.

It was already over. Timothy stood over his opponent, his sword yet held in the ready as he stared down the corridor, looking for more.

"Damn, but I hate watching you defend me!" Paul said to Juliana, then hugged her fiercely.

"Cannot . . . breathe," she managed, her face buried in his tunic.

He eased his hold. "Brilliant move, dousing the torch."

She shrugged and pushed away from him. Touching him was too painful. She didn't meet his gaze, couldn't let him see how she cared. Such caring was best put behind her. It wasn't important enough to him.

Timothy came toward them, and it was then that Juliana saw the blood that stained his chest.

Paul's face tightened as he went to his foster father. "How badly are you hurt?"

"My shoulder," Timothy said, reaching to hold his arm against his side. "It looks worse than it is." He looked at the men moaning on the ground, at the two Juliana had fought, who they could see limping away at the end of the corridor. He smiled at her. "Well done— to you both."

"I cannot remain such an open target while my people are hurt," Paul fumed. "After we've seen to Timothy, I will speak with the traitors."

Timothy's shoulder wound was of the flesh, and once the bleeding had been stopped, Juliana thought Paul's tension at last eased. She'd never imagined he would feel close to his foster father, and felt relieved to see it.

But her relief gave way to frustration in the great hall, when he had to leave her behind.

Paul crossed the hall, knowing many pairs of eyes stared at him with skepticism or curiosity or wonder. The traitors were scattered about, and he approached Lord Byrd, who had just left a game of dice.

"Lord Byrd, I wish to speak with you," Paul said between his teeth, hating his subservient role.

Paul expected Byrd to be angry at such a visible request, but the other man barely hid his agitated wariness.

"This is not proper," Byrd said.

"How can I care for propriety?" Paul asked plaintively. "My men and I were just attacked within these walls."

Byrd flinched. "You appear unharmed."

"Due to the skill of my men, of course, and I am grateful."

"If all is well, why do you risk speaking to me so openly?"

Paul lowered his voice. "It has been several days since you . . . revealed your plans to me. What more has happened? And when will we declare my identity, so that I'll have an army's protection?"

Paul kept waiting for the usual display of anger and arrogance, but Byrd seemed fearful, his beady eyes darting about even as he wrung his hands. Something was wrong.

"When I have news, I will let you know," the man said brusquely, then hurried away as fast as his bulk would allow.

Paul withdrew from the lance-throwing competition. Juliana had to wait until the midday meal, when the guests were dispersing into various pavilions overflowing with tables of food, before she could pull him behind the empty stands near the lists.

"Why did you withdraw?" she demanded. "You love to compete."

"The attacks are growing more frequent, and the traitors are nervous. I cannot let myself be distracted by a game."

She glared at him. "You mean you can't tear yourself away from your protection of me."

He only narrowed his eyes and said nothing.

"Do you think I'm weak? Did I *prove* myself weak this morn?"

"Weak?" he echoed in a low furious voice. "I was *proud* of you. I told you so. But . . . somehow things are different now. You're my—" He broke off.

"Your what? Your concubine?" she asked dryly.

"You're my lover, and I will protect you."

His lover, she thought, knowing that even those words were a concession from a man who guarded his emotions as Paul did.

"I am not your lover, not anymore."

Seeing Timothy bloodied had upset them both. Paul wanted to protect her, as she wanted to protect him. Surely he was reminded, as she was, of the fragileness of life, of the rare moments of pleasure they'd found in each other.

But they were finished now. Over. And she'd known when she'd seduced him that this was how it would end. But she was a mature woman—she would learn to live with it.

The love she felt for him had opened her eyes. She'd held herself back from real life, from being a woman, out of fear, but she needn't have feared love. Even such brief happiness had been worth the risk.

And as she contemplated what she was losing, it was as if she had been blind, and now could see again.

"Paul, everything we had together is slipping away, and do you know why?"

He crossed his arms over his chest. "I am certain you're about to tell me."

"Your parents were murdered, and you were helpless to do anything about it. It colored your whole childhood, put you in the path of the League—something you wish had never happened."

He said nothing.

"And then the murder was solved in your absence, a point of family honor that you had nothing to do with."

His frown grew even more forbidding. "Why do you keep bringing this up?"

"Because you cannot let it go! You're trying to avenge my father because you couldn't avenge your own."

"Because I know the regrets you'll face."

"As much as I understand this, I don't feel the same

way. If the name of the traitor comes out, children will suffer as I did, for even though they're innocent, all will believe them guilty by blood, another generation that the king cannot risk trusting. I don't want that. 'Tis over. Enough people have been hurt, including both of us."

Paul watched her stride away, telling himself that he was in the right, and she in the wrong. Whatever the mixing of his motives, the League needed to be reformed, so they would stop trampling innocents to reach their goals.

Innocents like his brothers and him, like Juliana and her family.

But wanting to be proved right, to have the truth aired, was only setting him apart from Juliana, the one person who mattered most. He'd thought avenging her father would make her happy, give her peace, but he himself seemed to be making things worse. He felt alone in his righteousness.

"Juliana, come look!"

She turned when she heard Margaret's voice and tried to smile at her friend. Margaret was sunshine itself, lightening her depressing day. Juliana had been standing alone in the shade of the outer curtain wall of the castle, watching the lance-throwing competition from a distance. She'd wanted to be alone, to accept that having a purpose would make up for never having Paul's love.

But she didn't want to wallow in it anymore, and was glad Margaret had found her.

"Did you see them?" Margaret asked.

"See who?"

"Sir Paul and my little brother. They're behind the viewing stands at the lists."

Where Juliana had left Paul alone. She shaded her eyes as Margaret pointed, and to her surprise, she saw Paul on his knees beside Edward, showing the little boy how to hold a light training lance in preparation to hurl it.

She wanted to stay angry, but was he helping the boy just for her?

"I never would have believed it," Margaret said, shaking her head in wonder. "Somehow, Sir Paul has won him over."

Juliana felt a lump in her throat. She never cried, and wouldn't do so now, even though Paul had won her love and was now trying to help a little boy for her sake. Yet he didn't deem their relationship important enough to do as she asked.

"He is a good man," Margaret said softly.

Juliana realized her friend was studying her. "Aye, he is. I was lucky."

"'Tis a shame he can't marry you."

"Won't," Juliana heard herself say, then realized she'd revealed too much.

Margaret's gaze focused on her. "I know there is the tragedy of what has happened to you, but . . . it doesn't seem enough of a reason for a man who feels so deeply."

He was a man who had wanted to succeed at everything he tried. But when he'd first emerged from the League cocoon, he hadn't been able to be as other young men. Had those insecurities followed him these last several years even though he'd proved himself a successful knight?

He was focusing on what he thought would help her, even though it was driving them apart. And the more she explained herself, the less he wanted to hear.

Because he was trying to do right by her the only way he thought he could.

"Juliana, you've become very quiet," Margaret said softly.

She gave a start, realizing she'd forgotten her friend was there.

Margaret touched her arm. "I am sorry if I brought you pain by mentioning marriage."

"Nay, you did not," Juliana said with a smile, "but might I ask a favor? Paul has withdrawn from the lance-throwing competition. Will you and Edward convince him otherwise?"

Margaret smiled hesitantly. "We can try . . . if you need us to."

"I do. But I'll remain here."

Margaret walked away, leaving Juliana to question everything that had happened to her recently. She'd misjudged Paul—had she misjudged other things? She'd told him she didn't want the traitor's children to suffer, but perhaps she was too quickly deflecting her own buried neediness. Paul had once questioned whether she felt she needed to prove herself to the League. Had he been right? Was she so desperate to have a home, a place to belong, that she was still trying to prove her loyalty, regardless of what the League had done to her family?

She put her face in her hands, wondering if she'd ever feel at peace again.

They came for Paul again in the night, and he was relieved. He wanted this mission to move forward, he needed it done. He needed to prove to Juliana that he was right and she was wrong—she'd thank him for it in the end.

When the blindfold was removed from him, he was in the same underground chamber hewn from rock— but the four men he faced seemed drastically different. Gone was the confidence, the superiority. They were whispering to one another, barely glancing at Paul.

"Are you going to listen to what I have to say?" Paul

demanded plaintively. "I was attacked again, and if it weren't for my own soldiers, I would be dead, and your plans ruined."

"Our plans are already ruined," the earl of Redesdale said between gritted teeth.

Paul narrowed his eyes. "What are you saying?"

"The king is on his way," Lord Byrd said, hands flat on the table as if he'd push himself to his feet. "He has sent word to Kilborn that he will be attending the grand melee, the final event of the tournament."

"He wishes to see the north's finest knights," Lord Gerard said. Rising to his feet, he began to pace, betraying his restlessness, his eyes darting about as if he looked for escape.

Paul had known the king was coming, of course, but not when. He'd thought they were supposed to clear the path for him, make the way safe. But the king had evidently grown tired of waiting, regardless of the danger. His Majesty knew the north was still in turmoil, and meant to settle it.

Paul played up his confusion. "I do not understand. You said the Scots and the Irish are coming—you want a battle. Surely 'tis time to reveal my presence and rally your supporters."

Redesdale and Byrd exchanged a glance. Sir Hugh Burton, the captain of the guard, folded his arms across his chest and looked inscrutable, as if he would put his trust in a battle. But apparently his lords didn't feel the same way.

"The will of the Lancastrians and Tudors was supposed to be broken before the battle," Redesdale said in frustration. "The king would have been dead before we met, and the battle merely to stamp out the last resistance to the inevitable."

"You intended to assassinate the king?" Paul asked in a bewildered voice. "Then why did you even need me?" He knew they still wanted to rule through a puppet on the throne.

Gerard picked up the story, even as he paced faster. "Our assassin was already hidden within the king's household."

Though Paul let himself appear confused, inside he knew that this changed everything, that he had to get word to the League.

"You were to be a distraction from the real plot," Byrd said dismissively. "The king would send his forces north, anticipating your threat, letting down his guard to an attack from nearby."

"Instead, he's come himself," Redesdale said bitterly.

"But . . . your assassin can—"

"Attack him here, right where we all are?" Gerard's voice rose shrilly. "We'll be implicated, beheaded!"

"Then stop him," Paul said, throwing his arms wide.

"We have tried," Redesdale said, glaring at Gerard,

who sank into a chair and hid his face in his hands. "We reached him yesterday on the march with the king's army. He believes himself called by God to bring England to its rightful place. He will not back down. He means to see the king dead, even if he himself loses his life. He killed one of our men, sent the other back to us wounded."

" 'Tis finished—we are finished." Byrd seemed to sink into his chair, a prisoner of his bulk.

"You know who he is. You can stop him."

"We will try," Redesdale said. He sounded as if he were convincing himself.

"What does he look like?" Paul demanded. "My men can help with the search."

"Why would you do that?" Gerard demanded in a querulous voice.

"Because I am implicated just as you are. I wanted to be part of a great battle—and instead you've all made us into cowards who sneak in the dark of night."

They said nothing for a moment, glancing among each other again.

"He is called Colfe," Sir Hugh said coolly, speaking for his lord. "He has no identifying marks, is so average in looks and height that you will not be able to find him. He is a dark Celt in coloring, but he is not fool enough to be so easily recognized. He is a fanatic, chosen because he does his work well."

"Then we will find him, and live to challenge the king in battle another day," Paul said.

He saw their disregard of him, but strode boldly out into the corridor. Since no one tried to blindfold him now, it was easy enough to remember how he'd gotten there in the dark. Even though one of his Bladesmen was probably following, he moved through the castle, flitting from shadow to shadow, remaining unseen. At last he reached Timothy's chamber and gave the right knock before he went inside. One man was always awake, and it was Theobald this time, sitting beside the small fire, his mask a dark shadow upon his face.

"Urgent news," Paul said, as the other men awoke on their pallets. "Alert the others and come to my bedchamber."

He knew Juliana hadn't slept since the traitors had taken him away. She wore her dressing gown, and she hugged herself when they stared at each other.

"What happened?" she demanded.

"The others are coming. I will tell you all."

She poured him a tankard of ale from a pitcher.

"Do I look like I need strong sustenance?" he asked wryly.

She poured another. "I do."

"Aye, the news is bad enough," he said.

When all seven of them were assembled, Joseph

standing near the door to listen for unwelcome guests, Paul calmly explained what he'd just learned.

Tiredly, Timothy said, "I was concerned that the king would not heed the League's advice to remain south until the threat was over. And now he is in far worse trouble than he knows."

The stubble on his foster father's face made him look even older, Paul thought, and wondered how long Timothy would continue accepting assignments. There was always the Council of Elders, whom Timothy had advised. The Council needed a voice of reason, someone who'd seen the harm that had been done when thoughtlessly focused on only the end result.

"The League will stop him," old Roger said. "We will see to that."

"Meanwhile, we will guard the king with our very lives," Timothy added. "We will fortify ourselves by requesting more Bladesmen. I have established myself among the servants both indoors and out. They will help us be on guard for the king's sake."

"Do not count on Redesdale and his retinue," Paul said.

"But they cannot depart, not without revealing their cowardice and the reason behind it," Michael added with satisfaction.

"I would offer to become close to the king," Juliana

said, "but I understand he is a moral man with a wife and babe in London."

Paul clenched his hands behind his back, keeping his expression impassive. The League had cost her father his life—and with her loyalty and duty, it could very well cost her her own. The ache in his chest was raw and painful, and at last, he understood the depth of his feelings for Juliana.

Chapter 23

The king arrived late the next afternoon, announced by trumpeters. Surely a thousand soldiers traveled with him, spreading across the fields surrounding Castle Kilborn to set up camp. Minstrels followed the trumpeters, moving among the guests who gathered along the edges of the road, anxious for a glimpse of the king.

Juliana stood at Paul's side, taking in the spectacle of the royal arrival. Lord Kilborn had seen banners of velvet and silk hung from the castle walls, and his own pennant now hung below that of the king, the red dragon of the Tudors, high above the battlements.

Somewhere in that sea of arriving men was an assassin.

But there were surely Bladesmen as well, to fight at their sides, to help protect the king.

At the banquet that evening, she was impressed by King Henry's cloak lined with white fur. He wore a simple gold crown upon his head. His face was long beneath his blond hair, with regular features except for a red wart upon his cheek. He could be any man, yet he'd persevered and made himself king—with the help of supporters. He would have to reign knowing that others believed him not the next in line to the throne. Perhaps that was why he had not allowed his wife's coronation yet—her father had been king, after all, not his. But he was descendant of kings through his mother. He had enough claim to satisfy those who'd backed him.

There were now soldiers everywhere, squeezing some guests out of the great hall for the royal banquet. Tasters ate the king's food before he did, making a poisoning unlikely.

Juliana realized that the best time for the king to be attacked would be during the actual melee itself, when men on horseback would be roaming the open countryside looking to defeat each other. And the king would be seated in the stands, mere yards away from knights with blunted weapons hoping to impress him with their skill and daring.

And someone would attempt an assassination.

Juliana and her fellow Bladesmen could not simply wait in front of the stands without calling attention to themselves. They would have to participate in the melee—all of them, she thought with satisfaction.

Late that night, Paul once again stared at the ceiling, Juliana lying as far from him as possible. He'd wanted to talk to her, try to explain the things, but she'd wanted to remain focused on the mission. She'd sharpened her daggers and sword, examined the armor they'd appropriated for her from the armory, and made herself very busy throughout the evening.

And Paul had felt frustrated. He'd waited too long; she was determined to avoid a relationship with him, and he felt helpless to do anything about it.

The fact that she could sleep on such an evening infuriated him. He was about to wake her up, demand that she hear his thoughts, when he heard the faint knock of a Bladesman at the door.

He climbed over her to get out of bed—she still insisted on protecting him—and knew by her tension that she was no longer asleep. But he said nothing, only went to the door, opened it—and gaped.

His brothers, Adam and Robert, stood there, grinning. Before he could warn Juliana, they pushed past him, then came to a stop. Paul shut the door and found Juliana already standing, her dressing gown tight to her chin, her body looking tall and lean yet somehow fragile without the bulk of her clothing.

But she was smiling at his brothers, and even smiling at him. "Gentlemen, I thought you might make an appearance," she said. "Come to see what your brother can do?"

Adam, Lord Keswick, smirked. "We've already

heard all about him in the great hall—his fondness for clothing, his mediocrity in the tournament—"

Paul groaned, and Robert elbowed him playfully.

"—the concubine he owns but will not marry," Adam continued.

Paul smiled stiffly at Juliana. "He must have been talking to Lady Margaret or Alex."

"And of course," Robert said, gesturing grandly, "he is the long-awaited Prince Richard. Strange how those rumors quickly died with the king's arrival."

"No one wants to be beheaded for treason." Paul shrugged. "But there are men here who wish that end for me."

"They've tried to kill him several times," Juliana informed the Hilliard brothers.

"But my personal guard has saved me more than once," Paul said.

Juliana didn't blush, only acknowledged her role with a nod.

Adam and Robert exchanged glances, then looked at Paul again, assessing him a bit too much. He didn't want his brothers saying anything to offend Juliana, and perhaps ruin his last chance to redeem himself in her eyes.

"Will she save you again on the morrow?" Adam asked.

"'Tis likely," Juliana said. "Someone has to."

Though Paul enjoyed the brief visit from his brothers,

they didn't stay long. And then Paul and Juliana were alone again. He expected her to climb back into the bed and turn her back.

And although she did return to the bed, she gave him a curious look instead. "You have brothers you love. 'Twill be difficult to leave England again."

"I do not intend to."

He thought that perhaps that would soften her stance toward him, but her eyes narrowed even as they searched his face. With a sigh, she turned away from him.

Juliana took her place in the charge line, visor lowered, body tense with the need to begin. She'd barely escaped her bedchamber that morn, dressed as a man, before Margaret had come to visit. In fact, she'd passed Margaret in the corridor, and although wearing her helm, her face had been visible. She'd bowed to the earl's daughter. Margaret had nodded politely, barely looking at Juliana as she'd hurried by.

Margaret was watching now, along with over a thousand soldiers, guests, and villagers. The entire countryside would be the battlefield as mounted knights clashed and tried to be the last man still in the saddle. Though facing each other in charge lines, the knights didn't fight on a team, but only for themselves. Every defeat meant the victor could lay claim to a man's armor or horse, or even ask for a ransom in coin. The best man here would be able to outfit his party many times over before the day was finished.

She could identify each Bladesman one by one, because of the small black smudge on the upper right of his shield and his helm.

And any assassin could identify the king. He sat on a special raised viewing stand, several noblemen—including the pale earl of Redesdale—on either side of him. Soldiers guarded three quarters of the dais, except where the king's view of the melee would be obstructed.

Juliana's horse moved restlessly beneath her, but did not stray from the line. Horses on either side neighed and shifted, controlled by their masters. She heard more than one man cheerfully call out that she would be an apt target, so small was she. Another answered on her behalf, to "let the squire have some enjoyment."

And then the horn sounded, the crowd cheered, and she urged her horse into a gallop, lance lowered, shield raised, eyes trained from within her helm on the galloping charge line of the enemy.

She'd long ago accepted that she did not have a man's thickness of muscle or brute strength. But the element of surprise, keen agility, and a well-trained horse beneath her could often defeat a far stronger man. She employed that now, dodging the first thrust of a blunted lance, and using the knight's motion to pull him off balance and off his horse.

She heard him swear, even in the midst of the crash of weapons and the screaming neigh of horses.

"Take yourself to the loser's pavilion," Juliana shouted in her deep voice. "I will find you there." Not that she intended to, but it would be expected of her.

And the man trudged off, leading his horse between small individual battles.

She used the terrain as best she could, dodging into a copse of trees or behind the occasional stands set up all through the fields. She took turns with other Blades-men, remaining near the king's stand. And always she looked for Paul, who had a far more difficult assignment than she did, for he had to appear untalented while still managing to remain on the field.

She unseated another knight by shattering her lance against his shield. But that weapon was destroyed, and she was down to her blunted sword and sharp daggers. She didn't want to hurt anyone if she could help it.

And then she saw an armed man just coming out of the trees she herself had used for protection. He was not looking for opponents, but kept his head focused on the royal dais. It had to be Colfe, the assassin.

He began to gallop toward the king, parrying one blow with his shield, using his sword to twist the weapon out of another man's hand. And still he kept coming toward the dais.

Juliana urged her horse into a gallop.

*   *   *

Paul saw everything begin to unfold—the knight coming out of the trees, letting nothing stop his charge toward the king; the soldiers idly watching, pointing out individual combats to each other, not paying attention as Colfe came inexorably forward.

Juliana, riding low over her mount's neck, was on a collision course.

And in that moment, Paul wanted to protect the woman he loved from every danger, even as he knew she was not a woman who needed protection. And that he'd lose her if he took her life into his hands.

The decision cast him upon the sharp edge of a sword, teetering each way as he fought the internal battle of his life. And although it cost him dearly, he held back, letting Juliana make her move.

He watched her gallop her horse across the field of combat, aiming for the assassin, who closed in on the king. Paul did not hang back, knowing he had to be within striking range if she failed.

Colfe stood up in his stirrups, never slowing his pace, and Paul realized the man meant to fling himself from his horse and at the king, sword first. The king's soldiers were too slow to realize what was happening, were too late to stop the man due to their position behind the king and courtiers.

But Juliana was there, and even as Colfe vaulted forward, she'd already done the same from the side, smashing into him armor to armor, her sword knocking away his, their horses screaming as they, too, collided. Juliana and the assassin crashed to the ground, rolling in a loud, metal-grinding heap. A fall while wearing heavy armor, from a horse moving at such a speed, could kill a well-muscled man.

A swarm of soldiers and Bladesmen descended on the two combatants writhing on the ground, and Paul was in the lead. He grabbed Colfe away from Juliana, and held the man up. The crowd jeered and roared, the soldiers stormed to grab him, and Paul was able to hide her escape.

Juliana needed no urging, knew she had to get away before her identity was revealed. Since she was close to the king's dais, she was able to roll beneath. Her armor caught more than once on a wooden beam, pressing against painful new bruises, but at last she reached the far side.

But her helm was too wide, and she ended up having to leave it behind as she crawled from beneath the dais. Everyone was concentrating on the assassin's threat against the king, and no one was watching her get to her feet, pulling her coif of chain mail closer about her face.

And then Alex came racing along the side, Margaret holding her skirts as she ran behind him. Juliana stopped, her head turned away, but they were blocking the direct path to the castle.

"I saw what you did!" Alex called triumphantly. "And I know who you are!"

Margaret almost skidded into his back. "Alex, what are you—"

She broke off, because Juliana had been forced to glare at Alex from beneath her coif, revealing herself. "Quiet!"

Margaret's mouth sagged open.

"Aha!" Alex cried, keeping his voice softer this time. Then he seemed to realize what was at stake, and looked about to see if they were overheard. "I saw you save the king's life, and I just knew!"

Margaret pointed at Juliana's armor, "You—you—" but could not come up with words.

"I told you of her talents on the tiltyard," Alex whispered to Margaret, whose hand he clutched.

"But . . . tossing a dagger is not the same as . . ." Again, Margaret's voice briefly failed her. "That was . . . *you*? Flinging yourself from the saddle? Saving the king's life?"

"I cannot explain," Juliana said, "I must change before I'm discovered by someone other than the two of you. Only know that you cannot reveal what you've seen, and trust that all will be well."

"But—but—" Margaret stammered. "Does Sir Paul know?"

"He was the one who grabbed the villain," Alex said, his face beaming with happiness. "We must let her go, Margaret. Juliana—I am proud of you."

Those words meant more than she could say. Feeling foolish tears dampen her eyes, all she could do was nod and turn away. She blended back into the streaming crowds who gossiped eagerly as they followed the bound assassin.

At last she made it to her bedchamber, only to find Michael waiting to assist her.

"Do you know what happened after Paul captured the assassin?" Juliana asked, as Michael began to work on the buckles holding together her chest and back plates.

"I did not linger, knowing you needed me. But I do believe Colfe was disgusted with his masters' cowardice, and was quick to spill names. The noblemen were apprehended trying to flee the stands."

She felt satisfied at the outcome, and at the moment, could not allow herself to think about the families of the traitors. "And Paul?"

"Everyone saw him lift the assassin out of the melee of pouncing soldiers. But most know he did not actually bring the man down."

Juliana felt suddenly cold, even though perspiring under all her padding and armor. "Some might think he was only turning the focus away from his own part."

"Perhaps. But Colfe did not call out his name. We shall see what the king decides."

Juliana did not exactly trust the king to do what was best for Paul, if what was best for England was something different. Paul had taught her these doubts, but they would keep her alive, and strip away the last of her naiveté.

After Michael stepped outside, Juliana donned her finest gown, and wore a veil to hide the fact that her hair was damp with perspiration. They met up again in the corridor and silently went down through the keep to the great hall, which was filled with the sounds of hundreds of excited voices. Soldiers searched Michael before they were allowed to enter the hall, and even ceremonial swords were being set aside.

Juliana spotted Paul's blond hair first, and made her way toward him. He still wore his armor, though he'd removed gauntlets and helm. No one spoke to him, as if until his fate was decided, the risk was too great. But Timothy and the other Bladesmen, his guards, were but a sword's span away.

Juliana took Paul's arm, and he smiled down at her.

"Where is the king?" she asked softly.

"Closeted in Kilborn's solar with the highest-ranking nobles and his councilors. Making decisions, I imagine."

"About you?"

He shrugged. "We shall see." And then he put his hand on top of hers and gently squeezed. "You were magnificent."

His admiration warmed her. "You saw the whole thing?"

He nodded.

"And since you apprehended the assassin, you must have been very close."

He nodded again.

"But you did not stop me."

His smile softening, he caressed her cheek briefly with the back of his fingers. "Make no mistake, I wanted to. But not because you couldn't handle it yourself."

"I know." She leaned against his shoulder, basking in the only praise that mattered. Whatever happened between them, she had his respect, and he had her love.

A hush spread out like a wave across the crowd, and Juliana stood on her tiptoes as soldiers entered the great hall in advance of King Henry. He strode to the dais reserved for Lord Kilborn's family and guests, and lifted both hands, signaling for quiet.

"A terrible deed was attempted this day upon our person," the king said, his voice ringing in the unusual silence. "But through loyalty and fearlessness, an assassin was apprehended. Know that we had already anticipated this event."

Murmurs raced through the crowd, then died again.

What did the king think to reveal? Juliana wondered, her body thrumming with tension.

"Loyal men worked on our behalf to bring forth traitors committing treason against the Crown. The Lords Redesdale, Byrd, and Gerard have been seized."

Gasps and cries briefly erupted, but once again, the king raised both hands.

"Others are no doubt involved and will be apprehended. But none of it could have been done without one man willing to risk his very life in a masquerade that made him a target of loyal men."

Juliana heard Paul curse under his breath, and smothered a grin.

"Sir Paul Hilliard, step forth," the king intoned.

Juliana let him go, and watched the way the crowd parted for him. He towered above most men, so handsome even in grimy armor and with his fair hair rumpled.

Paul went down on both knees, head bowed. "Aye, Your Majesty."

"Sir Paul Hilliard, brother of our long lost earl, Keswick, we owe you a great debt for your service to the Crown. We therefore name thee Baron Hilliard, and will enlarge your estate with a grant of lands and manors."

Paul lifted his head and spoke in a clear voice. "I thank you, Your Majesty."

Trumpets sounded, dozens of men surrounded Paul, and Juliana heard a low voice behind her curse. She turned in surprise to see Paul's two brothers grinning.

It was Robert who'd spoken, and he continued, "Damn, but now I'm the only one in the family without a title."

Paul was glad when at last he was left alone with a tankard before the hearth. The servants were setting up the trestle tables as men went off to change out of their filthy armor for dinner, their wives chatting excitedly in their wake.

He felt . . . exposed. He'd never in his life openly gone by his own name. But it felt good, too. And embarrassing. After all, it wasn't he who had caught the assassin, but Juliana. Yet the king could not reveal her or the League, and Paul could be the only one to bear the king's gratitude.

He watched Juliana even now, where she stood laughing at whatever his brothers had to say.

Timothy approached and bowed his head. "Baron Hilliard."

Paul rolled his eyes.

"Lord Hilliard?"

"I'm none of that to you," Paul said, smiling. "I prefer 'son' from your lips."

Timothy's smile faded and they looked at each other a moment, before Timothy cleared his throat awkwardly, and Paul looked away.

"Son," Timothy said in a husky voice. "I am very proud of you, and not just for your willingness to accept this mission, but for what I saw during the melee."

"Aye, acting incompetent is worthy of praise," Paul said dryly.

Timothy's expression remained serious. "Leaving Juliana to take on the assassin must have been the hardest thing you'd ever done."

"A choice that reverberated inside me for a long moment," Paul admitted. "I know now how you've felt in times past, when no choice seems to be the best, and every decision is fraught with peril."

Timothy only nodded.

"Can we put aside my animosity?" Paul asked. "'Twas hastily donned and held too long."

"No haste, Paul, but a lifetime altered through no fault of your own."

Paul stared at his foster father, but could only nod since Juliana and his brothers approached. Adam and Robert each clasped his hand, clapped his shoulder, and even ruffled his hair.

Paul ducked away. "I may be younger than you both, but there is no cause for that." Taking a deep breath, he sobered and said to his brothers, "I admire what you've both accomplished, the risks you took to see our father avenged."

Robert's smile turned wicked. "Isn't such a speech given *before* battle, in case there's not a chance to say it later?"

Paul shook his head. "It needs to be said aloud. Juliana helped me to realize how burdened with guilt I have been for not standing at your sides through such danger."

Juliana stared at him, saying nothing.

"Paul—" Adam began.

Paul held up a hand. "That is all I need to say, a truth you should know."

"So 'tis time to celebrate our pride in you?" Adam asked.

Paul looked at Juliana. "But first I must remove this armor. My personal guard makes an excellent squire."

She gave a faint smile, even as she followed him from the great hall.

Juliana's fingers trembled as she undid each buckle of Paul's armor in their bedchamber. He remained silent, and so did she, feeling awkward and sad and yearning and full of love, all at the same time.

He'd admitted aloud his envy of his brothers, and although he could not say it before others, she realized what he wanted her to know, that he agreed with her about his motives for avenging her father.

But other than that, their future was uncertain. Might he go with his brothers, leaving her to return to the League, leaving her only her memories of happiness in his arms?

The lump in her throat felt like it was swelling, like even swallowing couldn't rid her of the feeling that sorrow choked her. She would cry; she would make a spectacle of herself, she who prided herself on being as impassive and unemotional as any Bladesman.

When his upper body was bare of armor, but for his padded doublet, he surprised her by taking both her hands in his.

"Juliana." He seemed to breathe her name.

Stop! she wanted to cry, afraid to hear his words of regret.

"You were right," he said hoarsely, "about everything. My need to reveal the truth about your father was selfish in motivation, and it was as if my eyes were cleared by your words."

Relief was as warm as a blanket on a winter's day. "So you will keep the League's secret?" she asked with hope.

"I shall, because you ask it of me. But I still will hope to influence the Council of Elders so that nothing like this ever happens again."

"Influence the Council—" she began, then had to swallow before saying, "As a Bladesman?"

"Nay, through my foster father. Although I do not rule out the occasional emergency assignment of great importance," he intoned as arrogantly as the king.

She found herself laughing, and then was mortified as the first tear spilled from her eye. She tried to wipe it away, but he drew her into his arms and gently wiped it with his thumb.

"Why do you cry, sweet Juliana?"

"Because there is hope that I will see you again."

"Hope? 'Tis up to me to hope, for I offer you my love, and I do not know whether you will have me, after all of my foolishness."

She stared up at him, feeling shocked and full of disbelief. "But . . . but you've made clear that you never wanted marriage."

"And then I realized 'twas because I never thought I knew how to give of myself to a woman, after the poor examples I had in childhood. I tried to show you this. You deserve such a good life, after everything you've experienced. How would I ever be able to offer that? But I love you, Juliana, and I want the chance to prove it to you."

She put a trembling hand to his lips. "Please, Paul, please, let there be no more need to prove anything between us. That's all my life has been about, proving myself, though I couldn't see it. I denied my womanhood, and rejoiced on finding it again in your arms. Let

e be no more proving, but absolute faith. I love you,
Paul, and I will gladly be your wife."

He inhaled and closed his eyes briefly, then gave her
a crooked grin. "You helped me find peace with my
past, Juliana. Can we let love bring peace to both our
futures?"

And then he kissed her, and it was as if she was
reborn, all her cares and doubts banished, the future
bright with promise.

She leaned back in his arms. "But the League, Paul?
I do not plan to leave it."

"And I would never ask such a thing. I only ask that
you'll briefly retire when having my children."

"Children," she breathed in wonder. "Like young
Edward."

"I think a child of ours will be far from shy."

"He or she will be too busy seeing the world, watching their father compete in all the tournaments he likes."

"A life on the road? Nay, sweet Juliana. I have done
that, and 'tis in my past. A simple life with you and our
children is all I want."

"That sounds wondrous to me," she answered, standing on tiptoes to kiss him once more. "But no tournaments? I had planned to dress as a man and compete."

His expression changed from shock to horror to hard-
won resignation.

And she laughed her delight and happiness.

Author's Note

The late fifteenth century was rife with political turmoil, with many different kings coming to power. While reading extensively about this era, I became fascinated with the story of the little princes locked in the Tower of London. They gradually disappeared from public view and were assumed murdered. Their fate is much of the reason many people soured on Richard III, and welcomed Henry VII.

Several suspects had ample reason to want the princes dead, from Richard III to his onetime ally the Duke of Buckingham to Henry VII himself. In 1674, the skeletons of two children of approximately the correct age were found in a chest beneath a stairwell in the Tower and buried in Westminster Abbey under the names of the princes. Though photographed in 1933, the skeletons were incomplete, and no DNA tests have ever been done.

During Henry VII's reign, several people pretended to be young Richard, Duke of York (as did my hero,

Paul Hilliard), and all were eventually discovered and defeated. The trilogy of Paul and his brothers takes place in the 1480s, a time when Prince Richard would only have been in his mid teens. But I loved the story, and decided to play a bit with history, aging Prince Richard to match Paul. I hope you'll forgive me the liberty I took.

If you're interested in Paul's brothers, Adam's story is in TAKEN AND SEDUCED, and Robert's story is in WICKED, SINFUL NIGHTS. Thank you again for understanding, and I hope you enjoyed the adventures of Paul and Juliana.

Julia

Next month, don't miss these exciting new love stories only from Avon Books

Scandal of the Year by Laura Lee Guhrke
Julia always knew that Aidan Carr, the oh-so-proper Duke of Trathen, had a bit of the devil in him—a devil who secretly yearned for what he could not have. So when she decides she needs to be caught in a compromising situation, Aiden is the answer to her prayers.

Night Betrayed by Joss Ware
The Change that devastated the earth did not destroy Theo Waxnicki, it made him something more than human—eternally young…but not immortal. When he dies on a mission, he's lost in darkness…until a miracle lady brings him back.

Burning Darkness by Jaime Rush
Fonda Raine, a government-trained assassin, has her sights locked on her latest target: Eric Aruda, a rogue Offspring—a pyrokinetic who can create fire with just a thought. But Fonda has awesome powers of her own—and her ability to be in two places at one time enables her to put herself exactly where she wants to be…in Eric's bed.

Tainted by Temptation by Katy Madison
To escape the cruel false gossip of London, Velvet Campbell accepts a governess position in remote Cornwall. But when she finds, to her dismay, that her new employer—the darkly handsome Lucian Pendar—is himself the subject of whispered insinuations, she wonders: *has she found a kindred spirit, a destined love…or placed herself in peril?*

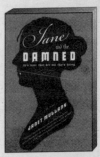

At Avon Books, we know your passion for romance—once you finish one of our novels, you find yourself wanting more.

May we tempt you with . . .

- **Excerpts** from our upcoming releases.

- Entertaining **extras**, including authors' personal photo albums and book lists.

- Behind-the-scenes **scoop** on your favorite characters and series.

- **Sweepstakes** for the chance to win free books, romantic getaways, and other fun prizes.

- Writing **tips** from our authors and editors.

- **Blog** with our authors and find out why they love to write romance.

- **Exclusive content** that's not contained within the pages of our novels.

Join us at
www.avonbooks.com

AVON

An Imprint of HarperCollins*Publishers*
www.avonromance.com